THE PINT
OF NO
RETURN

ALSO BY ELLIE ALEXANDER

THE SLOAN KRAUSE MYSTERIES

Death on Tap

THE BAKESHOP MYSTERIES

Meet Your Baker

A Batter of Life and Death

On Thin Icing

Caught Bread Handed

Fudge and Jury

A Crime of Passion Fruit

Another One Bites the Crust

Till Death Do Us Tart

THE PINT
OF NO
RETURN

ELLIE ALEXANDER

Minotaur Books
New York

THE PINT OF NO RETURN. Copyright © 2018 by Kate Dyer-Seeley. All rights reserved. Printed in the United States of America. For information, address St. Martin's Press, 175 Fifth Avenue, New York, N.Y. 10010.

www.minotaurbooks.com

Library of Congress Cataloging-in-Publication Data

Names: Alexander, Ellie, author.
Title: The pint of no return / Ellie Alexander.
Description: First edition. | New York : Minotaur Books, 2018.
Identifiers: LCCN 2018017605 | ISBN 9781250108654 (hardcover) |
    ISBN 9781250108661 (ebook)
Subjects: LCSH: Murder—Investigation—Fiction. | Women detectives—Fiction. |
    Microbreweries—Fiction. | Brewers—Fiction. | GSAFD: Mystery fiction.
Classification: LCC PS3601.L353755 P56 2018 | DDC 813/.6—dc23
LC record available at https://lccn.loc.gov/2018017605

Our books may be purchased in bulk for promotional, educational, or business use. Please contact your local bookseller or the Macmillan Corporate and Premium Sales Department at 1-800-221-7945, extension 5442, or by email at MacmillanSpecialMarkets@macmillan.com.

First Edition: October 2018

10 9 8 7 6 5 4 3 2 1

A toast to my editor, Hannah, for her insightful
eyes and love of craft beer!

THE PINT
OF NO
RETURN

CHAPTER

ONE

THE SOUND OF ACCORDIONS PLAYING "The Chicken
Dance," Leavenworth's most popular polka during Oktoberfest, filled the bustling square. All around me city crews,
dressed in matching baby blue T-shirts with this year's
Bavarian crest—two pewter beer steins, a pretzel, a black
bear, and a German sausage—were setting up for the weekend festivities. The town gazebo had been decked out in
strands of fall foliage wound together with yellow, orange,
and white twinkle lights. Hay bales and pumpkins flanked
the cement steps. Navy blue banners with golden leaves and
the word WILLKOMMEN hung from the lampposts that lined
Front Street. Even the trees burst with welcoming fall color.
It was no wonder that Leavenworth had become one of the
most popular places to visit during Oktoberfest.

I smiled and waved to a worker inflating a bouncy house
on the grassy area near the gazebo. Front Street would soon
be filled with vendor tents, arts and crafts booths, and an

entire kid zone (known as the Kinderplatz) with a climbing wall, clowns, and tons of games and activities to keep our youngest guests entertained while their parents imbibed the dozens of imported German beers that would soon be tapped. Over the next three weekends, thousands of visitors would make the trek through Washington's breathtaking mountain passes and winding roads to join in the revelry.

When Oktoberfest first began in 1998, four hundred people raised a pint glass in a toast to Germany's famed beer celebration. Through the years the festival had grown exponentially. Now events stretched over multiple weekends and drew crowds, brewers, performers, and beer lovers from all over the world.

It was impossible not to get caught up in the excitement, especially with every shop in the village getting in the spirit with elaborate fall displays. Collections of nutcrackers wearing lederhosen and baskets of apple strudel and kuchen (sweet cake topped with powdered sugar and toasted nuts) tempted passersby from the front windows of the square, where each storefront was designed to resemble a chalet in the German Alps. From half-timbered structures with ornate window carvings to balconies lush with blooming geraniums and white stucco siding framed with dark trim, every shop looked like a cottage from the German countryside.

Despite the craziness that had surrounded my life the past few weeks, I felt a sense of calm watching the familiar bustle that accompanied fall's biggest bash. Oktoberfest brought out the best in our remote village. Preparations had begun months in advance with shopkeepers ordering cases of

German flags and spending weeks washing their front windows and sweeping their sidewalks. The fact that the annual festival coincided with the official start of fall made it that much more spectacular. Our little Bavaria looked like a movie set. If I didn't live here, I might not believe that our pristine cobblestone streets and sunlit tile rooftops were real.

Could there be any place more beautiful? I thought as I stopped to admire a leafy oak tree, glowing gold with sun.

Alas, that thought quickly evaporated when I heard someone call my name in a nauseating singsong tone.

"Yoo-hoo! Sloan."

My stomach sunk. I knew the nasal voice all too well. *Play nice,* I reminded myself and turned to see April Ablin racing toward me. April was Leavenworth's self-proclaimed town ambassador and my nemesis. As always she was dressed in a barmaid costume that squished her ample bosom up to her neck.

I thought about making a run for it, but I knew that wouldn't do any good. April was persistent.

"Morning," I said, trying not to stare at her garish makeup.

"Oh, Sloan, I've been looking everywhere for you." She gasped for breath. "Have you heard the news?"

"No. What news?"

Her face, which was caked in three layers of foundation in an attempt to hide the wrinkles creasing her brow, gleamed with delight. "Oh, my goodness, I can't believe you haven't heard. I was under the impression that the Krause family knew everything there was to know about beer." She gave me a look of pity and fluffed her white ruffled apron tied over a red and white gingham skirt. "How rude of me. I'd

3

forgotten that you're not exactly part of the Krause family anymore, are you? I suppose that means you're out of the *beer* loop."

I didn't bother to acknowledge her dig. "What's the news, April?"

"Right." She twirled her fingers together. They were painted red, white, yellow, and black with the German flag adorning her thumbnails. Like everything else on April, from her hair extensions to her gaudy lashes, they were fake. "It's incredible. We are about to be movie stars."

"Movie stars?" I frowned.

"Yes! Can you believe it? A documentary film crew is arriving later this afternoon. They're shooting their film here. Right here in Leavenworth! Our little Leavenworth, or as we natives like to say—*Haus*." She butchered an attempt at an accent. "And during Oktoberfest no less. This is going to be huge for us—huge. This is going to put us on the map."

"Aren't we already on the map?" April brought out the worst in me. I thought about pointing out the fact that Leavenworth attracted thousands and thousands of visitors each year. It was hardly as if we were struggling to get people to come to our version of beertopia. Actually the opposite was true. Hotels, bed-and-breakfasts, and rental properties had been sold out for months. Oktoberfest was so popular that tourists who had booked late had to stay in nearby Wenatchee or Cle Elum (a thirty-minute or hour-long drive respectively) and get shuttled in for the day. The same was true for the Christmas markets. Families reserved hotel rooms and Airbnbs over a year in advance. Every season brought a new festival—the winter lights, Maifest, fall foliage, and many

4

more. There wasn't a moment that went by when our village wasn't brimming with out-of-town guests.

"Sloan, you know what I mean. Having a major film shot here is going to elevate us even higher on a national and international level." To emphasize the word "elevate," she placed both hands under her chest and shoved her cleavage up toward her neck.

"That's great," I said, starting to back away.

"Not so fast." April reached for my arm to stop me. She appraised me from head to toe and scowled. Then she leaned in. I could smell stale coffee that she had attempted to mask with a breath mint. "I've been meaning to talk to you about your . . ." She paused and gave me a once-over. "Attire."

My eyes betrayed me and followed April's gaze to my jeans.

"We need everyone in town on board for this film," April continued. "And those ratty jeans, ugly yellow boots, and beer T-shirt are not going to cut it. I've sold the film crew on the fact that we are the next best thing to being in Munich at Oktoberfest."

That was a slogan I had heard repeated many times. Villagers prided themselves on Leavenworth's famed festivals. Rightly so. Attracting visitors to the North Cascades had been a community effort. If it hadn't been for a small group of residents who banded together to transform their beloved town into the German mecca it is today, Leavenworth might not exist. The town had been on the brink of collapse after major mining and logging industries departed in the 1960s. Given its remote location in the Washington Alps, Leavenworth could have become a ghost town, but thanks to a resourceful and creative community, the town rebranded itself. Every shop and business had been spruced up and given a Bavarian face-lift. The community embraced the idea of modeling itself after a quaint German alpine village, as did tourists. Hence, Leavenworth, as we know and love it today, was born.

"What does that have to do with my outfit?" I asked April. In my work at Nitro, a new start-up brewery, jeans and a T-shirt were standard attire. Not to mention, every self-respecting brewer owned a sturdy pair of rubber boots. Waterproof, slip-resistant footwear is essential in the brewing process. My bright yellow boots had been special ordered from a brewing supply company in Wisconsin. They had reinforced steel toes and thick soles. When carrying or cleaning heavy kegs and equipment, you could never be too careful.

April rolled her eyes, which were outlined in black and coated in emerald green eye shadow. "Sloan, we have to show them that we're a real German village, and that means that *all* of us need to dress for the part." She did a twirl in the middle of the sidewalk to show off her dress. "As they say in the motherland, it is *wichtig* that we all embrace our heritage and duty. That's 'important,' in case you didn't know."

As always April butchered the German language. I could picture Otto and Ursula shaking their heads at her failed attempt to correctly pronounce the German word for "important." I wanted to remind her that in reality we weren't a German village and that I was pretty sure no one in modern Germany dressed in April's outlandish costumes. Of course, there were a handful of shop owners in town who outfitted their staff in German costumes as a marketing tool to attract more customers, but April was the only resident I knew who embraced the idea of dressing like a barmaid on a daily basis.

"Thanks, I'm good." I started to back away.

April's pumpkin orange lips thinned into a hard, narrow line. "As Leavenworth's official ambassador, I must insist that you rethink your anti-Beervaria stance."

"I don't have anti-Beervaria anything. I'm just not going to dress up. That's all."

Her cheeks burned with anger. "You haven't heard the last from me, Sloan Krause." With that, she stormed away on strappy high-heeled sandals that caught on the cobblestones and nearly made her topple over.

April wasn't going to ruin my morning. I crossed the street and rounded the corner to Commercial Street. Nitro, the small pub where I had recently been hired to help with brew operations as well as manage the bar and food service, sat just two blocks off the main strip near Waterfront Park. Garrett Strong, a home brewer and former engineer from Seattle, had inherited the building from his aunt Tess. When Tess died, she left what had originally been a brothel—in the late 1880s, during the height of the Great Northern Railway expansion—to Garrett, her only nephew. The two-story chalet-style building had served as a diner and bed-and-breakfast for years. Tess had been a fixture in the village and one of the driving forces behind Leavenworth's transformation from a run-down mill town to a thriving Bavaria. Garrett had made the space his own by tearing out the dingy vinyl booths and tossing his aunt's huge collection of German kitsch. The main floor had high ceilings and exposed beams. In the front, there was a collection of high bar tables and stools where customers could leisurely sip a pint. A twenty-foot distressed wood bar separated the dining area from the brewery equipment, kitchen, and office in the back.

Garrett's aesthetic was sparse and sterile. The walls had been painted a stark white, which made the brewery feel open, but also gave it a clinical feel. I had wrapped the exposed beams in twinkle lights and arranged vintage black-and-white photos along the walls to give Nitro a touch of home. So many of Leavenworth's shops and restaurants were packed with nutcrackers, cuckoo clocks, glockenspiels, and German souvenirs that I appreciated Garrett's clean, industrial vibe.

He was also extremely tidy. Cleanliness is close to godliness when it comes to brewing. There are so many things that can taint a beer or make it go bad. Good brewers know that keeping fermenting tanks and wort chillers in tip-top shape ensures a high-quality craft beer. Garrett was no exception. Nitro's shiny steel tanks sparkled, due to our regimented cleaning schedule and the fact that they were still new. As did the cement floors that we mopped down every night.

I opened the front door and weaved through the bar. Garrett tended to be a late sleeper, so I wasn't surprised to find the brewery quiet. I left my coat and purse in the office and went to check the tanks. We had been perfecting a new beer that we would be debuting just in time for Oktoberfest—Cherry Weizen. Leavenworth's proximity to the lush organic orchards of the Yakima Valley meant that we had an abundance of scrumptious handpicked produce at our fingertips. For the Cherry Weizen, we had ordered flats of bright, tangy Washington Bing cherries. I removed a taster from the tank with a turkey baster. Then I siphoned the Weizen into a tasting glass and took a sip. The beer was a gorgeous amber color with a touch of pink.

I swirled the liquid on my tongue. The Weizen had a perfect balance. It wasn't too sweet or tart. The refreshing summer flavor of sun-ripened cherries came through without being overpowering. I could already picture tourists sipping a cold pint of the picnic-worthy brew on our front patio.

One of my favorite parts of the brewing process was seeing a beer come to life. After fermenting for weeks in our tanks, this beauty was ready to carbonate and tap. I had a feeling that it was going to be a hit and sell out fast. Garrett and I planned to keg the Cherry Weizen this morning. As long as everything went according to plan, it would be ready later this evening, and would be flowing out of our taps by the time the crowds descended for Oktoberfest.

In addition to the fruity wheat beer, we would be pouring our regular lineup of brews—our signature Pucker Up IPA; Bottle Blonde, a light summer ale; and Perk Me Up Porter, a chocolate coffee brew. Unlike Der Keller, Leavenworth's oldest and largest brewery, Garrett preferred Northwest-style beers. Der Keller was one of the featured brewers at Oktoberfest and would be showcasing their signature German beers, like Kölsch, Hefeweizen, Doppelbock, and Dunkel. My in-laws, Otto and Ursula Krause, had brought their native beers to Leavenworth when they immigrated to the United States. It happened to be at the same time that the town was going through a major rebranding. They'd jumped on board with the idea of creating a Bavarian village, and within a few years, Der Keller had become one of the largest producers of craft beers in the state.

Without the Krause family, I would probably have been waitressing or bartending somewhere—if I was lucky. I grew up in the foster care system, which meant that I never had permanent roots. My early and teen years were spent bouncing between homes. Some were kind and welcoming, and many were worse than being abandoned. Once I finished high school, I paid for community college by working at a farmers' market and waiting tables. A twist of fate changed my future when Otto and Ursula happened upon my farm stand one day. They were regulars at the market, coming each weekend to source local produce for their new brewery, Der Keller. We got to talking about baking, and Ursula's eyes lit up. She regaled me with tales of sweet twisted bread brushed with butter and hand-spun honey from her homeland. Their enthusiasm for baking, beer, and life was contagious. I began to bake test batches of cookies and cakes and ask for their feedback. Their bighearted personalities made me long for a family like theirs.

The Krauses offered me a job at the brewery and wanted to set me up with their oldest son, Mac. At first I declined, but they were relentless in their quest. Not that they were pushy. Rather, Ursula would take my hand and pierce my soul with her kind eyes. "Sloan, the brewing world, it is changing. It needs a woman's touch. You will be perfect. Tell her, Otto."

Otto was equally insistent. "*Ja,* it will be good. You have the nose. It is a gift that not many people have. I will teach you how to use it. You will become a legend. Sloan, the pretty female brewer with the super sniffer." His eyes twinkled when he spoke.

How could I resist? I dove into craft brewing with Otto and Ursula as my mentors. Then they introduced me to Mac. It didn't take long for him to charm me, or for me to end up pregnant. In hindsight, it might have been a mistake to marry him, but I didn't regret becoming an official member of the Krause family. For the first time in my life, I had a place and a home to call my own. Otto and Ursula taught me everything they knew about craft brewing, German-style baking, and how to be a parent. I couldn't imagine my life without them. Or without Alex, my teenage son, and Hans, my surrogate brother. Sometimes I wondered if I would have fallen so hard and so fast for Mac if it hadn't been for his family.

When I had caught Mac cheating with one of Der Keller's youngest barmaids a few weeks ago, I had thought my life was over. All the years we had spent together carving out a home, raising Alex, working side by side in the brewing— were they a waste? I blamed myself. I'd been too lonely and let my heart loose. Growing up alone had taught me to stay guarded and closed. But once I met the Krause family, they cracked me open. I never should have allowed myself to love them.

Mac's cheating hadn't just been the end of our marriage—I feared it might mean that I was going to have to give up the only family I had ever known. Not that Otto, Ursula, or Hans felt that way. In fact, Otto and Ursula had recently given me a huge stake in Der Keller. They were preparing to retire soon and wanted to begin stepping back a bit. However, they were concerned about leaving the company in Mac's capable but impulsive hands, so had outlined a deal that gave Mac, me, and Hans each an equal share of ownership. They both had insisted that I was like a daughter to them and that, no matter what transpired between me and Mac, I always had a place at Der Keller. I believed them, but I had been tossing and turning, trying to figure out what was next for me. Part of me wanted to sever ties with the brewery, but I couldn't do that to Otto and Ursula.

The sound of movement upstairs shook me from my thoughts.

Garrett was awake. Time to focus on brewing and shelve my worries about my personal life and future for the moment. A minute later, he appeared in the brewery looking bleary-eyed. "You're here early, per usual." He winked. "Please tell me we have coffee."

I glanced toward the bar. "I'm pretty sure we have a fresh bag of beans. You want me to make a pot?"

"Good God, yes." He ran his hands through his dark and disheveled hair and followed me into the front.

We kept an assortment of soft drinks along with coffee and tea at the bar for anyone who wasn't a beer fan and for designated drivers, who could drink unlimited nonalcoholic beverages on the house. I found the bag of beans in one of the cupboards beneath the bar and poured them into the coffee maker. The scent of nutty beans made Garrett inhale deeply.

"How late were you up?" I asked, filling the carafe with cold water.

He blinked twice and stretched. Garrett was tall and thin with a casual style typical of brewers in the Pacific Northwest. This morning he wore a pair of jeans and a light gray T-shirt that read TALK NERDY TO ME. He was the exact opposite of Mac in almost every way. Mac was shorter and stouter with ruddy cheeks and blond hair. He could talk to a stranger for hours and convince them into doing anything for him. Garrett, on the other hand, was quiet and almost pensive. He chose his words carefully and tended to listen rather than join in a conversation.

"I can't remember," he replied, brushing a strand of hair from his brown eyes that reminded me of warm sand. "Maybe around one thirty or two? I wasn't keeping track of time."

"Were you brewing?" Many pub owners, especially those who owned nano breweries like Nitro, would brew at midnight after last call.

"I was playing around with a couple small batches of a pumpkin ale, but I'm not really feeling it." Garrett leaned over the bar to catch a whiff of the brewing coffee. "That smells so good. Why does it have to take so long?"

I laughed and glanced at the pot. Dark coffee dripped slowly into the glass carafe. "It's been brewing for two minutes."

"Exactly." Garrett pulled out a barstool and sat. "What do you think of pumpkin? Is it too much? I know that it's a huge trend in Seattle and Portland right now. But do we want to be trend followers or trendsetters?"

"Good questions."

He sighed. "Yeah, and getting the balance right is going

to be tricky. The first batch I brewed was way too heavy. It looks like sludge in the carboy." The carboy that Garrett referred to was a five-gallon glass tank used in the secondary fermenting process when we tested small batches. We brewed our signature beer on a larger scale in the stainless steel tanks in the brewery, but when experimenting with new recipes, we used Garrett's old home brewing setup in the kitchen.

"I think the second one is going to be too weak," he continued. "You'll have to give them a try."

He was right about beer trends. Pumpkin had been hot for quite a few years, with brewers offering seasonal holiday pumpkin ales in time for Halloween and Thanksgiving. Even though it was only the end of September, we were already planning and preparing our holiday line. Craft beer took a minimum of two to three weeks to brew, which meant that we had to get started on our next batch as soon as we kegged the Cherry Weizen and cleaned the tanks.

"Hmm," I said, reaching for two coffee mugs. "Personally I'm not a huge pumpkin fan, but could we do something in its place? I think having a late fall seasonal would be good, and then we can release our winter ales in time for the Christmas markets."

Garrett massaged his temples. "Yeah, a fall beer that would pair well with turkey."

I thought about it for a minute while I grabbed cream, sugar, and a stirring spoon. The coffeepot was nearly full. I poured a splash of cream into the bottom of one of the glasses, hit the pause button on the machine, and poured a cup for Garrett.

He clutched the mug with both hands. I offered him the sugar. "No thanks. This is perfect. Thank you."

"No worries." I added a half teaspoon of sugar and a healthy glug of the cream and poured myself a cup. "What about cranberries?" I asked, stirring the latte-colored coffee. As of late, I had taken to adding cream to my coffee. I blamed it on Garrett's influence. He had insisted that a touch of cream and a hint of sugar made for a perfectly balanced cup.

"Cranberries?" Garrett wrinkled his forehead.

"Yeah, what if we do an IRA with fresh cranberries? They would give the beer a nice bite and probably a gorgeous red color." IRAs, or India Red Ales, are a great choice for beer drinkers who like a malty finish with a touch of hops. The popular Northwest-style ale pulls a ruby color and has a slight bitterness married with notes of caramel and toffee.

Garrett nursed his coffee. "I like it." He nodded. "Cranberries are very fallish, right? And they go well with turkey, yeah?"

"Right." I took a sip of the coffee and tried to think if anyone around had done a cranberry beer lately. Nothing came to mind. "Sour beers are super popular right now, so it could almost be a mash-up of an IRA meets a sour."

"Yeah, let's try it. Can you get your hands on some cranberries?"

"I've got a guy." I chuckled.

"Of course you do." Garrett grinned. "Sloan, you have 'a guy' for everything, don't you?"

"Call it the curse of living in Leavenworth forever," I kidded. Although there was truth behind my words. In a town this size, it was impossible to go through a day without bumping into a friend or neighbor at the grocery store or post office. Living somewhere where everyone knows your name has its perks, and also a unique set of drawbacks. Like the fact that everyone in town knew exactly what had gone down between Mac and me.

We mapped out our plan for the day over coffee. The first order of business was kegging the Cherry Weizen. Then we would clean the clarifying tanks. I agreed to hunt down some cranberries for our test beer. When working on a new recipe, we only brewed five-gallon batches. I was confident that the grocery store would have enough cranberries in stock for that. After that, I would finish the food for the tapping party, and we would open the tasting room by four. It sounded do-able, and like we had a full day ahead of us.

I finished off my coffee, happy to have the distraction of Nitro to keep me from my thoughts.

CHAPTER
TWO

KEGGING THE CHERRY WEIZEN DIDN'T take long. Unlike at Der Keller, where a team of brewers worked on state-of-the-art, automated equipment, at Nitro we were a two-person team, which meant that nearly everything we created was touched by our hands. Like our barrels. A barrel is the standard measurement for breweries. At Nitro we have a five-barrel system, tiny in comparison to the big guys. Each barrel consists of thirty-one gallons. A standard keg is a half of a barrel. So our entire system could produce one hundred and fifty-five gallons, or ten kegs at a time. Plenty of beer to serve thirsty customers, but nothing like Der Keller's massive brewing and bottling operations. Their beers were distributed throughout the Pacific Northwest, and even as far away as the East Coast. Whereas at Nitro, we weren't even producing enough yet to have our beers on guest taps around town.

We had devoted three barrels to the Cherry Weizen,

giving us a total of six kegs. That roughly translated into just under seven hundred and fifty pints, if my math was correct. It was a challenge to estimate how long six kegs might last. Hopefully they would last through all three weekends of Oktoberfest, but there was a good chance that we might run out sooner.

Garrett and I had spent hours trying to predict how much traffic the pub would get, but it was almost impossible to determine. First, we were brand-new. Second, we weren't an authentic German pub. And lastly, Nitro sat off Front Street, the main drag that would lead tourists to the Festhalle and Oktoberfest tents. Businesses along Front Street prepped for months in anticipation of the throngs of tourists who would pass by their shops. Since Nitro was slightly off the beaten path and wasn't a featured beer vendor, we might not be busy at all. Then again, with over twelve thousand people expected to descend on our fair city, there would likely be spillover and those looking to escape the crowds and the never-ending oompah music for a while. In the end, we had opted to brew a little extra, but not go overboard.

The main draw for the next three weekends would be Oktoberfest itself. The massive street party required a ticket for entry. Once inside the tented area, beer lovers would knock back authentic German brews as well as a variety of beers from throughout the Pacific Northwest. The celebration would last into the early morning hours each weekend night, with bands, dancing, schnitzel, strudel, and constantly flowing taps. It was no wonder that people came from near and far to be part of the celebration. I could feel anticipation beginning to build in me.

When we finished kegging the Cherry Weizen, Garrett pulled on knee-high waders and elbow-length rubber gloves. "I'm going in," he said with a goofy grin as he covered his eyes with a pair of plastic chemistry goggles. The brewery's sterile white walls and cement floors reminded me of a science lab. Shiny stainless steel tanks stretched into the twenty-five-foot-high ceilings, making the sanitation process challenging, to say the least. Garrett would have to climb up a tank's ladder to spray down the interior. Then he would open a hatch at the bottom of the tank and allow the water to drain directly into a trough that ran the length of the floor. For every hour we spent brewing, we would spend double the amount of time cleaning.

"I'll soak the hoses and paddles in iodine and then go see if I can score some cranberries. Do we need anything else for tonight?" If only April were here now. I'd like to show her the grimy process of scouring the tanks. No self-respecting brewer would take on the task in a tight skirt and heels. Actually, scratch that. April probably would.

Garrett shook his head. "We're set for food, right?"

"Right." I had already finished our special Oktoberfest menu. To accompany the Cherry Weizen, we were offering a fruit, meat, and cheese tray with pomegranate and honey goat cheese, a tangy farmer's cheese, and an Irish white cheddar, rustic three-grain bread, salami, three types of local cherries, apple and pear slices, and mixed nuts. Our fall soup was a hearty vegetable soup laden with onions, garlic, carrots, celery, peppers, sautéed Brussels sprouts, and broccoli. We would serve that with a thick slice of the rustic bread and pat of hand-churned butter. Lastly we would grill specialty sausages that had been soaking for days in our beer brine. For the brine, I had combined water, salt, peppercorns, thyme, garlic, onions, brown sugar, and our Bottle Blonde beer. After boiling it until the brown sugar dissolved and the liquid became almost clear, I poured it over sausages and stored them in an airtight container. The brine would infuse the sausages and give them a juicy finish— perfect for fall grilling.

"I'm good, then," Garrett said, giving me a salute as he began scrubbing the tank.

I left to fill industrial-sized buckets with a mixture of iodine and water. We used a food-grade iodine product to sanitize the hoses. The brewing gear would get a good cleanse in the buckets and be ready for our next round of cranberry beer. Once I finished, I grabbed my purse and headed for the grocery store.

As soon as I turned onto Front Street, a smile spread across my face. The village was bursting with activity. Red, yellow, and orange geraniums exploded from wooden kegs turned planter boxes. Banners and twinkle lights stretched from the rooftops to the gazebo. Shopkeepers were putting the finishing touches on their seasonal displays. The air smelled clean and fresh, and the mountainside was aglow with sunlight.

How could anyone want to live anywhere but here? I thought to myself as I waved to the deli owner, who was stringing cured sausages together by hand.

I continued on to the grocery store, passing the park, where rows of bright white tents stood ready to house face painters and ice cream stands. Like everything else in Leavenworth, even the grocery store was designed to look like a German farmhouse. The front of the store had huge displays of Oktoberfest T-shirts, plastic beer steins, and green felt hats. Along with aspirin, Tums, and ginger ale—everything a partygoer might need to cure a hangover.

I chuckled to myself and made my way to the produce section. There were plenty of pumpkins and other fall gourds in wicker baskets, but no sign of cranberries. It must be too early in the season. I checked every row without any luck. I was about to give up when a young clerk walked past me. He was a few years older than Alex and a senior at the local high school.

"Hey, Jack, you don't happen to have any cranberries, by chance?" I asked.

"Hi, Mrs. Krause. How's Alex?"

"Good." I tried to ignore that he had called me Mrs. Krause. "He's in Seattle for the weekend."

"Cool. Yeah, I heard about that. Good weekend to be gone. You want me to go check the back for cranberries? I think I saw some earlier." He pointed to the employee area in the back.

"That would be great," I said with a smile and a sense of relief. Testing the recipe would take a few days, and I didn't want to have to wait to get cranberries shipped in from Seattle. On that note, I wondered if I should go ahead and put in a bigger order once I got back to Nitro. With the craziness of Oktoberfest, there was a good chance that the supply trucks would be loaded to the max. I made a mental note to call our supplier.

I wandered around the produce section, stopping to

admire the rosy red Washington apples and juicy fresh pears. Fall was most definitely the season of abundance here in the North Cascades. I was about to weigh a bunch of apples, figuring we could always use more and dreaming up an idea for an apple pie–inspired beer on the spot, but the sound of April's voice stopped me in my tracks. She was one aisle over, but her nasal voice carried so loudly that I was sure everyone in the store could hear her conversation.

"Now, everyone, if you will follow me, I'd love to show you a *vonderful* pastoral mural over this way. We had it commissioned by a famous German artist, who we flew in from Berlin. That's the level of commitment everyone in town has to ensuring that no detail goes untouched when it comes to authenticity."

I glanced to my left. The mural April had referenced was behind me. It depicted a quaint countryside farmers' market with bountiful produce, children dancing around a Maypole, and overflowing kegs. I agreed with April that the painting was lovely, but if memory served me correctly, it had been done by a local high school student as part of his senior project. Then again, I wouldn't have put it past April to lie about the mural's origin.

Before I had a chance to hide or duck into the next aisle, April and a group of people, who I assumed must be the film crew, given the fact that one of them held a portable camera and another a tablet, rounded the corner and ran straight into me.

"Oh, Sloan. What are you doing here?" April's face held a plastic smile, but her tone made it clear that she was less than pleased to see me. She had managed to embellish her ridiculous outfit even more since I'd seen her earlier. In addition to her skimpy barmaid costume, she wore a silky sash and a lacy white maid's cap.

"Shopping." I held up my empty basket.

She widened her smile, revealing a lipstick stain on her front teeth. "Now, I know that I mentioned earlier that everyone in our village embraces traditional German attire." She addressed the group. "Sloan is no exception. I'm sure you'll be changing later." She gave me a hard look. "Sloan is a brewer, and when she's working in the . . . warts or something?"

"Wort," I replied.

"Right. When she's working in that, she breaks the rules and wears this." April waved her hand across my jeans and yellow rubber boots.

Breaking the rules? The last time I checked there was no dress code for Leavenworth residents.

The only woman in the group, who looked to be about my age, clicked a tablet under her arm and stared at me. "You're a brewer?"

I nodded. "Yep."

April cleared her throat. "Well, Sloan has worked at Der Keller, where I'm taking you next, for many years. It's only been recently that she's struck out on her own and started working at a nanobrewery." She said the word "nanobrewery" in a hushed whisper.

The woman made a note on her tablet and then tucked it under her arm again. She extended her hand. "Payton Smith. I'm directing a documentary about beer, and I'd love to find some time to come watch you in action. We could do an entire angle about women in beer," she said, turning to an older man with thinning salt-and-pepper hair. "What do you think, David?"

He nodded. "I like it. It's a good hook to draw in a female demographic. That could help pull in some new interest." He wore an expensive gray suit, with a T-shirt underneath. The T-shirt reminded me of one of Alex's Superman comics.

April seethed. She dug her fake nails into the folds of her gingham skirt and forced a grin. "I must warn you that Nitro is not a German pub."

"But I thought you said that every business in town had to adhere to Bavarian design aesthetics," Payton noted. Her hair was cut in an angular bob and held back behind her ears with a pair of dark sunglasses.

"Yes, yes. That's true. We've been diligent in our efforts to ensure that any storefront—whether it's a chain like Starbucks or a small mom-and-pop shop—is in line with our standards. However there is some leeway in terms of what business owners choose to do with their interiors. I assure you that the vast majority of businesses have fully embraced our Bavarian culture, but there are a few stragglers who have been slower to adopt it." She glared at me.

"I don't think that matters. We want to document the entire beer process, and having a female brewer in town is fantastic," Payton said with a smile. She reached into an expensive leather purse hanging from her shoulder, removed a business card, and pressed it into my hand. "Give me a call, and let's set up a time to get together. We'll be here filming for the next three weeks. We have big plans for this project.

I'm already working on advanced screenings at Sundance, LA film fest, SOHO, Toronto International, South by Southwest, just to name a few. It's a huge undertaking and a ton of money, but we know the return on investment will be worth it. This is beer, after all. David and I are sure that Netflix or Hulu—one of the major players—is going to pick up the film. We're also considering rolling out a variety of screenings at breweries throughout the country."

I studied the cream-colored card. Payton's name and the word "filmmaker," along with her phone number, were embossed in gold. "Wow. That does sound like a big project. You're more than welcome to come by later this afternoon. We're tapping our newest beer, Cherry Weizen, and having a kickoff party."

Payton nodded enthusiastically. "Great. What do you think, David?"

"Cherry Weizen sounds good to me." He winked. "Not to mention having a lovely female brewer in the mix."

The younger guy, who had been balancing a camera on his shoulder the entire time we had been talking, shifted the camera and spoke up. "I'm Connor, by the way. Sorry to interrupt, but I had a cherry wheat beer once that was killer. Is a Cherry Weizen the same?"

I nodded. "Yes, Weizens refer to wheat beers. Some brewers opt to add berries or citrus to bring out the naturally sweet aromas in their Weizens, while others rely on different varieties of hops like the classic Hallertau Mittelfruh, used in German Weizens. It's a style that originated in south Germany. Traditionally they're unfiltered, giving the beer a cloudy appearance."

"Like a Hefeweizen?" he asked.

"Exactly. Think hazy." I glanced around the neat bushels of produce and pointed to a bunch of lemons. "Like the color of those lemons and served in a Weizen glass. You know the tall glasses with a narrow base and curvature?"

Connor nodded and angled his camera at my face.

I stepped back. "Anyway, the curved lip at the top of a Weizen glass helps trap the foamy head and allows you to really experience the aroma of a wheat beer."

"Okay we have to have you in this film," Payton said. She turned to David, the old gentlemen, who had picked up a lemon and was examining it. "I mean, we have to have her, right?"

He nodded and smoothed his charcoal gray suit. It was odd to see someone wearing a suit in Leavenworth, and even more strange that he wore it with a T-shirt.

At that moment, a younger man probably in his midthirties, wearing a pair of plaid shorts, a green felt hat with a ten-inch black feather, a crisp white shirt, and suspenders, burst around the aisle. "Hey! You aren't filming without me? Are you?" At first I thought he was kidding, but he lunged at Connor like he was going to hit him.

Connor almost dropped the camera. He muttered something I couldn't decipher and turned the camera on the man.

April swept forward. "Oh, Mitchell. Never." She batted her fake eyelashes. "I was simply introducing your crew to one of our—uh." She paused to give me another look of disapproval. "Local brewers, Sloan Krause."

Mitchell tipped his hat. "Great. I'll get you an autograph later, but for the moment we have B-roll to shoot." He ripped open a package of Band-Aids and plastered three of them over a nasty wound on his right forearm. "I leave for two seconds, and you start shooting. Connor, what the hell, man? I told you that you never shoot without the talent on set. Understood?"

Connor gulped. I noticed sweat beginning to form on the back of his T-shirt.

April reached out to touch Mitchell's arm. "Oh dear, are you hurt? We can't have our big star getting hurt here in our darling village. That just won't do."

Mitchell tossed the box of opened bandages at David. "Put that on your tab, old man." Then he flicked his suspenders, ignoring April, and motioned to the camera. "What's the angle, Payton? Why are we shooting in a freaking grocery store? And how many times do I have to tell you to fire this idiot?" He flicked Connor on the chest. "Does no one around here understand how this process is supposed to go? That camera can't be on if I'm not in the shot."

Payton and David shared a looked of frustration.

David's face remained passive, yet I noticed the tips of his fingers turn white as he pressed his hands together. "Enough. We're not shooting, Mitchell. We were just chatting with Sloan and learning about her brewing process."

"Why does the kid have his camera out, then?" Mitchell pointed to Connor, who lowered the camera. "I can't stand working with amateurs. You want to get this screened at Sundance, Payton—ha! Good luck with that."

What was the deal with this guy?

"When is the keg tapping?" Payton asked, turning to me and ignoring Mitchell.

"Tonight," I replied, wishing I could make a smooth exit.

"We'll be there. We'll absolutely be there. A female brewer. Wow. I couldn't have scripted this." She noted something on her tablet. Her sunglasses fell. She grabbed them with one hand and then tucked them into her purse.

April cleared her throat. "I don't know about that." She made a clucking sound. "We have a full afternoon ahead of us. As they say in Germany, we'll be '*beschäftigt*'—or 'busy' in our tongue. I'll be personally introducing Payton and David to each business owner in town. We're heading to Der Keller for a brewery tour and then Mitchell is going to shoot teasers throughout Front Street and in the tents."

"No worries," I said. "We're not going anywhere. Cherry Weizen will be on tap as long as it lasts."

Jack, the grocery clerk, appeared with three bags of cranberries. "Sorry it took me so long, Mrs. Krause," he apologized, handing me the berries.

I cringed at hearing my married name. "Thanks. I'm just glad you had them." I placed the berries in my basket. "Nice meeting you," I said to the film crew. "Hopefully we'll see you at Nitro while you're here."

Payton pointed to her business card. "Call me—please. Let's set something up. If you don't call soon, I'll hound you. They call me the Bulldog in LA. I get what I want, and I want you on camera. No, I need you on camera. This production is my baby, and I am committed to doing whatever it takes to make it an award winner. Having a female brewer could just be the frothy finish I've been looking for."

April pounded on her chocolate brown wristwatch. It was made of plastic with doves circling the face and two keg barrels hanging from a short chain. "Really, we must be on our way. I'm sure the next time we see you, you'll be dressed for the part." She gave me a hard stare before smiling broadly and nudging Payton, David, Mitchell, and Connor toward the front door.

I headed to checkout. I was eager to get back to Nitro to play around with a cranberry ale and to tell Garrett about the film crew. As a small start-up, we needed any publicity we could get, and it was all the better that April hated the idea.

CHAPTER

THREE

THE REST OF THE AFTERNOON breezed by. We opened the windows and let the crisp fall air mingle in with the smell of boiling grains and simmering cranberries. I appreciated that Garrett didn't feel the need to talk incessantly as we worked. He was as wrapped up as I was in watching the grain and documenting the process. His background in engineering was evident throughout the brewery, from the chemistry charts on the walls to his methodical approach to testing a new recipe. He created spreadsheets and was diligent in charting every step. We kept extensive notes about when we added the hops, the ratio of yeast to grain, and how long we boiled the wort.

We used all-natural ingredients and grains—barley, malt, oats, wheat, and rye—in our product. One of the many challenges facing smaller craft brewers was access to grains and hops. Big brewers often bought up hop varietals for decades at a time and stockpiled grains. Then they would turn around and use corn as filler. Craft beer geeks like Garrett and his home brew club were convinced the practice was a conspiracy to push cheaper-to-produce beer on the masses through unrelenting marketing campaigns.

Brewing on his home brew system was a completely different experience than working on the big equipment. It was much more hands-on. I liked getting to sauté the cranberries on the stove, adding in a splash of fresh lemon juice and a hint of sugar. I didn't even mind when I spilled spent grains on my boots or the fact that my ponytail was damp. There was something so satisfying about touching each step in the process. By midday we had finished five test batches, which were lined up and labeled in five-gallon carboys on the kitchen counter.

"One of these has to be a hit, right?" Garrett pushed his goggles up on his forehead and dabbed his brow with a napkin.

"Definitely," I assured him. I was confident that more than one of our test batches would be worthy of brewing on a larger scale.

"Fingers crossed." He glanced at the clock on the wall. "Do you need help with food prep?"

I mentally reviewed what needed to be done. The sausages had been soaking in the beer brine for two days. I needed to make the vegetable soup and arrange some fruit and cheese platters, which shouldn't take more than an hour. I shook my head. "No, I think I'm good."

"Okay. If you're sure, I'm going to go take a shower and change." Garrett tugged at his shirt, which was damp from the heat of the kitchen. "Then I'll get everything set up in the bar."

"Sounds good." I breathed in. The kitchen smelled like Christmas. "Won't it be great if the film crew comes by for the tapping?"

Garrett pulled the goggles from his head and tossed them on the far counter. The industrial kitchen with its stainless steel countertops and oversized fridge had served thousands of guests when Garrett's aunt ran her diner and bed-and-breakfast from the space. Technically Nitro didn't need a kitchen this size, but I was glad that Garrett had opted to keep it. It made food prep much easier and meant that if we ever wanted to expand and hire a professional chef, we had the room to do so. "I can't even think about having a film crew on-site. That would be amazing. My old home brew club in Seattle would lose their minds." He ran his hands through his hair. "Imagine a geeky home brewer TV star, huh?" His eyes twinkled playfully.

"Hey, you never know. They sounded pretty interested." I wished I had talked more about our brewing philosophy and about the differences between breweries our size versus the big guys like Der Keller.

"Fingers crossed." Garrett looped his fingers together and headed upstairs.

I shifted gears from brewing to cooking. For the soup I started by chopping garlic, celery, onions, carrots, and peppers. I tossed them into a sauté pan along with a huge glug of olive oil and turned the heat on low. While the veggies sweated on the stove, I cut Brussels sprouts in half and trimmed broccoli. Instead of simmering them in vegetable stock, I planned to grill them to a nice char. I would add them at the very end so that they stayed slightly crunchy. Almost like cooking pasta al dente. The blackened char should give the soup a nice hearty flavor. Often I would make soup in the morning and let the flavors mingle for the day, but since the star of this soup was the vegetables, I wanted them to maintain a slight crisp to give the dish a unique texture.

Soon the brewery smells were overpowered by the earthy scent of the veggies. I dumped the sauté into a soup pan and poured in veggie stock that I had made earlier. Next I added in fresh herbs—parsley, sage, thyme, and just a hint of rosemary. I finished the soup with a healthy shake of salt and pepper, and placed a lid over the top of the pot. With the soup bubbling, I grabbed a stack of plastic plates and began putting together colorful fruit platters. Food can really enhance the experience of tasting a beer, and I was excited for our customers to get an opportunity to see what flavors they might pull out of our Cherry Weizen when they sipped it after eating a slice of sharp cheddar versus a sweet pear.

Cooking had been an escape for me during my years spent hopping from foster home to foster home. Sometimes I wanted to pinch myself. It was hard to remember that life, and yet without experiencing loss and lack of connection in my early years, I might not have ended up in Leavenworth. Regardless of some of my past trauma and my current situation with Mac, I wouldn't have changed a thing. Cooking also made me think of Alex. No matter what transpired with Mac and me, we would always share our son. Alex was the best thing that had ever happened to me. I would do anything to make sure that he knew that he was well loved and stable, even if that meant having to suck it up when Mac was around.

I concentrated on arranging bright, organic fruits onto trays. Alex was on a field trip with his leadership class. Leavenworth schools tended to plan activities and outings around peak times like this weekend. The conference was in Seattle, and his teacher, along with a handful of chaperones, planned to show the team the sights for the weekend. They were taking a tour of the Space Needle, visiting museums, and shopping at Pike Place Market. I was glad that Alex could have a getaway with his friends, but the thought of not having him for an entire weekend made me almost teary.

Once the food was complete, I headed for the office to grab a new shirt and change out of my rubber boots. If the film crew did show up, April was going to be sorely disappointed that I hadn't heeded her warning to don a German costume. Instead I tugged off my boots and replaced them with a cute pair of wedge sandals. I took the shirt to the bathroom to change and to spruce up my appearance. The constant heat and steam from brewing and cooking had left my face dewy and my ponytail frizzy.

I untied my hair, which fell to my shoulders. When Mac and I were together, we always looked like a mismatched couple, with my dark hair and olive skin and his strong German ancestry, light hair, and pinkish skin tones. Since I'd never known my birth parents, I had to guess at my heritage. A foster mom had once told me that she was sure I was Greek. It would fit with my angular cheekbones and full lips.

Although Greeks aren't exactly known for their microbrews. Maybe at some point, I would have to make the trek to the isles and survey the beer scene.

While I brushed my hair and added a hint of blush to my cheeks, I imagined strolling along sandy beaches next to azure seas with a cold pint and Garrett by my side.

Stop it, Sloan, I scolded myself. Where had that come from?

My life these days was a roller coaster. The last thing I needed was to be daydreaming about my new boss.

I fastened my hair into a high ponytail, applied a shimmery lip gloss, and dusted my lids with a silver shadow that brought out the golden tints in my eyes. Then I pulled on a Nitro T-shirt. In keeping with Garrett's science theme, our staff shirts were black with white lettering. Our slogan, EVERYTHING'S BETTER ON NITRO, was written across the front. The motto was a play on the beer trend of adding nitrogen to a pint. A beer served "on nitro" has tiny bubbles, which makes it much smoother and creamier than traditional CO_2 beers. On the back of the shirt there was a retro logo in the shape of an atomic symbol, except the electrons had been replaced by hops. And the words of our other motto: NITRO— WHERE SCIENCE MEETS BEER. I liked the simplicity of the design and the fact that I could wear a T-shirt and jeans to work every day.

At Der Keller the entire serving staff dressed in German attire, barmaid dresses, lederhosen, suspenders, knee-high socks, and green felt hats. None of the Krause family wore the pub uniform. When Mac was in a working-out phase, he usually wore skin-tight T-shirts to show off his pectoral muscles. Thankfully Otto and Ursula had never asked me to don a frilly skirt. One of the perks of working in the brewery was avoiding having to look like April Ablin.

I stuffed my clothes and toiletries into my bag and gave myself one final glance in the mirror. I wanted to look put together for filming. My face had a nice, healthy glow, and tying my hair back accentuated my jawline. Wearing makeup and jewelry wasn't really my style. Probably in part because I didn't own anything when I was growing up. I never knew when my social worker would arrive on the doorstep of one of my foster homes to take me to a new home. I learned to travel light and not get attached to anything around me. While it made for a lonely childhood, it had also made me anything but a pack rat as an adult.

Pleased that at least I didn't look like I had been brewing all day, I grabbed my bag and stored it in the office. The sound of voices in the bar surprised me. We weren't due to open for another twenty minutes. I wondered if Garrett had opened the doors early.

When I made it to the bar, I was even more surprised to see Otto, Ursula, and Hans, Mac's younger brother, chatting happily with Garrett while he poured them each a pint. It was good to see Ursula out. She had fallen a few weeks ago and broken her hip. After surgery she had been on bed rest and had just recently been given the green light to start moving a bit.

"Ursula, you're here." I hurried over and wrapped her in a hug.

She barely came to my shoulder on a good day. With her injury she was using a cane, which made her posture slump. "Sloan, you look lovely." She returned my embrace.

37

"You should sit," I said, pointing to a table near the window. I couldn't imagine her trying to climb on a barstool.

"Exactly what I just told her," Hans said, nudging his mother's waist. "You go sit with Sloan. Papa and I will bring you your beer."

Otto's cheery face brightened as he watched me loop my arm through Ursula's and help her to the table. "Zat is our girl. Thank you, Sloan."

Ursula was steady on her feet and using the cane as if it were another appendage. "Wow, you've really got the hang of that," I said.

She beamed with pride. "*Ja,* I know. Ze doctor said I am ze best patient he has seen. I told him it was because of our beer."

I pulled out a chair for her and noticed a brief grimace as she sat. "Are you still in pain?"

"No, no. I'm fine." She patted the seat next to her. "Sit. Tell me how everything is going. Are you ready for the fest?"

I followed her advice and sat in the chair next to her, careful not to bump her injured hip. She didn't look like a woman who had undergone surgery. Her cheeks were warm with color, and her eyes bright. She wore a straight black skirt, sturdy ankle boots, and a hand-knit sweater the color of snow. It matched her hair and made her skin look as if it had been kissed by the sun. Ursula was the model of a German grandmother, not just in appearance but in her easygoing attitude and welcoming personality. It was nearly impossible to feel stressed in her presence. I could feel my shoulders relax and my breathing steady.

"Garrett let you in early, I see. How did you manage to get such special treatment?" I grinned. "Did you threaten him with your cane?"

She turned to the bar, where the three men were dissecting glasses of beer. Garrett pointed to striated layers in a foamy pint of dark chocolate stout. Otto dipped his pinky into the frothy head, and Hans savored a taste from another glass. "Beer. It brings everyone together. Garrett asked Otto if we might come by for a taste. As I'm sure you know, Garrett wanted to collaborate, but we couldn't ziz time because of my surgery. But Otto has promised him zat we will soon."

Ursula's sentiment was common in the craft brewing community. People often wrongly assumed that brewers were competitive. Sure, there were a handful of brewers who were competitive, but for the most part, brewers supported one another. The Krauses were famous for their fierce loyalty to the industry and burgeoning brewers. They supplied smaller brewers, like Nitro, with extra hops and grain, spent countless hours mentoring new brewers, and were continually willing to try new collaborations and partnerships. They believed that promoting the craft benefited everyone.

The brewing process is creative. Much like other artists—painters or chefs—collaborating with each other allowed brewers to share new ideas, flavor profiles, and techniques. Some of Der Keller's mash-ups had been such huge hits that they became regular offerings. It was yet another thing that I appreciated about our industry. It was about community, not competition.

"I hadn't heard that," I said.

"It will be good, I think," she replied, taking another glance at the bar. "I'm worried about Hans. I think maybe it is too much for him with Mac right now."

Mac and Hans were very different. Hans liked to work with his hands and do things behind the scenes. While he loved his family and the business, brewing wasn't his calling. He preferred woodwork and tinkering with the brewery equipment. Whereas Mac never shied away from the spotlight. He could almost always be found schmoozing customers and sampling the product in the front of the house. Otto and Ursula's restructuring plan for Der Keller had given Mac, Hans, and me equal shares of the company. We had been meeting more often than I enjoyed to discuss the brewery's future. Mac wanted to take over as general manager, but Hans had resisted the idea. I knew that Hans didn't want the responsibility of managing operations either. If anything, he probably would have been happiest to continue to pop in to check on the equipment and fix the occasional leak in the roof. However Hans, like me, knew that giving Mac total control of Der Keller could spell disaster.

Mac would never intentionally do anything to bring down the empire his parents had built from the ground up, but his tendency to leap in before doing any research and his need for attention and adoration could be Der Keller's undoing. Most recently he had invested in hop farms sight unseen. It had turned out to be a scam. The hops were nonexistent. If it hadn't been for Otto and Ursula's intervention, Mac's mistake could have bankrupted the company.

"What's going on?" I asked Ursula, keeping my voice low.

She met my gaze. "I think zat the pressure it is too much

for Hans. He has his furniture business to take care of, but he has been at ze brewery every day."

"He has?" I hadn't heard that. Then again, I'd been trying to make myself scarce. Mac and I weren't exactly on the best of terms at the moment. Hans had had to mediate our group meetings. I felt terrible putting him in the middle, but I was in no place to negotiate Der Keller's future with Mac when I had no idea what was happening with my own future. The one thing I did know was that I wasn't going to take on a bigger role at the brewery. I couldn't work with Mac—not now. Maybe never. Coming to Nitro had been the best thing for my mental state, and I enjoyed the smallness of our operation.

"*Ja*." Ursula folded her hands on the table. "It is okay, but it is not what he wants. You know?"

I nodded.

"What about you, Sloan? Have you thought about what you want? We have been worried about you, too."

That was a question that required more thought than I could give at the moment. "No," I sighed. "I mean I'm committed to Der Keller, and I promise I will help however I can, but I can't commit to being there every day. I'm happy here, and I have to do this for myself."

She reached over and put her hand over mine. Her palm was warm and the back of her hand was dotted with age spots. "It is okay. Otto and I understand. We want you to be happy, and we want you to know that you always have a home at Der Keller."

"Thank you." I squeezed her hand. "I know that." I could feel tears starting to well and fought them back.

"Mac will figure ziz out," Ursula said with a confidence that I didn't share. "He has gone through a midlife crisis, but he loves you and Alex. He knows his mistakes, and he will keep trying, I know."

I wasn't sure how to respond. Mac was her son. Of course she would defend him.

"Now, you know, I do not approve of his choices," she said, making me wonder if she had read my mind. "He must make many changes. We have told him ziz."

Cheating on me with a twenty-three-year-old barmaid called for more than "changes" in my opinion.

"I think it is my fault," Ursula continued.

"Your fault?" Otto and Ursula were the best parents I had ever met. They loved their boys and openly expressed their affection. Mac and Hans's childhood centered around the brewing community. They were fixtures at the pub and doted on by customers, staff, and vendors. Sunday dinners with the Krauses were filled with lively banter and platters of Ursula's homemade stews and German pastries. Otto and Ursula's love for their boys came through in everything they touched. How could Ursula think Mac's indiscretions were her fault?

"Ja." She looked to Hans briefly, then back to me. "We put everything into Der Keller. Maybe we should have paid more attention to ze boys."

"What?" My voice rose. Hans turned in our direction and gave me a funny look. I spoke in a more reserved tone. "No way. You and Otto are amazing. You did everything for your boys, and they know that."

She smiled, but her eyes held a sadness. "Maybe."

Hans and Otto joined us with three pints of beer. "Sorry, I didn't bring you one, Sloan," Hans said, sliding a pint of our Pucker Up IPA in front of him. "I thought you were probably serving tonight."

"Yep. I'm on the clock," I replied.

I caught a faint whiff of sawdust when he sat next to me. He looked much more like a carpenter than a brewer in his Carhartt pants and flannel shirt. "That's what I thought." He passed around tasters of the Cherry Weizen. "Contraband. Shhhh. Don't tell. Garrett hooked us up with an early taste."

"You'll have to let me know what you think," I said.

Ursula and Otto held their tasting glasses up to the light in unison. *Once a brewer, always a brewer,* I thought to myself.

"Ze color it is wonderful," Otto said.

While they tasted our new creation, Hans leaned closer. "Hey, I know you're busy, Sloan. It's going to be crazy with Oktoberfest, but I'm hoping we can find a few minutes to chat."

"About your brother?" I whispered.

Hans nodded, then his gaze drifted to the front window. I followed his eyes. My stomach lurched as Mac's sturdy frame passed in front of the window. What the hell was he doing here?

CHAPTER
FOUR

MAC BREEZED IN AS IF he owned the place. His polo shirt was one size too tight. I knew that he wore his shirts intentionally small to show off his muscles, but by the looks of his slightly sagging belly, he might need to reconsider. I couldn't be sure, but it almost looked like he had bleached his naturally blond hair. The tips of his short cut appeared frosted. Classic. Had he been tanning, too?

He and Garrett were far from friends, but Garrett took it in stride when Mac marched up to the bar and demanded a pint. Hans stiffened next to me.

I noticed Otto and Ursula exchanging a look. Mac took a swig of his beer and said something under his breath to Garrett before joining us at the table.

"No one invited me to the party, I see," he teased, yet there was an edge to his voice.

Ursula patted the empty seat next to her. She didn't need

to say anything. Her stern expression was warning enough. Mac sat and dropped the attitude, at least for the moment.

"This isn't bad," he said to me. "It's got a decent cherry flavor."

Otto waved both of his hands at Mac. "No, zis is wonderful. It is most excellent, Sloan." He gave me a nod of approval and scowled at Mac.

Mac changed the subject. "Have you heard the news?"

I braced myself. Mac was always scheming and making outlandish plans that he never followed through on.

"What news?" Hans tapped a weathered hand on the rim of his pint glass and stared at Mac with a weary frown.

"There's a big movie crew in town," Mac said with a touch of smugness. He liked being in the know. "They're filming a documentary about beer."

"*Ja*," Ursula broke in and stole Mac's thunder. "Zey stopped by Der Keller earlier. It will be good for Leavenworth and for our beers."

Otto held his cherry Weizen up in a toast. "Prost, to Der Keller and Nitro! A film about German beers and our town is nothing we could have expected when we came here so many years ago. True, Ursula?"

Ursula smiled. "True."

We all clinked our glasses. I was about to head to the bar to check in with Garrett. The doors were due to open any minute, and I wanted to be ready. Not to mention any excuse that took me away from Mac was welcome. As I pushed my chair back, the film crew arrived. Payton led the pack with her tablet and tight smile.

"Are we too early?" She paused with the door halfway open. Her leather purse hung over one arm.

"No, come on in." I motioned for them to step inside.

Payton held the door for David, Connor, and Mitchell. Then she looked from Otto and Ursula to me and then Garrett behind the bar. "You're here together?" she said with surprise. "How provincial. Leavenworth's brewers gathered together. To what? To discuss strategy for Oktoberfest? To assess the competition?" She nudged Connor. "Get the camera out. Let's shoot this. This is exactly the vibe I want to capture. The real-world view of brewing and what happens behind the scenes."

Mitchell sprang in front of our table. He yanked a forest green felt hat from his back pocket and stuck it on his head. The oversized black feather on the top of the hat flapped. It made him look like an ostrich. He rolled up the sleeves of his crisp white dress shirt, as if intentionally trying to look casual.

"Don't worry, Payton, I've got this." He snapped his fingers and shot his index finger at the camera. "Get this side, Connor. Keep up. How many times have I had to tell you that you have to be ready on the fly? That camera should always be on. Am I right, Payton? David? Anyone? I swear this production is a flipping joke. You would be laughed out of LA. Why did you hire this kid? What is he, like, twelve?"

Connor looked at his feet.

"That's an ironic statement coming from you," David said, giving Mitchell a hard look.

Ursula caught my eye. I shrugged.

Mitchell snapped both of his fingers. "We're losing the moment. Let's go! Let's do this, people."

Connor managed to set up the camera and focus it on us. I hadn't expected that we would be filming without any notice. What were we supposed to do? I didn't need to worry because Mitchell stepped in front of our table and launched into a spontaneous introduction.

"Mitchell Morgan coming at you from Beervaria, folks. That's right. We're here in the beer capital of the world to celebrate Oktoberfest America style. Break out your lederhosen and polish your pint glasses because the kegs are flowing and the vibe is off the hook!" He paused and pointed to his cap. "I'm ready to take you on a tasting tour that will make Munich envious, and it starts tonight at a nanobrewery that is knocking it out of the park every time."

Hans kicked me under the table.

Payton clapped one hand on her tablet. "Cut. Mitchell, what are you doing? You're totally off the wall. I want this to feel authentic, not scripted. This is a documentary. We're supposed to be storytellers—telling the truth. Our key demographic isn't college kids. We're going for the craft and the people behind it."

Mitchell ignored her and cleared his throat. "David, do you want to jump in here, old man? No? I didn't think so. Just stand there and say nothing like always. Good plan. Good plan."

David looked uncomfortable. He stuffed his hands in his suit jacket pockets.

"Listen, honey." Mitchell addressed Payton. "I understand you're new to the world of Hollywood, but I am the *talent*, and if the *talent* wants to go off script, then the talent will go off script. Capiche?"

Payton's upper lip disappeared.

David stepped forward. "Mitchell, why don't you take a minute? I don't think we've mapped out our plan for this location yet."

"Amateurs. Freaking amateurs." Mitchell yanked the feathered cap from his head and slammed it on the ground. He took a half swing at Connor, who had reached down to pick up the cap. "Leave it, kid."

Connor flinched and dropped the hat.

Mitchell kept his eyes focused on David. "I'll take a moment. You bet I'll take a moment. I'll go give my agent a call. I'm out in the middle of God knows where, and you people don't even have your shit together. I was told I would have a car waiting at the train station. I was told that I would have a top-of-the-line, luxurious rental property, and let me tell you, the place that woman Lisa took me to earlier is a crap hole. I told her to find me something new by tonight or I'm out of here."

David tried to interject, but Mitchell was on a roll. "Now this. We show up on location without a plan, and I do what I do best—improvise—and I'm shot down for that? This is what you hired me for. Total crap. There's not enough beer in this godforsaken place to keep me here." He grabbed his felt cap from the floor and stormed out the front door.

Leavenworth was definitely a bit off the beaten path, but a godforsaken place? Hardly. I wondered if the Lisa he had referenced was Lisa Balmes of Balmes Vacation Properties. She and her mother ran a property management company

49

in town and were known for their incredible eye for detail and personal touches, like leaving aromatic bags of locally roasted coffee, fresh flower arrangements, and a basket of German pastries at each rental. Their properties were high-end with mountain views, jetted tubs, luxurious linens, and all the travel essentials. If a guest happened to forget toothpaste or lotion, they could rest assured that Lisa and her mom, Chris, who co-owned the company, would have already thought of it or would hand deliver it. In addition to managing the rental properties, the two made sure that everyone who arrived in Leavenworth was treated like family. They arranged rafting trips on the Wenatchee River and wine tasting outings in the valley. I couldn't imagine that any of their properties would be unsuitable.

David tried to make a joke. "Talent. What can you do?" He offered a sheepish shrug.

"Is this a joke?" Hans whispered in my ear.

"Right?" I mouthed back.

Payton tapped on her tablet with her index finger. "David, you can either get him under control, or you can fire him."

Ursula reached for her cane. "I think we should be going." Otto helped her stand.

"No, wait, please," Payton pleaded. "I'd love to get a shot of you both here while they're tapping the keg. It's such a lovely sentiment that brewers rally around each other. That's not common in other lines of work, and I really want to capture that on film."

Ursula hesitated. I knew that she was as uncomfortable as I was.

"If you want, I can just film them without Mitchell's commentary," Connor offered.

Payton looked to David for approval. He shrugged. She gave a thumbs-up with her free hand. Then she set her purse on the table and reached inside. She pulled out a pill bottle and popped a few pills into her mouth. "Sorry. I have a pounding headache, thanks to Mitchell."

She scrolled through her tablet. "Okay, here's what I'm thinking. Let's just keep it casual. Go about your normal business and forget that we're here. What would you be doing now?"

Mac seized the opportunity. He got to his feet and proceeded to launch into a brief dissertation about Leavenworth's brewing past. Leave it to him to use the opportunity to step into the spotlight. His ruddy cheeks beamed with pride. A touch of a German accent that he didn't have worked its way into his speech. Payton nodded enthusiastically as he embellished his parents' history, claiming that they fled Germany in fear of religious persecution. That wasn't true. The Krauses loved Germany. They left when their sons were young in search of adventure, and because their hometown was saturated with pubs. They landed in Leavenworth due to its similarity to their beloved Alps. It wasn't until they were here for a few years that they realized the region was a prime location for a burgeoning beer community.

Neither of them corrected Mac. Hans kicked me under the table. I didn't dare look at him. Not with Connor's camera angled straight at us. I had a feeling the Krauses were remaining silent was because they too had grown leery of the documentary.

When Mac finished his exaggerated tale, Payton made another note on her tablet. "Perfect. That is exactly what we're looking for." She turned to Connor. "Please tell me you got that?"

He lowered the camera. "Yep. Got it."

They wore matching WISH YOU WERE BEER T-shirts. I hadn't noticed the shirts until now. "Love the slogan," I commented.

Payton looked confused.

"Your shirts." I pointed to Connor's chest.

"Oh, that's the film."

"What?"

"The documentary. That's the name of the film we're shooting. The film that all of you are going to be in. *Wish You Were Beer.*"

Otto and Ursula chuckled.

"Is it too much?" Payton's forehead crinkled. "Beer puns seem to be big in the industry. From the name of each brew to pub names. I've done extensive research to prepare for this film, and the puns seem to be endless."

"No, no, it is good." Otto gave her a nod of approval.

"If you want beer puns, I can go on forever," Mac said, raising his pint glass. "Like, Beauty is in the eye of the beer holder." He glanced in my direction. I glared at him.

Payton lit up. "That would be great. Maybe we can do a one-on-one. It could be fun to cut some puns in throughout the documentary."

Mac swelled with pride. "For sure. I'm here and I know everything there is to know about beer."

I could tell from the way he was looking at Payton that he had other ideas about where their "one-on-one" might lead. She was attractive, with an athletic frame and silky smooth hair that fell to her shoulders. I wanted to punch him. Instead I smiled sweetly and stood.

"It's time for us to open."

Payton nodded. "Of course. As long as it's all right with you, we'll go ahead and film your customers coming in and then the official tapping. I love that we scored a female brewer. What a lucky twist of fate, right, David?"

David had removed his suit jacket, revealing a WISH YOU WERE BEER T-shirt. He appraised me with his glassy dark eyes. "True enough. The camera is going to love her."

I wasn't sure how to respond, so I gave them a half wave and went to open the front door. A small line had formed outside. I noticed Mitchell standing on the corner of Front Street. He was waving his arms wildly and yelling at Lisa Balmes.

Poor Lisa, I thought as I ushered everyone inside. I wasn't sure which was worse. Dealing with Mitchell's ego or dealing with Mac.

CHAPTER
FIVE

I FORGOT ABOUT BOTH MEN once we opened. Nitro was buzzing with excitement. Blink 182 (one of Garrett's favorite bands and distinctly not German polka music) played overhead. Locals gathered around the high-top tables and pushed chairs together. Body heat and the smell of beer filled the small space. I propped open the front door and patio windows, allowing a cool breeze to waft in.

Garrett welcomed everyone. He talked about our brewing process and how we had used locally sourced cherries, thanking the Krauses for their hops and being sure to talk up Oktoberfest. Otto raised his glass in response and gave Garrett a friendly nod.

One of the shop owners stood on a barstool. "Listen up, everyone. Before they tap the new keg, let's make a pact. No one let the word out about this place to the tourists. Let them polka dance out in the tents to the never-ending sound of accordions. Nitro is going to be our little secret. Who's with me?"

This was greeted by a round of applause.

Garrett grinned. "Sure. We'll gladly provide respite for anyone who needs a break from Beervaria, but I for one am excited to try some awesome German brews in the tents." He scanned the crowd until his eyes landed on me. "Now, without further ado, I give you the amazing Sloan Krause." He winked at me. "Sloan, are you ready to tap that keg?"

The crowd whooped and hollered.

I felt a blush creep up my neck as I made my way to the front. I ducked behind the bar and reached for a commemorative glass. Then I placed my hand on the tap and began to pour the first pint. The ruby colored Cherry Weizen flowed into the glass. Pouring a perfect pint takes practice and patience. Pour too quickly, and you'll end up with a foamy mess. Once the beer reached the rim, I closed the tap and held the pint up for everyone to see.

"Ladies and gentlemen, we humbly offer you Nitro's first batch of Cherry Weizen," Garrett announced.

Everyone cheered. I handed the first pint to a guy at the bar and returned to pouring. I didn't even notice that Connor had made his way up to the side of the bar or that he had filmed the entire thing, until I turned to hand out more samples of our newest offering and he stuck the camera in my face. I nearly spilled the beer.

"You startled me," I said, placing the beers on the bar for the line of customers.

Connor pointed to his WISH YOU WERE BEER T-shirt. "It's

my job. I'm under strict orders from Payton to shoot every-thing. She says that they can cut everything on the editing room floor later, but right now if I don't get every single angle, I'm a dead man."

I chuckled.

"No, seriously. With Mitchell walking off, she thinks we might have to reshoot everything. She's thinking of com-pletely cutting out the host. Unless she can find someone new." He looked at me with a hopeful grin.

"Don't look at me. No way." I turned back to the taps. "This is where I'm meant to be. Pulling pints or deep in the mash tun. Not in front of the camera."

"It was worth a shot." He twisted the camera lens. "Would it be okay if I come behind the bar? I want to get a tighter shot of you pouring. It's like a work of art or something. Usually bartenders yank on the tap, but you're almost mas-saging it. Why are you holding the glass at an angle?"

"Come on in," I said, keeping my eyes on the lovely pink-tinted beer flowing out of the tap. I explained the right way to hold a glass—at an angle—to keep it from foaming too much. There were many factors that went into brewing, but one of the most important when it came to serving beer was carbonation. No one wanted an overly bubbly pint or a flat glass. Finding the right ratio of carbonation was a science and usually required multiple tastings. Some of which tended to come down to personal taste. For example, one of the lat-est trends in the Pacific Northwest was serving beers with very low carbonation. Personally, I wasn't a fan of the style. I liked a beer with a nice hit of fizz. But beers without tiny bubbles had become popular in pubs all around the region. They mimicked what you might taste if you sampled British beers—low carbonation and very little hops.

Northwest craft beer had been known for in-your-face hops. The hoppier the better. Brewers in the region had been crafting brews of one hundred IBU's (International Bittering Units, the scale used to measure the bitterness of hops in a beer) that no palate can even distinguish. Once a beer hits eighty IBUs, it's impossible to discern a difference.

Fortunately as of late, the hop-crazy trend had begun to slow in favor of malty flavor profiles and more balanced hop combinations. I had a feeling that was because brewers in our region were tired of IPAs and looking to try something new. As of late, I had noticed New England–style IPAs popping up on brewery tap lists. While similar in citrus tones, New England IPAs tended to be hazy and unfiltered, with a balanced and less light-your-mouth-on-fire-with-hops flavor.

It was important to me, as a brewer, to watch the shifting nature of the industry. Most traditional breweries kept their most popular beers on tap year-round, with a smaller selection of rotating seasonal brews. There were always brewers who pushed the envelope and helped sway trends. Recently sour beers had emerged on the scene, and some brewers devoted every keg to the fruit-inspired crossover. Sour beers originated in Belgium and were known for their distinct acidic taste. I had a feeling that the tart style was going to be popping up at more and more pubs as the craze caught on.

I tried to ignore the fact that Connor's camera was four inches away from my hands as I poured pints. Tapping a new keg brought an instantaneous, fresh energy to the space. Locals toasted one another and swapped strategies for surviving the next three weekends. Again, I wished that April could see the crowd. There was not a single pair of lederhosen in sight. Like me, Leavenworth natives were dressed casually in jeans, shorts, and T-shirts. There wasn't a single felt cap (except for Mitchell's) in a three-block radius.

I circulated the room, delivering bowls of my fragrant veggie soup and beer-brined sausages. The atmosphere was light and infused with camaraderie.

"Sloan." Ursula caught my arm as I passed by their table. "Ziz soup, it is wonderful. I must have ze recipe."

"I'm so glad you like it," I replied, steading a tray of full pint glasses.

Mac jumped to help me. His baby face was full of expectation. It took everything I had internally to keep my cool.

"I've got it." I glared at him and left to deliver the drinks.

Aside from Mac taking up space in my head, the keg tapping appeared to be a success, at least until about an hour later when Mitchell reappeared. His felt cap sat slightly askew. He pushed his way to the bar and leapt on top of the distressed wood that divided the seating area from the taps. Pointing at Connor, he flicked his wrist. "Get over here, kid. Get your head in the game, and point that lens at the bar."

Connor quickly shifted position to get a shot of Mitchell. Who was in charge of the film? Connor obviously took his orders from Mitchell.

"Pour me a pint of that Weizen," Mitchell demanded, turning around to face the bar.

I poured a pint and handed it up to him. What was he planning? This documentary was like nothing I had ever seen. Payton's vision of a glimpse into the world of craft brewing appeared to be at odds with Mitchell's need for the spotlight.

Mitchell held the beer with one hand and stuck two fingers in his mouth with the other. A piercing whistle silenced the room. "Drink up, Leavenworth! I'm your host, Mitchell Morgan, here to bring you the best of the best in brewing. We're going to be taking viewers on an intimate tour of this Bavarian village's mean streets and behind the scenes of breweries like Nitro, who are redefining the world of craft beer with beauties like this just-tapped Cherry Weizen." He raised his glass. "Cheers!" He waited for a reaction.

Everyone looked at each other, unsure what to do next.

David took a step forward and cleared his throat. "Mitchell, let's go take a walk."

"You have no power over me, old man, and you know it. Go take a walk yourself!" Mitchell gave David a look that made me shudder. David gripped the edge of a barstool.

Mitchell raised his glass higher. "Scratch that. Prost!"

A brief but awkward silence filled the tasting room. Mitchell held his ground on the bar and waited for the crowd to respond. Finally, a soft "prost" sounded from Mac. People took it as their cue to respond. Mitchell almost lost his footing as glasses lifted and everyone shouted, "Prost!"

"The mean streets of Leavenworth?" Garrett said under his breath.

"I know." We poured pints simultaneously as Mitchell continued to pander to his now attentive audience. He was explaining how he was the star and host of *Wish You Were Beer*. "I thought he left the film."

Garrett poured foam into the drip catcher. "Looks like he's had a change of heart."

That was the truth. Mitchell's schmoozing rivaled Mac's. He singled out people in the room, while constantly checking to make sure that Connor had him in the frame and was shooting from the right angle. "I'm coming for you next. I want to know everything about this beertopia and what makes Leavenworth tick," he said to the bookstore owner.

"And you." He set his sights on Chief Meyers, Leavenworth's longtime police detective, who was sitting at one of the tables near the front windows sipping a glass of water. "You and I are going to patrol these streets. Let's look into the dirty underbelly of the beer world. From urinating in public to skirt grabbing. What gets you tossed in the can here?"

Chief Meyers shot him a dirty look. I could tell from her scowl she had no time for his antics. It was nice to see her at the pub. I had a feeling she had come to support Garrett. Not long after our grand opening, there had been a murder in the brewery, and Garrett had worked alongside the chief to bring the killer to justice. Given that she was in her standard khaki uniform with a holster around her waist, I figured she probably wasn't here for our Cherry Weizen.

I noticed that Payton looked equally displeased. She said something I couldn't hear to David, but I could tell from her desperate gestures she was trying to get David to put a stop to Mitchell's display. David simply shrugged. Payton reached into her purse and pulled out three different pill bottles. She found the one she was looking for, opened it, and knocked back another pill. With a dark glare at Mitchell, she turned on her heel and left the pub.

I'd never seen anything like this. Granted, I didn't know anything about filmmaking, but I couldn't imagine that many documentary crews were this rife with drama.

"We should be charging admission," Garrett said.

Mitchell hopped off the bar and began circulating through the pub, but not before asking for a refresher. He had downed the pint of Cherry Weizen in about five minutes.

"I can't believe this is a documentary. It feels more like a bad reality TV show." I wiped my hands on a towel.

"Do you think it's an act?" Garrett glanced in Mitchell's direction. He was snapping selfies, tilting his feathered cap from side to side.

"Good question. It does seem over the top, doesn't it? Are you thinking this entire thing is an act? Him storming out earlier, too?"

Garrett shrugged. "I don't know. Maybe. I know there are some people who get crazy around beer. That guy is straight-up crazy."

Mitchell had finished his second pint, and he sent one of the bakery workers up to the bar for another refill. "Isn't he the coolest?" she gushed while I filled the pint glass. "I can't believe there's a real movie star here."

I wanted to remind her that none of us had ever heard of Mitchell Morgan. Instead I smiled and handed her a pint.

Mitchell barely noticed when she returned with a hopeful smile. His attention was focused on the front door. Lisa Balmes, the vacation property manager, had walked into

Nitro, followed by my least favorite person on the planet, April. I wondered if April pestered Lisa about her attire. She wore a pair of black skinny jeans, an ivory V-neck shirt with a matching thin sweater, and a fringy black scarf tied around her neck. Distinctly not Bavarian. April tagged after her, wearing the same dress from earlier, but she had taken off her maid's cap and tied her red hair in two long braids. She looked like she was trying to audition for the role of Heidi.

If Lisa noticed that Mitchell was staring her down, she gave no indication. She weaved her way to the bar, stopping a couple of times to chat with our patrons.

"Wow, what a turnout, you guys," she said to Garrett and me. "I think everyone in Leavenworth is here."

Garrett eyes perked up ever so slightly at the compliment. "Can I get you a pint of something?"

Lisa stared at the chalkboard menu on the wall next to the taps. "It has to be a Cherry Weizen, right?"

"Right." Garrett grabbed a clean glass and began pouring Lisa's beer.

"How are things with you, Sloan?" she asked, sounding genuinely interested.

"Good. I mean, the usual pre-Oktoberfest jitters, but I don't think we'll get too slammed. How about you?"

Lisa loosened her scarf. "I can't even think about it. I start to have a panic attack every time I think about the next three weekends. Starting tomorrow, every property that we manage is booked solid."

"That's great, though."

She nodded and then absentmindedly flipped through a bunch of keys hanging on a ring around her wrist. "Yes and no. You're right. We're thrilled with the business, but it's a lot to juggle. Everything in town and as far away as Wenatchee and Cle Elum is completely full. I spent the day delivering welcome packages to each cabin and house, and making sure the water and heat are running. This is the busiest season we've ever had, and there's no end in sight. Most of my properties are booked straight into the new year."

"Whew." I put the back of my hand to my brow. "You're making me tired just thinking about that. Remind me of that the next time I complain about brewing."

Lisa's warm smile instantly put me at ease. "Want to trade places? I know nothing about beer."

Garrett slid a cold pint in front of her. "Our mantra here is the only thing you need to know about beer is how to drink it."

"That I can do." Lisa raised her glass and took a sip.

"Is it just you and your mom managing all of the rentals?" I asked as I wiped up a spill on the bar.

"Yep. We have a couple of interns who help during the busy season, and I have a crew of help on standby. In fact, your brother-in-law . . ." She trailed off for a moment. I knew she wasn't sure how to refer to Hans.

"Hans?" I offered.

"Yes, Hans has even offered to jump if my regular repair guy can't. You just never know what can go wrong. We try to plan and anticipate, but inevitably a pipe will burst or a furnace will go out. There are some things that we can't control."

"I never thought about that."

Lisa drank her beer. "Yeah, and then there's the logistical nightmare of getting cleaning crews in and out before the next batch of guests arrive, booking transportation and shuttles for people, making sure that none of the properties are damaged. Last year a set of identical twins decided to plug up the bathtub in one of our most expensive cabins. They flooded the entire house. That one I didn't see coming." Her key ring jangled as she reached into her purse and checked her phone. "My to-do list is like a mile long right now."

Before I could ask her if there was anything I could do to help, Mitchell slid up next to her and put his arm around her shoulder.

"How's my upgrade coming?" He squeezed her narrow collarbone as if he were giving her a massage.

It must have hurt because Lisa winced. She stuffed her phone in her purse and tossed Mitchell off her. "Like I explained earlier, we can't upgrade your rental house. Everything is sold out for Oktoberfest. I had to pull some big strings and convince my neighbor to take a trip to visit her grandkids in Seattle just to get you in a place. I moved the family who was supposed to be staying in your property to my neighbor's. There's nothing else I can do. Every hotel within a hundred miles has been booked for months."

Mitchell moved his hands to her shoulders. "You know who you're talking to, right? Our film is going to bring huge money into your podunk town." His speech had started to slur slightly.

It was everything I could do not to reach across the bar and sock him.

April squeezed in. She intentionally pressed her chest against the back of a barstool to show off her cleavage. "Did I hear you two talking about a housing problem?"

Lisa glared at her.

"That's right. Yeah. I've got a problem. A huge problem." Mitchell took off his felt cap and slammed it on the bar. "They've put me up in a ridiculous cottage. It's full of German kitsch. It has a terrible smell—like cabbage or worse—and it's filthy."

April gasped and put her hand to her heart. "What? Lisa, this is unacceptable! Mitchell is a movie star and should be treated like one." She stroked his arm. "Don't worry. We'll get this fixed immediately. Won't we, Lisa?"

Lisa threw her head back. "No, April. *We* won't. Mitchell is staying in the Edelweiss cabin. It's one of the nicest rentals in town. And I assure you that none of our properties smell. That's the most ridiculous thing I've ever heard—even from you." She glanced at me and rolled her eyes. "That cabin has been professionally cleaned and was torn down to the studs and completely remodeled last year. Mitchell is full of it."

For a second I wasn't sure what April was going to do. She sputtered, trying to put together a coherent sentence. With a huff, she brushed Lisa off. "Listen, Mitchell, don't you worry. I have a lot of pull around town. I am Leavenworth's official ambassador."

Lisa nearly spit out her beer.

April shot daggers at her. "I'm sure that Lisa has overlooked something. This isn't exactly her area of expertise. I happen to be the most senior real estate mogul in town. Why don't you just sit tight tonight, and I promise by tomorrow morning I'll have a luxurious rental waiting for you."

Mitchell's body swayed. He pointed to Garrett. "Hey, get me another, man."

Garrett hesitated.

April snapped. Then she flung her braids from side to side. The motion made her skirt, which barely covered her ass, creep up even higher. "Get him another. He's not going anywhere tonight. He only has to cross the street, and need I remind you that he's our special guest?"

Garrett poured Mitchell another. I couldn't wait for Mitchell to return to his "crummy" cabin.

"Maybe we should send him on his way with a growler," I said to Garrett, as April pulled Mitchell away from the bar. I wasn't surprised that she had set her sights on him, and for once I didn't feel the least bit sorry for her prey.

He chuckled. "I like the way you think, Sloan."

"What a pompous jerk."

"You can say that again." He handed me a tray of glasses. "Can you deliver these?"

"Of course." I took the tray and passed out more pints. On my way back to the bar, Ursula reached for my arm.

"Sloan, we must be going soon."

"Thanks for coming." I stopped and knelt next to her. Hans, Mac, and Otto were wrapped up in a discussion about fermenting techniques.

"For you, anything." Her porcelain skin wrinkled as she frowned. "Sloan, I must ask something of you."

I swallowed. Ursula's face was serious. What did she want to ask me? Something about Mac? Was she worried about Alex?

"I heard that you have been looking for your mother," she said, so softly that I could barely hear her.

"You did?" How? Leavenworth was small, but I hadn't

shared my quest to find my birth mother with anyone other than Garrett, and I knew he wouldn't have betrayed my request for secrecy. He had found a photo a while ago of a woman and a young girl who bore an uncanny resemblance to me. Ever since I'd seen the photo, I couldn't let it go. I'd been dreaming about the picture. Tiny flashes of my years before foster care would fly through my head, like a cloud on a windy day. I could never capture the entire memory. Just snippets of a birthday cake with pink candles and the scent of jasmine and minty toothpaste. I didn't trust the fleeting images. They could be nothing more than my imagination playing tricks on me.

"*Ja.*" Ursula folded her hands in her lap. "I think it is better if you leave the past in the past."

I wanted to ask her more, but April interrupted us. "*Guten Tag,* Krause family." She motioned to Mitchell, who stood to her right, chugging his beer. "Have you had the pleasure of meeting Leavenworth's *haupt* star?"

"*Haupt* star?" Ursula wrinkled her brow.

"Yes, yes, I believe that's how you say 'movie star' in your native tongue," April replied in a condescending tone.

"No. Ziz is not how you say movie star. You would say *Filmstar.*"

April's nostrils flared. "Your German must be rusty."

Ursula looked dumbfounded.

"Anyway, it doesn't matter." April waved. "Have you met Mitchell Morgan? He's a dreamy actor from LA."

"*Ja.*" Ursula gave Mitchell a nod. "We have met."

Without further comment, April yanked Mitchell on to a new table. I had to stifle a chuckle. What poetic justice that

Ursula had corrected April's abysmal German. I was about to ask her why she thought it was a bad idea for me to look into my past when I saw Garrett waving to me from the bar.

"I better go," I said to Ursula. "Can we talk later?"

"*Ja*. Of course," she said with her warm smile.

I stood and returned to the bar. "Sorry. Is it nuts up here?"

"I thought you said things might be kind of slow around Oktoberfest." Garrett loaded used pint glasses into a plastic bin. "I think we're going to need to fire up the dishwasher soon."

"We're going through the beer tonight, aren't we?" I did a quick mental count of the used glasses. There were at least one hundred glasses in the bin. "I do think it will slow down, but not until tomorrow."

"You can blame most of it on Mr. Drama." Garrett nodded toward Mitchell, whom April was parading from table to table.

"Mr. Drama, perfect." I laughed.

"He appears to be enjoying our Cherry Weizen, and everyone else is enjoying his performance." Garrett's hickory eyes darkened. "I'm cutting him off, though."

"Good idea." I glanced to the tasting room. Most eyes were focused on Mitchell, as if everyone was waiting to see what he would do next. He didn't appear to be classically drunk, but his body was certainly unsteady, and his eyes looked glassy. I appreciated that Garrett wasn't taking any chances in overserving. "Let me take those," I said, grabbing the tub.

Any reason to get away from April was good with me. I took the dishes to the kitchen, rinsed them in the sink, loaded the dishwasher, and then hit start. Fortunately the commercial machine would wash and power dry the glasses in a matter of minutes. The only problem was that no one wanted to be served a beer in a hot glass. After the dishwasher ran through its cycle, we immediately put the pint glasses in the freezer and let them chill. While I waited for them to cool, I thought about what a success the keg tapping had been. Now if I could manage to avoid Mitchell, April, and my soon-to-be-ex for the next few days, perhaps Oktoberfest would be a breeze.

CHAPTER

SIX

MITCHELL CONTINUED TO STIR UP trouble until Garrett finally sent him (followed closely by April Ablin) out the front door shortly before last call. Only a handful of regulars remained. The Krauses were long gone, as was Lisa. I had to admit that seeing Lisa's reaction to April made me feel better. At least I wasn't April's only target. Not that I would wish her on anyone, but at least there was safety in numbers.

Garrett picked up behind the bar. I wiped down the empty tables with a mixture of soap, water, and a splash of vinegar. The natural cleaner mingled with the scent of beer. My feet were sore and my muscles were tired, but it was another successful keg tapping. I was happy for Garrett. He deserved every ounce of praise that he had received.

When the last customer left, we closed and locked the front door. I still wasn't used to locking up. In Leavenworth people rarely locked their houses. With just over two thousand residents and nestled into the high Cascade Mountains, our village didn't see much crime. When Garrett arrived from Seattle, he had insisted on security measures. At first I thought he was being paranoid. That quickly changed after we had a break-in and a murder at the brewery.

He poured us each a pint of our celebrated Weizen. "Well, cheers to us." He clinked his glass to mine.

"We made it. Another night. Another pint."

"Even with a crazy movie star around." Garrett scratched his stubbly cheeks. "Can we really call that guy a movie star? Since when does narrating a documentary about beer give you diva status?"

I laughed. Bubbles went up my nose. The cherry scent was immediate and reminded me of Ursula's cherry strudel. "I was thinking the same thing. The beer culture is so laid-back. He does not seem like a good fit for the project."

"No way." Garrett gave me a thumbs-down. "Something is off with the entire production. It doesn't feel right to me."

"Yeah. Did you happen to notice Payton, the director?" The floor was sticky under my feet. Another trademark of pub life.

Garrett shook his head. "No. What about her?"

"I think she's fed up with Mitchell. I couldn't hear their conversation, but I got the sense that she doesn't want him on the film anymore."

"Why would she? He's a nightmare."

"A nightmare who loves your beer—don't forget that." I took a sip of the bright Weizen.

"His only redeeming quality." He held up his glass in a toast.

The sounds of a polka band drifted through the open windows. *One of the bands must be rehearsing on the main stage,* I thought.

"How did you manage to get him to leave?" I walked to shut the windows.

"You can thank your friend April for that." Garrett tipped back his glass. "She ordered a growler of our Cherry Weizen and dragged him out of here. Good luck to him. I can only imagine trying to escape April's clutches."

I laughed so hard I almost spilled my beer.

"Those two were made for each other. Although the thing is, he didn't seem knock-down drunk. He had a few pints too many, but he's a big guy. I think that's just his everyday *lovely* disposition." Garrett grinned and took another taste of the beer. "This turned out better than I expected. Now if our experimental cranberry batches turn out this good, I'll be happy."

"I agree. How much did we go through tonight?" I was concerned about our stock with the influx of tourists about to arrive.

"Maybe half a keg. We should be in good shape."

"What's our plan for tomorrow?" I wanted to check my phone to see if I had an update from Alex. He had promised that he would text me pictures of his trip.

Garrett furrowed his brow. "I was going to ask you that. That last time I was in town for Oktoberfest was at least ten years ago. It's bigger than it was back then, right?"

"Without a doubt. Probably double." I glanced at the angled parking illuminated by the street lamp out front. "I'm planning to get here early. Parking anywhere around here is going to be at a premium. They shut down the streets by midmorning. I was thinking I would just come early and stay all day."

"That's a long day. Are you sure?" Garrett twisted the tap handle to make sure it was locked in place for the night.

"No problem. Welcome to Oktoberfest in Leavenworth." He smiled.

"On that note, I'm going to head out. I'll see you in the morning."

"At beer dark thirty." Garrett winked.

"You got it." I went to retrieve my things from the office. Sure enough, a text from Alex had come in. It was a picture of him and his friends at the top of the Space Needle. "Look, Mom. No hands!" he had written, and then sent me three red hearts. "Love you. Hope Oktoberfest is a blast. Don't work too hard."

I clutched my phone to my heart. Then I sent him a reply telling him to have fun and try and get some sleep.

Yeah right, teenage boys sleeping, I thought to myself as I stepped outside into the cool night. I could smell the shifting season in the crisp leaves and the hint of hay in the air. I tossed my bag in my car and was about to get into the driver's seat when shouts broke out. At first I thought maybe it was a group of early arrivals who had already begun imbibing, but the screams turned almost manic. I shut the door and ran in the direction of the sound.

Rounding the corner onto Front Street, I spotted two people running toward me from the entrance to the Festhalle. The glow of the street lamps cast hazy shadows. Moonlight reflected off the top of the bright white tents. Work crews were still setting up the tents for tomorrow's festivities and had barricaded the last two blocks. It was too dark to make out who was fighting, but their argument was escalating. I hurried down the dim sidewalk, running past the nutcracker shop, the bakery, and the deli. Cold air hit my lungs as I raced toward the commotion.

A woman I didn't recognize was chasing after Lisa. "You killed him! You killed him! Get back here!" the woman shouted, racing to catch up to Lisa.

They were heading straight for me.

"I have no idea what you're talking about," Lisa yelled over her shoulder. She sprinted down the middle of the street.

What was going on?

The woman was hysterical. "You killed him!" she shrieked again, catching Lisa and almost tackling her to the ground.

"You're crazy! Get off me!" Lisa yelled, trying to free herself from the woman's grasp.

I caught up to them just as the younger woman tried to lunge at Lisa. "Hey, what's going on?" I shielded Lisa from her. Dry leaves clustered in piles on the edge of the sidewalk.

"She killed Mitchell! Mitchell Morgan is dead, and she killed him," the woman wailed. "Mitchell is dead."

"I have no idea what she's talking about," Lisa said, giving me an incredulous look and fending the woman off with one hand.

"What do you mean, Mitchell's dead?" I asked, continuing to play referee. I wasn't sure what the woman's issue was yet, but from her wild eyes and shallow breathing, I wondered if maybe she was under the influence of something stronger than beer.

"Mitchell is dead!" She threw her hands over her face and sobbed. "I saw her!" She pointed a shaky finger at Lisa. "She did it."

I looked to Lisa, who shrugged. She was obviously as confused as I felt. "Try to breathe and calm down." I took a slow, deep breath to model this for the young woman.

She tried to breathe through her tears, but it only made her chest quiver.

My mind spun. Was this woman telling the truth? There were at least a couple dozen workers moving between the tents, and I could still hear a band playing. We were about twenty feet from the main entrance to the Festhalle. If Mitchell was dead, why was no one else reacting?

"I just saw Mitchell an hour or so ago, and he was fine. What makes you think he's dead?"

"Because he is! He's dead. Over there!" She pointed toward a huge tent at the end of Front Street. Three lines had been gated off with temporary fencing. Banners hung above each line for vendors, prepurchased tickets, and ticket sales.

"How do you know?" I pushed.

"I saw him. I thought he had had too much to drink. He does that sometimes, you know. I went to check on him, and he wasn't at his cabin, so I decided to come down to the square to see if maybe he was still at one of the pubs or even in the tents filming." Her voice became steadier as she spoke. "I looked everywhere. I was going to give up and go back to my hotel but then I spotted him in the . . . the . . ."

"The bar?" Lisa asked, glancing the opposite direction. Bavarian chalets lined each side of the road. Icicle lights had been hung from baroque balconies and glimmered in the dark.

"No, over there." She pointed to the ground. "He's dead. I'm sure of it."

She sounded more coherent.

"If he's dead, we have to call the police," I said, heading for the tent.

The woman ran after me. "You should call the police. You should call them right now, because she killed him." She thrust her finger at Lisa.

Lisa shook her head. "I don't know what's going on, but I didn't kill Mitchell."

"Let's leave that for the moment," I suggested. "Can you show me where you found him?"

"Okay, but I don't think I can get close to him again. I'll probably pass out."

"You don't have to. Just show me where he is, and I'll take it from there."

She wiped her nose on the back of her arm. "Okay."

Leaves scattered like confetti as we followed her toward the tent. She stopped when we got a few feet away from the gated area. "I can't go any closer. I can't look." She covered her eyes with her hands. "He's over there on the ground." She pointed to the section that read TICKET SALES.

I looked to Lisa, who gave me a nod of solidarity. We pressed on. "Mitchell," I called. "Mitchell, are you okay?"

No response.

Could this woman be telling the truth?

Lisa paused.

I didn't blame her. Part of me wanted to run. I had a sinking feeling that the woman wasn't crazy. At that moment, I looked down at my feet and spotted Mitchell Morgan sprawled out on the cement. I knew instantly that the star of *Wish You Were Beer* was indeed dead.

CHAPTER

SEVEN

"CALL THE POLICE," I COMMANDED, looking up at Lisa.

She reached into her oversized handbag and pulled out her cell.

The young woman wailed and dropped to her knees. "He's dead. He's really dead, isn't he?"

I didn't have time to console her. Instinct took over. I checked for a pulse while I waited for Lisa to update the police. "He doesn't have a pulse," I told her, trying to find any sign of a pulse on Mitchell's other arm.

"Is he breathing?" Lisa asked.

I placed my hand under Mitchell's nose. "No." I wasn't sure if it was my independent upbringing or a typical stress reaction, but my voice sounded clinical and like it was originating outside of my body. The smell of beer assaulted my senses. How much had the man had to drink?

"Any sign of trauma?" Lisa repeated questions from the

911 operator. "Chief Meyers and the ambulance are on their way."

I assessed Mitchell from head to toe. Shattered glass enshrined his head like a crown, yet he wasn't bleeding. There wasn't a weapon nearby, but then again, it was dark. "Not that I can see," I said to Lisa as the sound of sirens filled the bleak silence around us.

Lisa continued to talk to the operator while I checked the street. Why had the young woman automatically assumed that Lisa had killed Mitchell? What had made her leap to murder?

The felt cap that Mitchell had had on earlier was gone. It didn't look like he had suffered a blow to the head, but I wasn't about to turn him over and check. A terrible thought invaded my head. What if Mitchell had succumbed to alcohol poisoning? What if we had overserved him? Or could he have been so drunk that he fell and knocked himself out? Maybe Garrett had been wrong about how much Mitchell had had to drink.

I removed my phone and clicked on the flashlight. Shining it on the ground, I got a better look at the glass shards. No wonder Mitchell smelled of alcohol. The growler of our Cherry Weizen was shattered. My stomach dropped. Where had April disappeared to?

I was about to go talk to the sobbing woman when Police Chief Meyers zoomed up behind us with her sirens echoing and lights flashing. I shielded my eyes with my hand.

"Sloan?" Chief Meyers moved with agility despite her bulky frame. "What happened?" She removed a flashlight from her belt and shined it on Mitchell's body.

"He's dead." I heard the lack of emotion in my tone.

Chief Meyers didn't take my word for it. She started what I assumed was standard police protocol, assessing Mitchell and the scene around us. A minute later the ambulance arrived. It didn't take long for the EMS workers to confirm my suspicions. Mitchell Morgan was dead.

"No one leave." Chief Meyers addressed us. "I want the three of you over on that sidewalk." She pointed to the right side of the street, to one of Leavenworth's most popular shops—The Gingerbread Cottage.

The quiet moonlight had been replaced by the sound of sirens, stirring the handful of tourists and locals from the bars. I hadn't even realized that a small crowd had begun to gather until I walked over to the sidewalk.

The young woman continued to sob and convulse. I wished I had a tissue or something to offer her. I ushered her over to a white picket fence in front of The Gingerbread Cottage. "Let's wait over here."

She didn't resist.

"I'm Sloan, by the way. I don't think we've met."

Her breath was shallow and choppy. "I'm—I'm—Kat. Kat Kelly."

"Are you part of the documentary team?"

She wiped her nose with one hand and then the other. "No. I wish. I'm Mitchell's biggest fan. I would follow him anywhere."

That sounded odd. I couldn't help but raise my brow.

"He's the most amazing actor I've ever met in my entire life," Kat continued, oblivious to my reaction. "Have you seen *Crazy House*? It was my favorite childhood show. I've seen every single episode at least five times. I'm the president of his fan club, and you wouldn't believe the things he's done for us and given us through the years."

Actually what I couldn't believe was that Mitchell had a fan club. "Really. Like what?" I asked.

"Like this." She waved a trembling arm toward Front Street, where blue and white flashing lights bounced off the charming storefronts. "He invited me up for the weekend. As president of his fan club, I was going to get an exclusive look at his new film. He paid my way and everything."

Prior to today I had never heard of Mitchell Morgan. How big was his fan club?

"I'm from Salem, Oregon, so he had to pay for my train ticket and a hotel room." Her voice was full of pride.

I wondered how Mitchell had found a hotel room, especially when he'd been so vocal about his subpar vacation rental. "That was nice of him," I commented, trying to keep her talking. Her petite frame quivered, but at least her guttural sobs had stopped.

"That's the kind of guy he is—I mean *was*." She started crying again.

I put my arm around her shoulder. Kat fell into me.

A few feet away Lisa was talking to the group of gawkers who had come to see what was going on. The quaint white stucco buildings and dark timbered awnings seemed to give off an eerie vibe. Could this really be happening in our village?

"Did you see anything before Mitchell collapsed?" I asked Kat.

She trembled. "What do you mean collapsed? He didn't collapse. She killed him."

"You saw her kill Mitchell?" I stared at Lisa, who was making a call on her cell. She paced in front of Shoe Haus, a cobbler's shop that had been in business for over thirty years. A wooden sign carved in the shape of a shoe swung above Lisa's head.

Kat wiped her nose again and pulled away from my shoulder. "No. I mean not exactly, but it had to be her. She was the only one around."

"I'm not sure I follow."

"Mitchell asked me to meet him here. We were going to hit a bar and then he was going to give me my hotel key and a pass to Oktoberfest."

We both paused when the EMS workers covered Mitchell's body with a sheet.

"Oh my God! Oh my God. Oh my God. This is really happening? Is it really happening, or am I in a bad dream or something? Maybe you should pinch me." She rocked back onto the white picket fence. Giant gingerbread cutouts dotted the front lawn. It was a strange juxtaposition—sweet decorations against a backdrop of death.

"Sadly, it's not a dream." I looked away. The thought that I had touched Mitchell's dead body a few minutes ago made my stomach queasy. "Okay, so you came downtown to meet Mitchell. Then what happened?"

"I got here, and I couldn't find him. He was supposed to be at some pub around the corner, but they were already closed." Her voice was shrill. She rocked back and forth onto the tips of her toes. *Her feet must be freezing in flip-flops*, I thought, rubbing my arms. Had the temp started to drop, or was I feeling the effects of shock?

I figured she was talking about Nitro.

"This is my first time in Leavenworth, so I went around to every place that was open to try and find him. The bartender in the bar across the street told me that he had seen Mitchell heading for the tent, so I tried there next."

"Is that when you saw Lisa?"

She shook her head. "No. I looked everywhere in the tents, but he wasn't there. I tried calling and texting, but he didn't respond. I wasn't sure what to do next. Then I heard him yelling at someone, so I ran out here. It all happened so fast. There was the sound of shattering glass. The next thing I knew, I saw that woman over there." She caught her breath and pointed at Lisa. "Running away from Mitchell's body and Mitchell lying dead on the ground. He didn't collapse. She killed him, and she was fleeing the scene," she repeated.

I inhaled through my nose. Was Kat distraught, or could she have seen something? I glanced at Lisa, who was digging through her purse for something. She didn't look like a killer. Not to mention, what possible motive could she have for killing Mitchell? Aside from him complaining about her rental properties. Lisa was a professional. She was used to dealing with client demands. I couldn't picture her snapping.

Kat chomped her nails. "This was supposed to be the best day of my life. Now it's the worst." She buried her face in her hands as more tears spilled out.

Chief Meyers directed a team of police officers and EMS

workers. I watched as they loaded Mitchell's body into the ambulance. Although I didn't share Kat's deep affection for the man, the fact that he was dead gave me a moment of pause. As the ambulance backed away, a hush fell over everyone. The frenetic energy of people coming out to see what the drama was had been replaced by a mournful stillness. Even Chief Meyers gave the ambulance a two-fingered salute.

Next to me, Kat collapsed on the sidewalk. She used the fence to support her back as she hugged her knees to her chest. Part of me was envious of her emotional outburst. My coping strategy as a foster kid had been to keep my feelings bottled up. Being overly tearful or seeking physical comfort from strangers wasn't in my DNA. I had learned to go inward in times of stress, and for the most part, it worked. The exception had been meeting the Krauses and having Alex. They had cracked a piece of me open, and I had never been the same since.

Kat's ability to release her raw grief made me acutely aware of my rigid body posture and the fact that my mind was ticking through possible causes of Mitchell's untimely demise.

Chief Meyers moved in our direction. She had one hand on the front pocket of her tight uniform, and the other held a flashlight. "Sloan, a word." She motioned with the light for me to step away from Kat. Her imposing frame reflected on the street. She was a tall and solid woman with a commanding presence. I sensed that even had she chosen another profession, she would have embodied respect wherever she went.

I followed the illuminated halo on the sidewalk. "What's

her deal?" Chief Meyers asked. I didn't need clarification to know that the chief was talking about Kat. "Is that the wife? Girlfriend?"

"Fan club president."

"You've got to be kidding me." Chief Meyers whipped a small spiral notebook from her back pocket and scratched a note in it. "Fan club president?"

"That's what she told me. You'll have to interview her, but she said that Mitchell paid for her to come up for the shoot."

"Anything else?" Chief Meyers clicked her ballpoint pen on and off. "Walk me through what you saw, step-by-step."

I explained about hearing screams and coming to see what had happened. "Lisa called 911. I checked for a pulse, but Mitchell was already dead."

"What time was this?"

"Sometime after eleven. We closed then and cleaned up. Probably eleven thirty."

She made a note. A walkie-talkie attached to her chest crackled. She removed it, clicked a button, and then rattled off a code. "Continue."

"There was broken glass nearby. I smelled beer. I'm pretty sure that the glass was from one of our growlers. I don't know if Mitchell had too much to drink and collapsed, or maybe he tripped and hit his head? It's weird because Garrett and I were just talking about Mitchell and how much he'd had to drink. He was a jerk to everyone at the pub, but I don't think that was induced by alcohol."

A hint of a frown tugged at her round cheeks. "I'll take it from here, Sloan. My team is bagging up the evidence as we speak. I want to hear what else you might have seen, heard. Did you see any movement in the distance? Someone fleeing the scene, perhaps?"

I shook my head. Her questions made it sound like she was operating under the assumption that Mitchell had been killed. "No. It was too dark. I know that he left Nitro with April Ablin, but I haven't seen her anywhere. And Kat keeps insisting that Lisa killed him."

Chief Meyers perked up and swiveled her head in Lisa's direction. "Lisa Balmes?"

"According to Kat," I said with a nod.

"Did you see Lisa near the body?" She waited with her pen poised, ready to strike the notebook.

"Not near Mitchell. She was by the tent, I think." I racked my brain to try and remember exactly what I had seen. I thought of myself as being a good witness, but now that Chief Meyers pressed me on specifics, I felt like my mind had gone blank.

"Sloan?" Chief Meyers prompted me when I trailed off.

"She was around, but not by Mitchell's body." I retraced my steps from the car. "His arm felt cold when I picked it up, but then again I was in shock so maybe my hands were just cold."

"Hmm." She nodded.

The more I thought about it, the more I was sure that had to be true. "Do you know how he was killed? Could someone have hit him? Is that why there was glass around his body?"

Chief Meyers held out her pen. "Slow down, Sloan."

I thought that was all she was going to say, but her gaze

drifted from Kat, who was still sobbing on the sidewalk, to Lisa, who was huddled with a group of locals.

"Just between us, we won't know for a while, but I spotted a shard of glass in the back of Mitchell's skull. I'm operating this investigation as a murder. I want you to call me if you think of anything else, and keep your eyes open."

"Will do."

She walked over to Kat and crouched next to her. Chief Meyers suspected foul play. In some ways, that news didn't surprise me. Mitchell hadn't exactly endeared himself to our community, but at the same time, that meant that someone I knew, potentially someone I cared about, could have killed him.

I waited around until the police gave us the all clear to leave, along with instructions that they would be in touch for further questioning if necessary. My body shuddered as I returned to my car. My feet ached from standing on cold cement, and my mind whirled. Had someone in our easygoing village brutally ended Mitchell Morgan's life? And why?

CHAPTER

EIGHT

WHEN I WOKE THE NEXT morning, I wondered for a moment if I'd had too much to drink last night. It felt like I had a hangover. My neck was stiff. My head pulsed with shooting pain, and my mouth was dry. I rolled out of bed and stumbled into the bathroom, where I downed two Advil and a glass of water. Memories of finding Mitchell's body flooded me. Was that why I felt so crummy?

I splashed cold water on my face. My eyes were bloodshot. How much sleep had I had last night? From the looks of the puffy bags under my eyes and the dry taste in my mouth, I had a feeling not much. I never slept well when I was home alone. Alex had been taking turns staying at the family farmhouse with me and at a hotel with Mac. I hated waking up to an empty house, even though I knew that Alex was safe and having fun in Seattle.

I wondered if news of Mitchell's death had already spread

around town. The con of living in a community as small as Leavenworth was that it never took long for everyone—literally everyone—to know your business. Today was the official start of Oktoberfest, which usually meant a palpable excitement hung in the air. Given what had happened last night, I had a feeling the atmosphere might be a bit more somber.

Time to get moving, Sloan, I told myself. I pulled on a pair of jeans, a Nitro T-shirt, and my favorite pair of well-worn black Converse low-tops. Since we weren't brewing today, there was no need for my boots. Then I brushed my hair and pulled it up into a ponytail. I applied moisturizer to my face and a thin, shimmery lip gloss. The combination of waking up a bit and the Advil were already making my headache disappear. After a cup or two of coffee, I should be as good as new.

A text from Alex brightened my spirits: "Up and at 'em, Mom! You won't believe this. Check out the view we got from the front row. Mr. Mathewson knows one of the organizers and asked if we could sit in the front. Stay tuned for Seahawks and Sounders pictures soon. Love ya."

I grinned. Alex's leadership workshop was a dual effort by Washington's two professional football and soccer teams, designed to teach high schoolers throughout the state how to build community. I could feel his enthusiasm through the text. In the picture, he and his classmates posed on the floor of the convention center. Alex stood almost two inches taller than his teacher. He had inherited his height from me. I replied back, insisting on pictures and encouraging him to try and get some autographs. Knowing that he was safe and having fun helped calm the intrusive thoughts looping through my mind.

In the kitchen, I blasted classical music while I brewed a strong pot of coffee and made myself a bowl of oatmeal. Our kitchen had always been the gathering place, with its airy beamed ceiling and wall of windows that looked out onto the hop farm that Mac had cultivated on the property. This morning it felt sterile and cold. I tried to distract my lonely thoughts by replaying everything that happened last night. It felt like a bad dream. Had Mitchell really been killed?

The coffee beeped. I poured a splash of cream into the bottom of a mug and watched as the dark coffee blended with the cream. The smell made the pulsing in my head slow to a dull throb. I pulled out a barstool and savored my coffee and steel-cut oatmeal. Was I overlooking something? What had Lisa been doing downtown that late? I'd been so focused on trying to calm down a hysterical Kat that I hadn't had a chance to talk to Lisa. I still doubted that she had a motive for harming Mitchell, but it was convenient that she happened to be at the scene of the crime. If I had time later, maybe I could track her down and get her perspective.

I felt strangely responsible. And I needed answers.

For the moment, I needed to finish my breakfast and get to Nitro. Once I had polished off two brimming mugs of coffee, I felt completely back to normal and ready to tackle the day. I grabbed my purse, locked the front door, and headed for the car. Dew coated the grass and my windshield. A telltale sign that fall was here.

The drive from our farmhouse took me past a long stretch of organic vineyards and orchards. Sunlight flickered on the hills, illuminating the lush color of the changing deciduous trees. Leavenworth's beauty was unmatched year-round, but during the fall our landscape put on a magnificent show of color. Gold, green, red, orange, yellow, and brown leaves highlighted the hillside. Two red-tailed hawks circled above, gliding on the gentle wind. Picturesque mountains rose like steady giants. Dew kissed the lush grasses and sparkled on the tips of flowering fuchsias. *No wonder people will flock here for the next month,* I thought as I turned off the highway and into town. Mother Nature had painted the North Cascades better than any impressionist painter could.

I drove down Front Street, turned, and found parking around the corner in front of Nitro. Once things really got going later in the day, finding a space to park in the square would be nearly impossible. I couldn't resist taking a peek to see if there was any activity near the tents, so I grabbed my purse and walked to the end of the block. To my left was a wooden water trough, designed to look like an old-fashioned horse-watering station. In reality it was a modern drinking fountain and a topic of conversation amongst tourists.

Sure enough the area where we had found Mitchell's body was roped off with bright yellow police tape. Two police officers stood guard on either side of the perimeter. If the area remained off-limits tonight, that would make for another conversation starter and might mean that Oktoberfest revelers would funnel past Nitro on their way out of the tents. That could be good for business. Or dry our kegs in a matter of days.

What are you thinking, Sloan? I scolded myself for focusing on how we might profit off of a tragedy. That wasn't like me. Mitchell's death and the stress over Oktoberfest and my relationship with Mac seemed to be getting the best of me. I shook off my feelings with a shrug of my shoulders and a deep inhalation. Time to do what I did best—beer.

I was about to turn around when I heard Chief Meyers's husky voice. "Sloan, is that you?" She came out from the tent in her khaki uniform with a brown tie. The gold badge pinned to her chest glinted in the sunlight. I raised my hand to my forehead to shield my face.

"Yeah. Sorry. I guess I came back to see the scene of the crime, so to speak. I couldn't sleep last night after finding Mitchell."

She was a woman of few words. Instead of trying to console me, she adjusted her polyester pants and pointed to the chalk outline where Mitchell's body had been. "My team's about done here. Any new thoughts this morning?"

"New thoughts?" I noticed small yellow markers placed near the shattered glass.

"Anything else you can remember? Sometimes it's the small details that give us the biggest leads." Her words reminded me of something Garrett had once said about needing a big space to work out his problems. Had I been too mired in the small details in my life? Were the tiny decisions keeping me stuck? Weighing me down?

Chief Meyers cleared her throat. "Sloan?"

"Yeah, sorry." I concentrated on everything that had happened since Mitchell and the *Wish You Were Beer* crew had arrived. "What about the gash on his arm?"

93

"Gash?" Chief Meyers had removed her notebook and was gnawing on her pen.

"When I met Mitchell at the grocery store yesterday, he was putting Band-Aids on his arm. It looked pretty bad. Could that be related?"

"Could be." She continued to chomp on the pen. "We noted the injury. Could be that the deceased had an altercation with the killer prior to the actual murder. You didn't hear how he happened to injure the arm, did you?"

"No." I shook my head. "He didn't say, but he didn't exactly endear himself to anyone. If anyone had asked, I bet he would have bitten their head off." I paused for a moment. "Actually, that's not true. He and April were hanging out last night. You should talk to her."

"Already on my list."

"There was definitely tension between him and the crew." I told her about Mitchell's terrible treatment of Connor, crazy demands, and how Mitchell had stormed out of Nitro only to return shortly after as if nothing had happened. And about how Mitchell's behavior had obviously rattled Payton. "She kept popping pills last night, and then she stormed out. She and Mitchell were clearly at odds with how the documentary was taking shape. The production is strange. I've never been part of a documentary, but for a Hollywood film, it doesn't seem very professional."

Chief Meyers held up a finger. I waited for her to flip through her notes. "What about Kat Kelly? Claims she's president of his fan club."

The smell of gingerbread hit my nose. I turned to see that the door to the Gingerbread Cottage had been propped open.

A smart move by the shop owner. The fragrant, spicy scent of molasses and cinnamon made me hungry for one of their delectable cookies slathered with vanilla icing.

"That's another thing," I said to the chief. "How does he have a fan club? According to Payton, the director, he used to be a child actor, but no one I know has ever heard of the guy. His attitude was worse than any stories I've read about Hollywood divas."

One of the officers walked over to Chief Meyers and whispered something in her ear. "Gotta wrap this up, Sloan. I have a date with the county coroner. Should have the toxicology report back soon."

I didn't want to ask the next question, but knew I had to. "Do you think he could have had alcohol poisoning? I saw him nearly chug three pints, and he was definitely slurring his speech." I couldn't stomach the thought that we could have contributed to Mitchell's death. Garrett had cut him off, but if the report showed high levels of alcohol, could we be in any trouble?

"Won't know until I talk to the coroner." Chief Meyers stuffed her pen into her breast pocket. "Before you go, Sloan. Do me a favor and just be on the lookout for anything unusual, especially if this crew is hanging around Nitro."

"Will do." We parted ways. Chief Meyers gathered her officers together. I couldn't resist the scent of gingerbread, so I strolled into the Cottage to pick up some cookies to share with Garrett. The inside of the bakeshop was like a scene straight from the pages of a fairy tale. Tiered gingerbread castles dripping with royal icing and too pretty to eat were displayed in showcases. There was a Halloween village made entirely from the spicy cookies as well as a re-creation of the Seahawks' stadium with miniature gingerbread football players and a referee. I snapped a picture for Alex.

"Wow, you've outdone yourself this year," I said to the girl behind the counter.

She was packaging dozens of gingerbread cutouts of the Oktoberfest crest in cellophane bags. "I know. Isn't that the cutest? We get so many Seahawks fans in from Seattle."

"They're going to love it." I perused the pastry case. "I'll take a dozen cookies. Half iced and half dipped in chocolate."

"Good choice. The chocolate dipped are my favorite."

We chatted for a few minutes before I left with my bag of treats. I wasn't sure if Garrett had ever tried Leavenworth's famed gingerbread. I was more than happy to introduce him to my favorite cookies.

As I inserted my key into the lock on Nitro's front door, I heard someone whispering my name. I turned around, but no one was there. Was I hearing things now? Great.

"Sloan?" The voice sounded again.

I clutched the bag of gingerbread, but dropped my keys on the sidewalk. When I bent over to pick them up, a shadow flooded the sidewalk. My heart skipped a beat. Typically it takes a lot to rattle me. If I'd heard someone calling my name on Leavenworth's charming streets any other morning, I would have taken it in stride, but I reacted instinctively, standing up and holding my keys like a weapon.

"Hey, sorry." Kat stared at me with wide eyes. "I didn't mean to scare you."

I relaxed. "What are you doing up so early?"

She wore a yellow-and-green-striped stocking cap and a

puffy bright yellow parka. One hand was clutching her suitcase and the other was shoved into her coat pocket. "I didn't know what to do last night."

"What do you mean?" I repositioned the key and unlocked the front door. Why did she have her suitcase with her?

Her cheeks were blanched as if all the color had been drained from them. She shivered.

"Why don't you come in?" I said, holding the door open for her.

She hurried into the pub, dragging her suitcase behind her.

"Can I get you a cup of coffee or something?" I asked. "Gingerbread?"

"That would be good," she said through chattering teeth. "I'm so cold."

"Have a seat." I pointed to a barstool. "I'll brew some coffee, and help yourself to a cookie. They're delicious."

She set her suitcase next to the table while I went behind the bar to brew a pot of coffee. "You're up and moving early," I commented.

"I didn't know where to go." Her voice cracked as she spoke. She opened the bag of gingerbread and peered inside.

"Really, have one," I insisted.

"If you're sure?" She hesitated before reaching into the bag and picking a chocolate-dipped cookie. "I just didn't know where to go, and you were so nice last night, that I thought . . ."

"What?" I dumped ground beans into the coffeepot and stared at her. "What do you mean?" I recognized the look of panic on her face. I was all too familiar with her wild eyes and the feeling of not knowing where your next meal is coming from or where you're going to sleep.

She nibbled on the cookie. "Well, it's been kind of a mess. After the police interviewed me, I went to the hotel where Mitchell said he had a reservation for me, but they didn't have one. They said they were full. I went to every other hotel in town, and no one had space. I didn't know what to do, so I ended up sleeping in the gazebo."

"The gazebo?" No wonder the poor girl was ghostly white and shivering. Nighttime temperatures had been flirting with freezing with the shift into fall. Soon the morning dew would turn into a hard frost. Leavenworth sat at over one thousand feet, which meant that evening temps quickly plummeted, even in the middle of summer.

She rubbed her parka. "I didn't know what else to do. I don't know anyone here, and Mitchell made all the plans. The hotel said they'd never heard of him. I made them check three times."

"You slept outside?"

"What else could I do? I came on the train." She broke the cookie in half and took another small bite. Was she savoring it because she was worried it might be the only thing she would have to eat today?

I filled the coffeepot with water and set it to its strongest brew. Then I joined her at the high-top table while the coffee percolated. "What hotel did Mitchell say he booked you at?" I sat next to her and helped myself to a cookie. The cookies that I had chosen were soft and were sprinkled with sugar before being dipped in royal icing and dark chocolate.

They were nicely spiced with delicate hints of nutmeg and cloves. Soft with chewy centers and just a touch of sweetness. I might have let out a little moan when I took the first bite.

"The big one across the street. Hotel Residence." She reached into her parka and removed a crumpled brochure. "I was so excited because they have a huge German breakfast every morning where they serenade the guests with an authentic alpenhorn." She pointed to the picture of the hotel's founder in traditional German garb waking up the village from the fourth-floor balcony.

The hotel was one of Leavenworth's most popular. Its ornate wooden beams had been carved by hand by the owner and his son. Guests were treated to German hospitality, like evening cocktails in front of the massive rock fireplace and homemade strudels and cooked-to-order omelets at the Hotel Residence's famous breakfast buffet. But what made a stay at the hotel unique was the morning alpenhorn concert. For decades, the hotel owner would thrust open the balcony doors, climb onto a precarious ledge, and greet the entire village with a morning salute. Like clockwork at 8 A.M., the familiar sound of the alpenhorn would reverberate through our quiet streets.

"They didn't have a room for you?" I polished off my cookie.

She shook her head and pressed her finger on the brochure. "No. They said no one made a reservation under Mitchell's name, my name, or even anyone associated with the film."

"Let me call over there for you. I know the owners. Maybe there's been a mistake."

"No," she wailed. "There's nothing. Trust me, I've tried. I begged. I asked if I could sleep in the lobby. They kicked me out. I think they thought I was making it up or something. The same for all the other hotels. They all said they've been sold out for months. I don't have any money to get home, and Chief Meyers told me not to leave town. I don't know what I'm going to do." She hid her face in her hands.

The coffee beeped. I patted her arm. "Relax. We'll figure something out." I stood up and went to pour her a cup. "Cream or sugar?" I asked from behind the bar.

"Yes, please."

"Do you want something more to eat? We have some pastries in the kitchen."

"I'll take the coffee for now." She wiped her nose with the back of her parka. "The cookie was amazing. Thank you."

I stirred thick cream and a teaspoon of sugar into the steaming mug and delivered it to the table. Immediately she wrapped her hands around the cup. "What did Mitchell tell you about the weekend?"

She clutched the mug tightly. "Not much. I guess I should have asked more questions, but I was so excited about winning this trip and getting to see how a real movie is made that I didn't think about it. I just packed my suitcase and hopped on the train."

Her words jumbled together as she spoke. Last night she had looked young, but this morning she looked even younger.

If I'd had to guess, I would have put her in her very early twenties.

She took a sip of the coffee. "What am I going to do now? Where am I going to stay? There's nowhere to go, and I don't know anyone in town. The only person I knew was dead."

"You can stay with me until we figure something out."

Her eyes widened. "I can? Thank you, thank you!"

I smiled. I couldn't let the poor girl sleep on the streets. Not when I had a huge, empty farmhouse. She was right about Leavenworth being at capacity for the weekend, but it wouldn't hurt to have a conversation with the owner of Hotel Residence. Kat was obviously distraught. Maybe she hadn't articulated her situation clearly. I couldn't imagine anyone in Leavenworth kicking a young girl to the streets if she had really pleaded to sleep in the lobby. Plus, I could talk to Lisa and see if Kat could take Mitchell's rental cabin once Chief Meyers completed her investigation.

"It's fine. I have a big farmhouse. You can sleep in the guest room, and I'll talk to a few of the hotels in the meantime and see if I can find something."

"But I don't have any money." She bit her bottom lip. "This trip was supposed to be all expenses paid. Mitchell was covering the hotel and even my food. Even if you can find me a room, I can't afford it."

I placed my hand on her forearm. Her shirtsleeve felt like ice. "Don't worry. We'll figure it out. In the meantime you can stay with me."

"That's so nice of you. I can help. I can work for my stay."

"You don't need to worry about that."

"No, really, I want to. I want to earn my keep."

It was probably due to my vagabond upbringing, but I had a soft spot for her. The fact that she was willing to help out in exchange for a room endeared her to me. Then again, was there an outside chance that I had just invited a murderess to be my guest?

CHAPTER

NINE

I GLANCED AT THE SLEEK, modern clock hanging on the far wall. "I can run you home now, if you want. You're welcome to take a nap or a bath. Whatever you want. You can make yourself at home, but I need to be here today."

"No, that's okay. I'll stay here. Put me to work. I promise I'm a good worker and I won't get in your way." She tugged off her parka and hung it on the back of the barstool.

I studied her. To be honest, we could have used another set of hands around the pub that day, but I didn't know anything about this girl. What was Garrett going to say about me taking in a stray?

She must have sensed my hesitation, because she sat taller. "No, really, I would feel worse to make you take me out to your house and then come back to work. I swear I'll do anything. Mop floors, wash dishes. Anything." The color had returned to her cheeks. That was a good sign.

It would be easier to stay in town. There was so much work to do before the evening keg tapping and the official opening ceremonies for Oktoberfest. Not to mention, it was probably smarter to keep her where I could see her. For all I knew, if I dropped her at the farmhouse, she could rob me blind. I hated thinking that way. That was what families used to think of me when they took me in. No one ever said it aloud, but I could tell by their ever-watchful eyes and the fact that I never was allowed to be left alone. I wanted to trust Kat, and yet I had to be a realist.

"Let me check with Garrett, the owner, and make sure he's cool with you hanging out. As long as it's okay with him, then I'll put you to work."

"Great." She grinned. "Thank you so much. I promise I won't let you down." Her curls spilled out from the stocking cap.

"It's fine." I pushed back my stool. "Finish your coffee. I'll grab you something to eat and be back in a few."

She dutifully sipped the coffee as I went to the kitchen. Garrett was just coming down the back stairs. He ran his fingers through his sleep-styled hair. "Am I hearing things, or were you talking to someone?" Per usual, he wore a pair of faded jeans, sandals, and a beer T-shirt. This one with the slogan REAL MEN WEAR LEDERHOSEN.

I laughed. "You're not actually going to wear that, are you?"

"Only for April." Garrett perked up at my reaction. "Actually you inspired me with your REAL WOMEN DRINK BEER shirt. When I saw you in that, I hopped online and ordered this beauty." He ran his hands over the cheesy shirt.

"Oh, great. I'm glad that I inspired you to order that." I pointed to his shirt and winked.

His face shifted. "You inspire me every day, Sloan."

My throat tightened. His eyes pierced through me. I couldn't swallow. What was wrong with me? I attempted to laugh off his compliment. "Glad to be of service."

He looked slightly injured, but squared his shoulders and then scratched his chin.

Garrett was a night owl. It had taken me a while to get used to his lazy morning routine. Unlike Mac, who was always obsessed with his appearance, Garrett would stumble downstairs in the morning without brushing his hair or caring about what he was wearing. "You weren't imagining things. I was talking to someone. We have a guest."

"A guest." He rubbed his eyes and followed me into the kitchen.

I explained Kat's situation and told him what happened last night while I put together a plate of fresh fruit and muffins.

"A murder?" Garrett reached for a bunch of grapes. "Not that I'm surprised in some ways. The guy managed to make enemies of almost everyone in town in the matter of one night."

"It looks that way." I broke a chocolate chip muffin in half and took a bite. *Stress eating,* I thought to myself. "Mitchell wasn't dangerously intoxicated, was he? I mean, I know you cut him off, which was the right thing to do, but he didn't seem completely out of control."

"No. He wasn't. Although he was definitely acting strange. I wanted him out of here before he caused an actual fight."

"That's what I told Chief Meyers." I bit my bottom lip. I was glad that Garrett agreed.

"Who is the girl?"

"She's the president of his fan club. He was supposed to book her a hotel room and pay for her trip. She won it as a prize, but it sounds like he flaked out."

"That's a shocker." The sarcasm in Garrett's voice was thick.

"My thoughts exactly. I can't let her roam around town without anywhere to go. What do you think about letting her help out?"

He shrugged. "It's fine by me. She can't work in the bar, obviously. Not without paperwork. Is she even twenty-one?"

"I don't know. I'll find out. I was thinking we could have her on growler-washing duty, send her to pick up supplies, and what do you think about having her pass out flyers at Oktoberfest?" Garrett and I had discussed disseminating marketing materials. Many restaurants and shops in town offered special discounts for Oktoberfest weekend. We had talked about putting together a flyer for a free tasting flight. It would be a great way to pull new clients into the brewery.

"Sounds good to me." He helped himself to a muffin. "So Mitchell was killed? The guy had an attitude, but that's terrible."

"I know." I pushed the image of Mitchell's lifeless body from my head.

"You okay, Sloan?" Garrett stared at me with concern.

"No, I'm fine." I wasn't sure that I was, but I didn't want to relive last night. "Do you want to come meet Kat?"

He chomped the muffin and nodded. "I guess I better."

Kat was equally effusive with her thanks to Garrett. He brushed it off. "No big deal. That's how we roll around here. Happy to have your help."

He left to get caught up on paperwork in the office. I showed Kat around and tasked her with cleaning. "By the way, how old are you?" I asked as I handed her a pair of rubber gloves.

"Twenty-two," she said with a touch of pride.

"Can I see your ID?"

She reached into a hidden pocket on the inside of her parka and handed me her ID. I checked the license. It looked legit to me. We still wouldn't have her pour or help in the front, but I felt better knowing that she was of legal age. There was no way I would take a chance like that with the Washington State Liquor Control Board. I was sure that officials would be in town to monitor Oktoberfest. If anyone stopped by the brewery for a spot check, I wanted to make sure we were in compliance with the law.

"Once you finish cleaning, come find me and I'll give you your next task," I told her.

She pulled on the gloves. "Okay. Thank you again. I don't know what I would do without your help."

"Don't worry about it," I said with a wave, and went to find Garrett in the office.

He had a spreadsheet open on his flat-screen computer monitor. "What's the verdict?" he asked, clicking one of the columns.

"We'll see. She seems enthusiastic and earnest, but I'm going to keep an eye on her."

"That's probably wise." Garrett pointed to the monitor. "How long do you think we should wait before we dry hop this test batch of cranberry?"

Garrett's scientific approach to beer fascinated me. He spent hours analyzing spreadsheets and tracking minuscule changes in each batch.

"I don't know. Maybe tomorrow?" I suggested.

He clicked a key on the keyboard and made a note. "Yeah. I like that. Two days into the fermentation process. Let's stagger the remaining batches, and maybe we do a couple without dry hopping?"

"Sure." I was used to Der Keller's automated process, and appreciated the chemistry and testing involved in creating new blends for Nitro. "I'll let you keep working, but what do you think about a flyer for Oktoberfest? I know we talked about it a while ago. Then I dropped it because I wasn't sure how we would pull it off with the two of us. Now that we have Kat's help, I can create something this morning and send it over to the printer. They're usually quick. I'm sure they could get us a stack of flyers this afternoon."

"Let's do it." Garrett sounded enthusiastic.

"A tasting flight?" I asked. "Do we want an expiration? The end of the month? The end of the year?"

He scratched his chin. "Sloan, you always make me think, and it's way too early in the morning to think." To prove his point he reached for his coffee and took a huge sip.

"Sorry." I winked. "This is why you pay me the big bucks, though."

He threw his head back and laughed. "Big bucks. Don't we wish."

One of the most unexpected things about working with Garrett had been the way we had quickly fallen into a comfortable rhythm around each other. I had to admit that I looked forward to our easy banter.

"It will happen. Someday. Trust me."

"Oh, I trust you, Sloan." He held my gaze for a moment, making my heart rate speed up and my palms start to sweat.

I cleared my throat. "If you trust me, then I suggest we extend the offer through the end of the year. That way if people don't have a chance to stop by during Oktoberfest, we can catch them during the holiday markets and winter light fest."

"Do it." He gave me a nod of approval and clicked something on his spreadsheet. I took my laptop and went to the bar to work on designing a flyer. I wished that Alex were here. He had a natural eye for design and had been considering a career in marketing. We had tasked him with designing Nitro's menus, and he had done a brilliant job of capturing Garrett's scientific slant. Without our in-house designer, my best bet was to send the local print shop our logo, a copy of our menu, and text for the flyer. They could put something together for us. I wrote some copy about tasting Leavenworth's newest Northwest-inspired ales with a free flight. Then I shot off an email with everything to the print shop. They responded right away, letting me know that they would have a design ready for approval within the hour and that our flyers would be printed and waiting for us at the shop no later than noon. Yet another thing to love about life in a small town. The business community was tight-knit. Unlike in a big city where it might take weeks or months to turn around a project like ours, in Leavenworth it could happen in a matter of minutes.

With that complete, I checked on Kat to see how the cleaning was coming. Her face was flushed, and sweat beaded on her smooth forehead, but she looked lighter than I had seen her since our first meeting.

"I'm off to run a couple of errands. It looks like you've got the swing of things."

The smell of bleach had overtaken the brewery. She dabbed her forehead with the back of her elbow. "It feels good to do something, you know?"

I did know. One of my go-to coping strategies was to keep busy. "Yep. It's true." I pointed behind me to the office. "Garrett's here if you have any questions. I shouldn't be long."

"No problem. You can count on me. I'll keep scrubbing until my fingers bleed." She squeezed an industrial sponge into a bucket of bleach.

"Don't do that." I grimaced. "Just give everything a good wipe down."

At least something is working out this morning, I thought as I stepped outside into the crisp fall air. The vibe felt different. Despite the chatter of crews putting the finishing touches on the square and wrapping the Maypole with stunning garlands of red and white carnations, I couldn't shake the memory of seeing Mitchell's body sprawled on the street.

Shop owners deadheaded geraniums in window boxes and hung WILLKOMMEN signs on their front doors. A few hours from now, tourists wearing lederhosen and dirndl dresses would spill onto Front Street en route to the Festhalle and the giant Oktoberfest tents that flanked the end of the square.

Tomorrow at noon, everyone would crowd the sidewalks to watch the keg procession. Villagers would join in the parade waving flags and tossing bundles of colorful flowers and packages of German chocolates. Would anyone even know that a man had died right here?

Mitchell's death loomed heavy on my mind as I stopped at The Nutcracker shop to chat with the owner, who was dusting his impressive collection. There were nutcrackers for any occasion imaginable from Halloween to Easter. Every profession, hobby, and craft was represented in the wooden statues like one dressed in doctor's scrubs and another in park ranger's khaki uniform. An entire ten-foot wall was devoted to Christmas.

"Morning, Sloan," the owner, Stan, said, stepping into his open doorway as he dusted the top of a nutcracker wearing suspenders and a green felt hat. "You ready for the games to begin?"

"As ready as we'll ever be." I looked around the electric storefront that Stan and his wife had owned for as long as I could remember. Signs had been posted throughout the shop advertising Oktoberfest special discounts.

"Hey, at least you're not at Der Keller this year. It's always a mob scene." He must have worried that he had offended me, because he stopped and quickly changed the subject. "I heard there's a film crew in town. They asked if they could stop by later and get some shots of my merchandise. I told the director this is the largest assortment of nutcrackers this side of the Mississippi."

"Is that right?" I stared into the store. Every inch of wall and counter space showcased a nutcracker with a paper price tag. Some were tiny, while others were almost four feet tall.

"You bet." Stan returned the nutcracker he was holding to the front display and brushed off his hands. "I also heard there was a murder last night. Over behind Nitro."

That didn't take long. Word had already spread, just as I had imagined.

"Sadly, that's true," I replied.

"One of the film crew, huh? Heard he got his head smashed in. That's a bad way to go."

I placed my hand on my stomach in an attempt to center myself. "No. It wasn't pretty."

"You were there?"

Talking about Mitchell's murder wasn't high on my list, but I knew that if I tried to skirt away, that would only make it worse. If everyone had already heard the news, gossip would be spreading like wildfire. I gave him a condensed version of last night's events in hopes that he could fill in our fellow villagers and leave me out of it.

"That's weird," he said when I finished. "I saw that guy across the street late last night."

"You did?" My senses perked up.

"Yeah. Over by the gazebo. I stayed late to clean and do one last inventory count. You know how it is before Oktoberfest. Have to have all our ducks in a row." Stan nodded toward a nutcracker holding a bottle of bubble bath, a back scratcher, and a rubber ducky.

I nodded and waited for him to continue.

"It must have been sometime after ten. I heard voices over in the gazebo. That guy was fighting with a woman."

"He was?"

"Yep. Sounded like a lover's spat to me. But I wonder if maybe it was more." He picked a piece of lint from a nut-cracker wearing a Scottish plaid kilt.

"Did you see who he was with?" My mind went straight to Kat. She had claimed that she never found Mitchell, but what if she was lying? Had they had a fight in the gazebo and then she chased him to the tents?

"No." He shook his head. "Couldn't see. It was a woman for sure. She had a real high-pitched voice, and she sounded pretty pissed."

"You should let Chief Meyers know. If you saw Mitchell at ten, it wasn't that much longer until he was killed."

"Will do. I'll give her a ring right now." He gave me a nod and returned inside.

So much for feeling relieved. Had I just invited a mur-derer into our pub? Who else could have been fighting with Mitchell in the gazebo shortly before he was killed? Every-thing was pointing to Kat. I had to get back to the pub and warn Garrett.

CHAPTER

TEN

I NEEDED A NEW PLAN—STAT. I would pick up the flyers and then swing by Chief Meyers's office. Police headquarters were located outside of the square, but the chief kept a small office in the village, which was mainly used when tourists had imbibed too much.

What had I been thinking, offering to take in a stranger? I had felt sorry for Kat, but had I made a major mistake? What if her sob story was fake? Maybe she had constructed an elaborate lie to hide the fact that she had killed Mitchell. Usually I felt like I was a good judge of character. My dissolving marriage made me feel like I was losing it. Should I return to the pub and give her the boot? Or would that inflame her? If she had killed Mitchell, she obviously wasn't stable.

"Sloan, wait up!" I heard Hans's familiar voice and felt an immediate sense of relief. Hans would know what to do.

"Hey, how's it going?" he asked, catching up to me in three long, easy strides.

"Not great." I winced and launched into what I'm sure sounded like a jumble of incoherent sentences.

Hans wrapped his arm around my shoulder in a protective, brotherly move. "Come on. Let's go sit." He smelled of cedar shavings. I caught a faint hint of furniture oil from his coveralls as we crossed the street.

We sat on a bench not far from the Kinderplatz. By the afternoon, the grassy hill would be a sea of happy children running with pumpkin balloons and dancing to the joyful sounds of the accordion. Crisp leaves piled next to the bench, another reminder that season was shifting.

"I already heard about Mitchell," Hans said crossing his legs and keeping his arm around my shoulder. "How are you holding up?"

Sometimes I couldn't believe that he and Mac were actually brothers. Hans's steady, calming eyes instantly made my heart rate slow. "I'm kind of a mess. You know me, I'm not ever a mess."

He squeezed my shoulder. "I know. But to tell you the truth, Sloan, it's nice to see you vulnerable. It looks good on you."

Hans was one part carpenter and one part therapist. I often wondered if my childhood would have been different with a brother like Hans. He also had an uncanny ability to read people and pull them out of themselves.

"Thanks a lot."

"I'm serious, Sloan. We've talked about it before. You don't always let people in." His golden brown eyes were pleading.

I didn't respond. His words were true. There was nothing more to say.

"I know that you're going through a hard time, but I have to say that I like seeing you crack a bit. It's good." He cracked his knuckles as if to make his point.

"It's good? How am I supposed to work and keep my personal life together when I'm like this? And what about Alex?"

"What about Alex?"

"He's not used to seeing me like this either. I'm supposed to be the strong one."

"Being vulnerable is being strong." He stared at me as if trying to hammer home his point. "The two are one and the same."

I wasn't sure I agreed with him, but I didn't have the energy to debate the point at the moment. Why was the stress getting to me now? I'd been in similar situations in the past and been able to keep my emotions in check. What was different now? The reality that my marriage was ending? The stress about staying at Nitro or returning to Der Keller? All of it?

Hans softened his tone. "Listen, I just don't want to see you beat yourself up. It's okay to feel like this. Most of us feel unsettled pretty much every day."

"Well, not me," I kidded, breaking the tension.

"No, not Superwoman Sloan. Never let them see you sweat, right?"

"Exactly." I kicked the pile of leaves at my feet.

"Fine. Have it your way, but we're not done with this conversation." He removed his arm from my shoulder and uncrossed his legs. "I hate to add to your plate, but we're going to have to talk about Der Keller."

A monarch butterfly with golden yellow wings fluttered past the bench. I wanted to fly away and escape with it. "I know."

"Mac wants to do things his way. I've been trying to be there as much as I can, and I told my parents that I would work every weekend of Oktoberfest to help out, but we're going to need more help long term." The stress was beginning to show on his face. Like Garrett, Hans tended to let things roll off him. He didn't typically clench his jaw and burst into brief moments of anger like Mac, but I noticed a thin purple vein bulge on his temple as he spoke. "Sloan, neither of us want Der Keller, but unless something has changed with you, I don't think either of us want to see my brother run it into the ground either."

"Right." I sighed.

Hans reached down and picked a blade of grass. He twisted it around his pinky. "I think our only option is going to be hiring help—more help for the pub and brewery—maybe even a manager. It's going to mean forking over some money, but I don't see any other way."

"I'm sorry that you're in the middle of this mess." I leaned my head on his shoulder.

"Family is messy, but it doesn't mean it's not worth it." Hans tossed the blade of grass onto the ground. "We can revisit this conversation once we get through Oktoberfest."

"Deal."

We paused our conversation when a troupe of jugglers walked past on their way to set up their vendor tent. One of the jugglers tossed Hans a purple beanbag. He caught it on his foot and tossed it back to them. "You want to talk about the murder?"

"Yes." I let out a sigh. Then I told him about Kat and what I had learned from Stan, the owner of The Nutcracker. "What do you think I should do?"

"Go to Chief Meyers. That was your first instinct, right?"

"Right." I nodded.

"I suggest you start there."

What was wrong with me? Why did I need Hans to validate something as simple as talking to the police for me?

"Sloan?"

"Huh?" I shook off the feeling of self-pity. "Sorry. Yeah. That's where I was headed anyway."

"Good." He paused. "And you're sure you're okay?"

"I'm fine." I stood. "Shaken up from last night. That's all."

"Right." Hans gave me a half smile. "I'll come by later and see how it's going."

"That would be great." I left him on the bench. As I headed for the police office, I could feel Hans's eyes on my back. I knew he was worried about me. I was worried about me, but dwelling on my problems wasn't going to solve Mitchell's murder or help me survive the weekend. I needed to figure out who had killed the actor, pour pint after frothy pint, and wait to deal with my personal life once the crowds had returned home.

Like everything else in the village, the station looked like a German cottage. There were two wooden beer barrels on either side of the front door and the word POLIZEI carved on a hanging sign.

Inside, the small building had been modernized. Three desks housed computer equipment, scanners, and phones. Chief Meyers sat at one of the desks surrounded by two uniformed officers.

She looked up when I cleared my throat. "Sloan, long time no see."

"I wanted to fill you in on a couple things that I've learned about Mitchell since I saw you earlier."

She whispered something to one of the officers, who gave her a salute. He motioned for the other officer to follow him. Chief Meyers stood and adjusted her khaki pants. Sounds from the scanner crackled. She flipped it off. Then she picked up a pen with deep tooth marks in it and a notebook. "Shoot. What do you got?"

Her face didn't flinch when I told her about Kat sleeping in the gazebo last night or about the fight that Stan had overheard.

"You invited this girl into your workplace and your home?" she said in a disinterested tone when I finished.

"It sounds rash when I hear it repeated back to me, but I have a feeling about her."

"It sounds like something the Krauses would do." Chief Meyers raised her brow. She wasn't classically pretty, but there was something compelling about her face. I wondered if it was her quick wit. As a lifelong resident of Leavenworth and our longtime police chief, Meyers knew everything about everyone in town, including my in-laws. She wasn't effusive, and yet her concern for community permeated everything she did, from stopping to pick up a stray piece of trash on the sidewalk to checking in on some of Leavenworth's most senior residents and bringing them bags of groceries each week. We were lucky to have her.

I couldn't debate her on her assessment of Otto and Ursula. The Krauses opened their home and brewery to everyone. The only difference was the circumstance. I didn't think they'd ever invited a suspect in a murder investigation to dinner.

"You've got a feeling about this girl?" Chief Meyers pursed her lips and stared at me.

"She seems genuine, and yet she could be lying. Maybe it's an act."

"Maybe." She considered this for a moment. "You know, I like this idea. Why don't you and Garrett keep an eye on this girl. Let her get comfortable with you. Maybe she'll let something slip. They always do. We're pulling records on the entire film crew and running names through our database. If we get a hit on this girl, I'll let you know. But in the meantime, keep a close eye on her."

"Will do." I started to leave. "Did you get the coroner's report back?"

She scowled. Then she looked over her shoulder. With one finger, she motioned for me to come closer. I leaned over the counter. Her voice was grumbly as she spoke. I had often wondered if she had once been a smoker, but I'd never seen her light up. "Got it about an hour ago. Mitchell had something else in his system. A roofie. Usually used in date rape cases."

"Really? So the shards of glass?"

Chief Meyers shook her head. "Not our murder weapon. The coroner thinks that between Mitchell's blood alcohol level and the drug, he passed out. Hit his head. The growler might have been the final fatal blow, or it could have shattered when he fell." She coughed loudly. "This stays between us."

"Understood." I wasn't sure what this news meant in terms of Mitchell's death. Someone had slipped him a roofie? Who? I started to back out of the station, probably with a dazed look on my face.

"And, Sloan." Chief Meyers stopped me.

"Yeah?"

"I mean a close eye. I wouldn't let this girl out of my sight, and I'm not sure you want her at your house alone." The police scanner crackled again. Chief Meyers flicked it off with one motion.

"What do you think I should do?"

"Is there someone else who can come stay with you?"

From her expression, I could tell she was hinting at Mac. "No. Not really. I guess I could ask Hans to come and stay for a couple of nights."

"I think that would be wise if you're going to bring this girl home. Remember someone has been killed. Murdered, right here in our town."

I tried to swallow, but my mouth went dry. She was right. Was I putting myself at risk? Or, worse, Alex? I could watch over her at Nitro, but did I want her sleeping in our guest room? Before I returned to the pub, I was going to stop by the Hotel Residence and see if they had misplaced her reservation by chance. And if there was no space for her there, I was going to check in with Lisa to see if she could stay at Mitchell's empty cabin. I was willing to help Kat, and I wanted to believe her. But never at the expense of my son.

CHAPTER

ELEVEN

I PICKED UP OUR FLYERS at the print shop and headed for the Hotel Residence. The hotel was one of Leavenworth's grandest properties, with its sloping red tile roof, stone chimneys, and wooden turrets. Each guest room had its own private balcony with a view facing the mountains or looking out over the village. Hanging baskets cascading with bleeding hearts and trumpet vine greeted me as I entered the lobby. The interior of the hotel had been decked out for Oktoberfest. Garlands of German flags were draped over the massive wooden chandelier, and rows of bright red, yellow, and black welcome packages lined the reception desk. It smelled of baking apples.

"Sloan, nice to see you," Brad, the hotel's younger owner, said from behind the desk. Like his father, he had embraced German tradition and was a master craftsman when it came woodwork. He had mentored Hans when Hans decided that the brewery life wasn't for him. "How's that kid-brother-in-law of yours? He's supposed to stop by and help me with a holiday project."

"Funny. I just left him in the park." I glanced toward the ornately carved lobby doors. "What smells so good?"

"Hot apple cider," Brad said, nodding to a self-serve cart with baskets of mini doughnuts and a carafe of steaming cider with cinnamon sticks. "It's our signature welcome for our Oktoberfest guests."

Touches like this were just one of the reasons that the Hotel Residence was highly sought after. Brad was in his early fifties and had worked in the family business for his entire career. I had heard that his father had recently begun teaching him how to play the alpenhorn so that Brad could carry on the morning serenade when he retired. I didn't think his dad would make an exit anytime soon. The almost eighty-year-old was still spry and a fixture in town. Then again, a few weeks ago, I would have sworn that Otto and Ursula would work at Der Keller until their final days.

"That sounds like Hans, hanging around in the park while the rest of us work our fingers to the bone." He winked. "Are you ready for the madness?"

"I hope so." I crossed my fingers.

He waved his hand over the rows of gift bags. "The first guests should be arriving in the next couple hours. I love the calm before the storm."

"Actually, that's why I'm here."

"Don't tell me that you want a room." He rested his face on his hands. I looked around the stunning lobby. No detail had been overlooked. Brad and his father had left their mark with hand-carved woodwork chiseled with love. From the spiraling balcony above me to the solid-core wood doors with wrought-iron handles, every beam of wood had been carefully designed. Huge windows offered views of the deep green mountainside, and a piano with comfy seating welcomed guests to gather in front of a stone fireplace.

"No. Not exactly. I'm guessing you heard about the murder last night?" I straightened the stack of flyers in my hands.

He gave me a solemn nod. "Terrible news. I can't believe it."

"One of the women attached to the film crew said that Mitchell—the actor who was killed—reserved a room for her here." I placed the stack on the recently oiled reception counter, and tucked a stray strand of hair behind my ear. "Apparently when she tried to check in last night, they couldn't find the reservation."

Brad scowled. "Really?" He moved closer to one of the computer monitors. "What's her name?"

"Kat Kelly."

He typed in the name. "Nope. Nothing comes up under that name."

"What about Mitchell Morgan?"

He tried Mitchell's name too. "I don't see anything under that name either."

"Okay. That's what she said." I picked up my stack of flyers. "She said she tried to get a room last night, but since you were booked, she ended up sleeping in the gazebo."

Brad's eyes went wide. "What? We had plenty of room last night. She slept on the streets?"

I nodded. "She said that she begged your staff to let her have a room for one night, but that they turned her away. I didn't think that sounded like something any of your staff would say, which is why I wanted to check in."

"I'm glad you did." Brad looked concerned. "Hang on a minute. My front desk manager just went to lunch. She was here all night. I want to see what she has to say."

"Sure." Brad's reaction was what I had expected. Kat's story didn't add up. A guest stopped to help herself to a cup of the ambrosial cider. The smell was intoxicating—sweet and spicy, my preferred flavor profile. Maybe Garrett and I would have to experiment with an apple-cider brew.

Brad returned a few minutes later. "I spoke with the front desk manager. She said that no one came in last night asking for a reservation. We were only at thirty percent capacity with a few early arrivals, so there were ample rooms available should anyone have come in."

So Kat had lied. "Thanks for asking. That's really helpful."

"No problem." Brad offered me a caramel toffee from a bowl on the counter.

I declined. "I have to get back to the pub. You should come by and try our new Cherry Weizen if you get a free moment."

"You had me at Cherry Weizen." He grinned. "I'll try. Good luck!"

"Same to you." I left with a wave. Chief Meyers's warning rang in my head. Kat had lied about trying to find a hotel room last night. The question was why? Had she been embarrassed that she didn't have the cash to cover the cost? Or had she been involved in Mitchell's murder?

My conversation with Brad made me more convinced that bringing Kat home was a bad idea, so before I returned to Nitro I decided to see if I could track down Lisa. She and her mom had an office on the opposite side of town. I retraced my steps past the gazebo and headed up the hill toward the bookstore and The Carriage House, where the restaurant's old-fashioned horse-drawn carriage was being outfitted with streaming silky ribbons and carnations for tomorrow's parade.

Continuing on, I passed a pretzel stand, wine shop, and Spielzeug, a toy shop that imported European toys and games. The Wenatchee River flowed past Blackbird Island to my left. A canopy of gold-hued trees clustered on the island. Straight ahead lay Icicle Ridge. Soon its peak would be dusted with fresh snow.

I came to two adjoining A-frame chalets. Flyers for vacation homes and acreage for sale were posted in the front windows. A wraparound deck connected the two cabins. One side housed April's real estate firm, and the other, Balmes Vacation Properties.

Please don't let April see me, I said internally as I climbed the short flight of wooden stairs and made a beeline to my right. The door to Balmes Vacation Properties was propped open.

"Hello?" I called, peering inside to see Lisa slumped on the floor crying.

"Lisa, is everything okay?" I stepped into the doorway.

She reddened and stood up immediately. "Oh God, Sloan, this is so embarrassing. Sorry." Blinking rapidly, she patted her eyes with the tips of her fingers. "I'm so sorry to be so unprofessional."

"No need to apologize. I didn't mean to sneak up on you."

She pressed her knee-length skirt back into place. A strand of honey-colored hair had fallen out of its short ponytail. She twisted her finger around it. "I can't believe you saw me crying. I never cry."

"Is it because of last night?"

"Last night?" Lisa thought for a moment and then it hit her. "Oh, the murder. No. I mean that's terrible, of course, but the guy was such an ass. He deserved what he got."

I was surprised by her response and how easily she dismissed Mitchell's murder.

She fiddled with three silver bands around her wrist. "You have to see this review."

"A review?" Now it was my turn to be confused.

"A bad review. A horrid review. The kind of review that could destroy my business." She walked to her desk and handed me a sheet of paper.

It was a printout of a popular travel review website. According to the site, Balmes Vacation Properties had over one thousand four-star reviews. The most recent review, however, was scathing. FILTHY, RAT-INFESTED! read the headline. It went on to complain about customer service and false advertising, and ended with "This company is so bad that I won't even give it one star. If I could I would give it a negative star. I'll never stay at a Balmes Vacation Property and suggest that unless you like living like a homeless person you don't either."

"Ouch." I handed her back the paper.

"Did you see who wrote that?" She pointed to the bottom of the page.

I stared at the spot where she placed her finger. "Mitchell Morgan?" I said aloud.

"Can you believe it? Why? Why would he do that? He had only been in his cabin for an hour, and I can promise you the place was spotless. He went straight to the internet and posted this under his real name. What a troll.

"We've never received a one-star review. Never. It's a good thing that he's dead, because otherwise I would have killed him myself." Her almond eyes flared with anger.

I wasn't sure how to respond. The review was terrible. I had no idea why Mitchell had decided to take to the internet. But I couldn't help wondering if this was the first time Lisa had seen the review. Could she have seen it last night? If she prided herself on her business's reputation, could she have killed Mitchell in retaliation or in a fit of rage?

I wanted to tell her not to sweat it. Bad reviews were part of working in the service industry. Even Der Keller had received a handful of snarky reviews over the years. Otto and Ursula made it a point never to respond to negativity.

"Ziz is not about us," Otto had once said at a staff meeting when a server showed him a less-than-glowing review from a popular website. The commenter had filled paragraph after paragraph with details about German beers, claiming that Der Keller was a fraud.

Our staff burst into laughter when Otto read one of the lines from the review aloud. "Has anyone who works at this place ever been to Germany? I think not!" He folded the sheet of paper. "I think, *ja*—we have." Everyone chuckled. Otto continued in a calm tone. "If one of our customers has something to tell us that can make us better and improve, then *ja*, we will listen, but ziz is nonsense." Then he proceeded to shred the nasty review.

"You can't let it get to you," I said to Lisa. "I make it a point never to read reviews."

"What? You have to read your reviews. Clients today make purchasing decisions based on reviews. This is a new century, Sloan. Customers are savvy. They read reviews. They read comments. They have the ability to learn tons about a business before making a purchase or booking a reservation. This one review could costs me thousands and thousands of dollars."

"Really?"

"Yeah. God, I can't believe Mitchell. After everything I did for him. That is one of the nicest properties we manage. I just can't figure out why Mitchell was so awful." She opened her desk drawer and pulled out a ring of keys. "In fact I have to walk over there now to let the police in. Mitchell locked every door and window. Can you believe it?"

I shook my head. "Mind if I walk with you?"

She motioned to the door. "Be my guest."

"Had you ever met Mitchell before?" I asked, waiting for her to close the door behind us and trying to keep my body close to the building. It would be just my luck to see April pop her head out of the office next door.

"Never." She pointed up the street. "We're going that way. Why?"

"I just wondered if he had some sort of grudge."

"No. Why would he? I never even interacted with him. Everything was set up through the film company. Payton organized it all. From the minute that man arrived in town, he started complaining. You would think he was an A-list star or something. He sent over a list of demands when my mom let him in."

"He did? Like what?" Lisa was shorter than me by at least

four inches, but she was on a mission. I practically had to sprint to keep up with her.

Her heels slammed on the sidewalk with each step. "It was ridiculous. He said his skin type demanded a sheet thread count of no less than eighteen hundred."

"Do they even make sheets with that kind of thread count?"

She shrugged. "Probably. I assured him that our linens were of the highest quality. We buy sheets made of Egyptian cotton that are soft and luxurious and great for any skin type, but that wasn't good enough for him."

"Seriously?" Mitchell was sounding more and more like a diva by the minute.

"Oh, that's just the tip of the iceberg. He wanted the fridge stocked with imported bottled water, demanded a visit by an in-house masseuse, and wanted a driver to take him around town." Her arms pumped back and forth as we crested the hill and headed toward a row of charming cabins nestled above the river.

"Where? Up to the mountains?" I pointed to the ridgeline. "You can walk everywhere in Leavenworth—literally."

"I know!" Lisa become more agitated as she spoke. "The guy was a first-class jerk. Mom and I are used to filling requests for guests, but not like Mitchell's and not at the last minute. This isn't New York. Where did he expect us to come up with a masseuse? Or we were supposed to drive to Seattle to find his brand of imported bottled water?"

"And you're sure he was serious about these requests? Do you think he could have been putting on an act?"

Lisa shook her head. "No way. You should see my cell phone. I must have a log of fifty calls from him. He was dead serious."

She emphasized the word "dead," making me wonder again just how far Mitchell had pushed her.

Why the demands? Mitchell wasn't well-known, at least around here, and he was narrating a documentary. Had he been overcompensating for something? Or was he just an ass, like Lisa claimed?

We arrived at the rental property. It was the largest on the street—three stories, with dark walnut trim and balconies on each level. A set of stairs led to a landing on the ground floor where a deck split, taking guests inside through an arched doorway or around to the back side of the cabin. I peeked onto the deck while Lisa flipped through her key chain. The twenty-foot deck stretched the length of the cabin and offered a sweeping view of the Wenatchee River below. Lisa hadn't exaggerated about the property. It was a private oasis.

She opened the door and let out a gasp. "Oh my God, Sloan, get over here!"

"What is it?" I ran to the archway.

Lisa dropped the keys and pointed inside.

The cabin looked as if it had been hit by a tornado. Garbage—black and slimy banana peels, candy wrappers, used tissues, and something that looked and smelled suspiciously like old fish were piled on the hardwood floors and on bookshelves and windowsills. Every couch cushion and pillow had been ripped open, and the stuffing torn out. The furniture had been overturned.

I threw my hand over my mouth and nose to block the overpowering smell.

"What did he do? He destroyed my property!" Lisa shouted, looking at me in disbelief.

CHAPTER
TWELVE

"WE BETTER CALL CHIEF MEYERS right away," I suggested, waving my hand in front of my face to try and brush away the awful smell.

"He destroyed my property!" Lisa yelled. "This is worse than when a Seattle fraternity came to town a few years ago. They didn't do anywhere near this much damage. And, my GOD, what is that smell?" She pounded her fist on the exterior wall so hard I was worried that she might snap her wrist.

While she ranted, I called Chief Meyers, who promised to be right over.

"How could he have done this in one night?" Lisa asked, starting to go inside.

I caught her arm. "I don't think that's a good idea. Chief Meyers is on her way. She said that her team is already aware of the damage. Apparently, the police were here last night and she made it clear that they're still looking for any evidence connected to Mitchell's murder. We shouldn't touch anything."

Lisa nodded but didn't take her eyes off the mess. "Just wait until I post pictures of this. The guy gives us a terrible review after trashing the place. What nerve."

She stared at the cabin in disbelief. My thoughts went to his murder. Had Mitchell torn up the rental property or had his killer? It seemed unlikely that Mitchell would have shredded the pillows and couch cushions. It looked more like someone had been searching for something. The garbage and rotting smell were another thing altogether. Had someone tried to make it look like Mitchell was living in filth, or was Lisa right? Maybe Mitchell had gone on a rampage and trashed the cabin on purpose to spite her. Could there be a connection to the drug that the coroner had found in his system?

I sighed and tried to console Lisa while we waited for the police. The day was getting more confusing by the minute.

Chief Meyers arrived within minutes. She moved with intention, but obviously not fast enough for Lisa.

"Hurry," Lisa pleaded. "My property has been destroyed."

If Chief Meyers heard Lisa's comment, she gave no indication. Instead she climbed the stairs one step at a time and blocked access to the cabin. "I can't let you in. My team has already done an initial sweep." She pointed to numbered yellow markers like the ones I'd seen around Mitchell's body last night. "We'll take it from here, ladies." She directed one of her uniformed officers inside and dismissed us.

As much as I wanted to stay, I had to get back to the pub. I left with Lisa arguing about needing to come inside to assess for insurance purposes how much damage had been done. Chief Meyers held her ground. "This is a police investigation. Step away from the door."

I didn't want to get on her bad side. "Come by later, if you can," I said to Lisa.

She gave me a half-hearted thumbs-up.

I took the pathway along the riverfront back to Nitro. The sound of the river and the squawks of mountain crows kept me grounded in reality. The more I thought about it, the more convinced I became that Mitchell must have gone into some kind of drug-induced rage. What other motivation could he have had to trash the cabin?

Garrett was setting votive candles on the bar tables when I arrived. "Hey, I was about ready to call a search party."

"Sorry." I set the flyers on a table. "Where's Kat?"

He looked over his shoulder. "She's doing inventory in the kitchen, why?"

I quickly filled him in on my conversation with Chief Meyers. He listened with a passive face. "You know, I'm with you, Sloan. I have a good vibe about her. She doesn't seem like a killer. It sounds to me like she was obsessed with the guy."

"Right, but what if he didn't return her feelings? You know that old saying, 'Hell hath no fury like a woman scorned.'"

"True. But from the way she's been shaking and sobbing all morning, she looks more like she's in shock." His well-defined muscles flexed as he lifted a large box of vases and candles onto the bar.

I was glad that Garrett shared my perspective. "Well,

regardless, Chief Meyers wants us to keep an eye on her. Do you think we should send her to the Festhalle later to hand out flyers?"

"Why not? What's she going to do? Run off with a stack of coupons for a tasting flight?"

He had a point.

Like Hans, Garrett had a pragmatic approach to life that made me think more rationally. He was right. Kat was probably harmless, and I knew that she was broke. If she couldn't afford a hotel, she wasn't likely to get far.

Garrett stared at the wall of photographs. "Sloan, I hate to tell you this right now because I know you have a lot going on."

"Okay." I could hear the trepidation in my voice.

"A woman called while you were gone."

That sounded benign. I wondered why Garrett kept running his hand across his chin as if trying to find the right words.

"She asked for you."

"Okay?" I repeated.

"She's called a bunch of times." He didn't make eye contact.

"Why didn't you say anything?"

"Every time she calls, she asks for you. You remember the calls, right? The two times that I've come to get you and then you've picked up the phone and no one was there?"

I nodded.

"It's the same woman. I'm sure."

My stomach dropped. "Okay."

"When she called today, she asked if you were going to

be here tonight. She said that she keeps missing you by phone and that she's going to try and stop in tonight."

I clutched a barstool. The room went fuzzy. I had a feeling I knew who the woman might be. When Garrett had discovered the old photo in his aunt's collection of me when I was a young girl with a woman, we both assumed she must be my mother. The picture had set off a chain of thoughts and memories that I couldn't shake.

I had no recollection of ever being in Leavenworth, but I must have been at some point. I didn't know why Garrett's aunt had the picture or if she had known the woman. I had asked Ursula about it once. On opening night at Nitro, Ursula had gravitated to the photo wall. I watched her delight in seeing old friends and the Leavenworth she had helped grow and cultivate. I also noticed that her face clouded at the sight of some of the photos. At the time, I had thought it was nostalgia for her younger days, but then when Garrett found the photo and I showed it to her, the same look crossed her face.

"I do not know zis woman, Sloan," she had said, turning her head away from the photo.

"But doesn't she look like me?" I had asked. "Don't you think this could be me as a young girl?"

Her eyes welled with tears. She left the table to pour herself a cup of tea.

I pressed on. "Doesn't this look like me?"

She huddled near the stove. "I do not know. Maybe. It could be. That was so long ago."

I tried to ask her more, but she had refused to speak. I was convinced that Ursula knew the woman. Did that mean she knew me, too? If Ursula knew anything about my past, why wouldn't she tell me? And why had she encouraged me to drop the subject?

Since our conversation, I'd been trying to find out anything I could about my past. I'd written to the state adoption agency and looked up my old social worker. She had since retired, but I had tracked her down. She was living on Vashon Island. I'd written her a pleading letter asking for any information she might have about my parents and how I'd come into the system. It had been three weeks, and I had yet to receive a response.

Why hadn't Garrett told me about the calls earlier?

"Sloan." His voice shook me into the present.

"Yeah." I exhaled.

"I probably should have told you the first time she called, but I didn't think much of it. People call the pub all the time. But the calls have kept coming, and now if she's going to stop by, I thought you might want a heads-up."

"Thanks. I appreciate it." I loosened my grip on the stool.

"Have you heard anything from the state yet?"

I shook my head. "Nothing." I had filled Garrett in on my quest to figure out the mysteries of my past. He'd been helpful without being pushy. I had appreciated his support.

"Is there anything I can do?" He brushed something off his ridiculous REAL MEN WEAR LEDERHOSEN T-shirt.

"No. I mean if she shows up, I'll roll with it. We're going to be busy anyway. The first weekend of Oktoberfest isn't the best time to make an appearance, you know."

He chuckled. "True. Maybe that's her plan."

"Maybe." I put on what I hoped was a neutral face and

turned the conversation to prepping for the afternoon. In reality my head spun like a Tilt-A-Whirl. Was the mysterious woman my mother? And if so, why had she finally decided to make contact now? After all these years of silence. The timing was too coincidental. I had found an old photo, made a few inquiries, and suddenly someone was trying to reach out to me. I had a bad feeling about it.

"What's next on the agenda?" I asked with a smile.

Garrett frowned. He looked like he wanted to say more, but instead he placed another votive on a table and told me that April was coming by within the hour to discuss Nitro's décor.

"You can't be serious."

"Would I kid about April?" He tapped the text on his shirt. "She's going to love this, don't you think?"

April had been pestering Garrett since he opened the brewery to bring it more in line with Leavenworth's aesthetic. Not a week went by when she didn't "pop in" to see how things were going and leave a basket of German decorations behind.

"Just when I thought this day couldn't get worse."

"I can deal with April," Garrett said. "You want to check in on our helper?"

"Will do." I picked up the flyers and headed for the kitchen. If my mom had decided she was ready to meet me, why did she have to pick today to make it happen?

CHAPTER

THIRTEEN

I FOUND KAT IN THE kitchen surrounded by stacks of old dishes. "How's it going?"

She tucked her hair behind her ears. Her roots were dark, fading into lighter tips. I knew the ombré style was popular, but wondered if it was intentional or if Kat couldn't afford the upkeep on salon highlights. "You guys have a lot of dishes here."

"This used to be a full-scale diner," I replied, pointing to a set of China. "Garrett's great-aunt ran a bed-and-breakfast and popular restaurant. These dishes are left over from her." We had been using the mixed flatware in the pub. Garrett didn't see any need to spend money on new dishes or silverware when we had an entire kitchen full of his aunt Tess's collection. Her style didn't exactly match his sleek, modern taste, but to be honest, no one cared. They came for our beer, not our dishes.

"You know, some of these are collectors' items," Kat said, picking up a salad plate with fluted edges and a delicate blue flower pattern.

"Really?"

"My dad owns an antique shop that I used to work at. I've seen this pattern before. It's by a famous German designer."

"Hmm. You'll have to tell Garrett." Kat's knowledge of vintage China surprised me. If Aunt Tess's collection was valuable, that was yet another reason to keep an eye on her.

"Thanks again for letting me stay and help out. I don't know what I would have done."

I decided that it was time to confront her. With Mitchell's rental property in shambles and the Hotel Residence fully booked, she was going to have to come home with me later, and I wanted to gauge her reaction to what Brad had told me.

"Listen, I want you to be honest with me, okay?"

She gulped. "Okay."

"I talked to Brad, the owner of the Hotel Residence, a while ago, and he said that no one came in asking for a room last night. In fact he said that the hotel wasn't even at fifty percent. You could have easily gotten a room."

She hung her head and nodded. "I know. That's true."

I walked closer to get a look at her eyes as she spoke.

"I'm sorry. I shouldn't have lied."

"Does this have something to do with Mitchell's murder? I know you're lying, but what I'm worried about is that you're lying about killing him."

She threw her hand to her heart. Her green eyes looked genuinely stunned at my suggestion. "You think I killed him? Oh my God, no! No. I didn't kill him. I needed him. He was my shot at breaking into the industry."

I folded my arms across my chest.

"I swear. You have to believe me." Her cheeks blotched with color.

"Explain it to me, then. Why were you sneaking around last night, and why did you lie about not being able to get a hotel room?"

She rubbed her temples. "It doesn't sound good when you say it like that."

"I know. That's why I want you to tell me the whole truth. I want to believe you, Kat, but right now I'm not sure what to believe."

"You can trust me. I should have told you the truth from the start. It's just that I never expected that Mitchell would die." Her voice sounded shaky. "The truth is that he didn't invite me here. He barely even knew that I existed. Once he sent me a thank-you note for starting a fan club, but I'm not sure if it was even signed by him. His agent probably signed it."

"He didn't know you?"

"No. I mean, I send him email every day. That's part of my duty as president of the fan club."

"How many people are in the fan club?"

"At last count, we were over ten thousand. We even have fans from Canada and New Zealand, which makes us international."

I couldn't imagine ten people joining a Mitchell Morgan fan club, let alone ten thousand, but I kept quiet and let her continue.

"You see, I've been dying to meet Mitchell in person. He posted on his Instagram page about how he was going to be on location in Leavenworth for the next few weeks. I knew this was my chance, so I quit my job, packed my suitcase, and bought a train ticket."

"I don't understand. Why did you lie about winning a getaway? What was your plan?"

Her cheeks flamed. "Well, I wasn't exactly sure. The train ticket was more expensive than I thought it was going to be. I guess it's peak season." She reached into her jeans and pulled out a wad of bills. "I have ninety bucks."

"How did you think you were going to get a hotel and pay for food with ninety dollars?"

Was she really that naive?

Bright red spots spread to her neck. "I thought Mitchell would take me in. You see, we have so much in common. I know his entire filmography. I knew that if I could just meet him in person, he would see my potential and get me an in. My parents told me I was crazy. They refused to give me any money and told me that if I did this, not to come home."

"What?"

She started to cry. I moved to comfort her. I couldn't imagine telling Alex something so harsh.

"They think I'm too flaky. They told me it's time to stop this nonsense and grow up. They don't understand me. They think that running Mitchell's fan club is just a hobby. I've told them a million times that it's more, but they never listen. I've wanted to work in the business for as long as I can remember. Mitchell was my inspiration. *Crazy House* was the best show on television, and I would have done anything to be on set. You name it—grabbing coffee, scrubbing floors—anything. That's how a lot of kids get their break, you know? You work hard and work your way up."

I didn't want to tell her that I had to agree with her parents. I wasn't sure that following after her childhood idol would lead to an industry job.

"They want me to go to college or get a real job, but that's not for me. I'm destined for more. I'm destined for Hollywood, and Mitchell was going to be my break."

Her logic was flawed. If she wanted a career in the industry, I couldn't figure out how a path as a B-lister's (or for that matter C- or D-lister's) fan club president would get her there. Why did everyone keep talking about Mitchell being an actor? He wasn't acting. He was hosting. And he was an unknown. It didn't make sense to me.

"I can tell that you think I'm crazy. My parents look at me like that. It's not like it used to be. It's all about your social following. Like I said, my social media fan page has over ten thousand followers. I'm not stupid. I had a plan. I just needed to finally meet Mitchell to prove that I had a relationship with him. From there I was going to leverage my social profile to get a position at one of the film companies."

Ten thousand followers sounded impressive, but I didn't know much about social media. I made a mental note to ask Alex about it later.

"When I found Mitchell dead, I panicked. I didn't know what to do. The lie just kind of slipped out."

"Why make up a story about a paid trip? Especially if you didn't have the money for a hotel room?"

She dug her fingers into her temples. "I didn't want to go

home. I couldn't. Not with Mitchell dead. I thought maybe if the director and film crew thought that I was friends with Mitchell and he had invited me, they would give me a chance. I know it probably sounds crazy, but I was desperate. I have to get a job in Hollywood. I have to."

Her story was outlandish, and yet I found myself believing her. Even feeling sorry for her.

"I don't know how it came out. Maybe it was the shock of seeing Mitchell on the street like that." She paused and shuddered. "It kind of spilled out of me, and then once I said it, I couldn't take it back. I had no idea how expensive it was going to be up here. I thought maybe I could crash at a youth hostel or something."

That much was certainly true. If you could find a hotel room in the near vicinity during Oktoberfest, you could expect to pay double, if not triple, the price. It wasn't unheard of for tourists to drop upward of five hundred dollars for a one-night stay.

"I wanted to tell you the truth but thought you would tell me to head to the train station and go home. I can't go home. Not yet. Not until I have a solid lead in LA or a real job. I have to prove this to my parents."

I patted her arm. "I get it."

"You do?" She stared at me with dewy eyes.

"I do, and I appreciate you telling me the truth. You're going to have to tell Chief Meyers everything you've told me, okay?"

She nodded. "Okay, yeah." The splotches on her cheeks and neck began to fade.

"And you can stay under one condition."

"Anything. Anything you say."

"No more lies." I gave her my best mom look.

She held up her pinky. "I swear. Pinky swear on my life. No more lies."

"Good. Let's get back to organizing this mess, then."

She returned her attention to counting dishes and marking them on the inventory sheet that Garrett had printed. Maybe it was a mistake, but I wanted to believe her. She seemed earnest. Plus, why would she make up such a crazy story? I had the sense that she had made a rash decision to pack up and come to Leavenworth without a plan. But she didn't strike me as a killer. Quite the opposite. If she was telling the truth, then she was the last person who would have wanted Mitchell dead. She needed him to validate her social persona, and her entire trip hinged on the fact that she was going to talk him into letting her stay with him. I felt relatively confident that I was safe around Kat. If anything I felt sorry for her. Did she know what she was getting into with Mitchell? He had to have been at least fifteen years older than her. Had she come to Leavenworth to sleep with a much older and powerful man in hopes of furthering her career? I shuddered at the thought.

However if she wasn't the killer, that put me back at square one. Who else could have killed Mitchell Morgan?

CHAPTER

FOURTEEN

THE REST OF THE AFTERNOON breezed by. Having an extra set of hands certainly helped. We decided to open early when Garrett noticed a small crowd of tourists congregated outside. They were dressed in German costumes. Red-and-white-checkered shirts, knee-high wool socks, lederhosen, and green felt hats with feathers for the men. The women were dressed in tiny skirts with layers of white ruffles, bodices with plunging necklines, and striped socks. Obviously they were ready to hit the Festhalle, which didn't open for another two hours.

"Should we let them in?" Garrett asked.

"Why not? Might as well let them get a head start and spend their money here, right?"

He motioned to a growler at the end of the bar that was filled with handheld German flags. "We can get rid of some of those."

"Let me guess. April brought those?"

"The one and only. Fortunately I got out of the conversation by agreeing to hand out flags."

"That's pretty painless."

"Especially considering that she left me that." Garrett pointed to a pair of dark brown lederhosen, green suspenders, and a red-and-white-checkered shirt that reminded me of a picnic blanket. "She wanted me to wear that."

I laughed. "That is so you. You should do it."

He gave me a challenging look. "Really, you want me to wear it?"

"It would be pretty funny."

"Tell you what. I'll wear that if you wear what April left for you." He walked to the other side of the bar and reached under the countertop. Then he stood and held up a milkmaid's costume that would barely have covered my derriere. Its frilly lace skirt looked like it would fit a doll, not a grown woman.

"No way." I held my arms up in surrender. "It's not going to happen."

Garrett laughed so hard that he choked. "If you could only see your face, Sloan."

Kat appeared from the kitchen, carrying a tray of sparkling pint glasses. "That's so cute!" She set the glasses on the bar and went over to get a better look at the costume. "I've always wanted to wear something like this," she gushed.

Garrett caught my eye and winked.

I nodded.

He handed Kat the costume. "It's all yours."

"Really? Are you serious? I can't wait to try it on. This is perfect. My friends on social media are going to love this. If you want, I can wear it to hand out your flyers. You know, get in the German spirit."

"In the German spirit, you bet," Garrett said, with a touch of sarcasm in his voice that was lost on Kat.

She skipped away to put on the costume, and Garrett and I exchanged a laugh. At least someone at Nitro was embracing our Bavarian heritage. April would love it. I opened the doors to our first round of tourists while Garrett began pulling pints. Within the hour, every table was filled. Music pulsed overhead, and beer flowed freely from the taps. Oktoberfest was off to a great start.

"Need anything from the kitchen?" I had to raise my voice to be heard over the crowd.

"Doritos," Garrett shouted in reply.

We had discovered that we had a mutual love of the cheesy snack. In addition to keeping bowls of pretzels and nuts on the bar, Garrett had insisted we stock Doritos too. He didn't receive any argument from me.

I found giant bags of the chips in the kitchen, along with Kat, who had transformed into a quintessential German barmaid in the costume that April had left for me.

"You look great," I said reaching for a bag of Doritos. I ripped open the bag and dumped them into a plastic bowl, helping myself to a handful.

She did a quick spin. "Isn't it so cute? I feel like I should be dancing in the streets of Munich or something."

From her glowing expression, I guessed that was a good thing.

"Should I start handing out flyers?" she asked, fluffing out her petticoat.

I chomped the Doritos. "Sure. It's picking up in the bar, which I'm sure means that crowds are starting to gather." I gave her clear directions about passing out our marketing materials without being too pushy.

She threw her arms around me in a hug. "Thank you. Thank you a million times. I'm going to do the best job for you. And I'm going to plaster my social media with as many pictures as I can."

"You can thank me by doing a good job."

"I promise, I won't let you down." She grabbed the stack of flyers. "I'll check in in an hour, is that okay?"

"Actually, I'll come find you." I tried to keep what Alex calls my "Mom tone" from my voice.

She nodded and waved. I watched her prance toward the front with layers of fluffy tulle flapping at every step. I figured checking up on Kat would be a good excuse to see what was happening at Oktoberfest and try to get a moment to talk to the rest of the film crew. And speaking of checking up on Kat, I shot Alex a quick text asking whether or not ten thousand followers was substantial and if he could take a look at Mitchell's online profile for me when he had a chance. He was probably still at the conference, because he didn't text back right away.

I returned to the bar with the bowl of Doritos. Garrett and I poured pints for another hour before things started to wind down. It was obvious that everyone was in town for Oktoberfest. As soon as the sound of Leavenworth's most popular polka band sounded on Front Street, people closed out their tabs and headed outside to join the party.

Garrett crunched a Dorito and stared at the empty bar. "Wow, talk about mass exodus."

"Don't take it personally." I soaked a sponge in soapy water and began wiping down the bar.

"It's a good thing you warned me. Otherwise I'd be worried that our beer drove them away."

"Not our beer. Just the promise of lots more beer and hours and hours of dancing."

"What should we do?" he asked through a mouthful of chips. "Close up? Do you want to go hit the party?" He motioned to two lanyards with Oktoberfest passes hanging next to the taps. "April dropped off tickets for each of us. Apparently every business owner gets free passes as part of our dues to the downtown business association."

"Why don't we take turns?" I suggested. "It'll be good for you to go mingle with some of the other breweries in town, but there's a chance we'll get a straggler or two tonight. Kat is passing out our flyers, so maybe if people tire of hearing 'The Chicken Dance' five hundred times, they'll find their way here."

"Good idea." Garrett reached for more Doritos. "Why don't you go first? I'll pick up and gorge myself on chips for a while."

I laughed and stared at his orange fingers. "Take it easy on the chips, man. You have to save yourself for beer."

"Don't worry; I always have room for beer." He licked his pinky. "By the way, I had an idea earlier. Why don't we let

Kat stay in one of the rooms upstairs? I think she's harmless, but I'd feel better having her here rather than sending her home with you."

"Are you sure?" I stacked pint glasses into a tub.

"Yeah. There are a bunch of empty guest rooms upstairs. They might as well get some use." He cracked his knuckles. "I worry about you being so far out of town and alone."

I felt my heart speed up. Was Garrett worried about me? "Thanks. I'm fine, really, but as long as you're cool having Kat stay here, that would be a relief."

"Consider it done."

I took a load of pint glasses to run through the dishwasher before grabbing my sweatshirt and making my way outside. Colorful German costumes filled the streets. People linked arms and swayed to the sounds of the polka band. A line snaked from the entrance to Oktoberfest for five blocks. No one seemed to mind. The atmosphere was thick with buzzing energy. Every shop along the route had its front doors and windows flung open. Merchants handed out coupons and free samples of milk chocolate bars, gingerbread, and apple strudel. The entire village had turned into one giant block party. It was impossible not to get caught up in the atmosphere.

A group of college students in matching plaid shirts, knee-high socks, and felt caps stood at the end of the line. I fell into place behind them.

They discussed their strategy for meeting girls and how to avoid a hangover tomorrow while the line inched forward. I scanned the crowded streets for any sign of Kat. *She must be up closer to the tents,* I thought, not spotting her in the near vicinity.

More and more people queued up behind me as the line continued to move forward slowly. I used the time to contemplate everything I had learned about Mitchell's murder thus far. With Kat seeming less and less like a suspect, I tried to imagine who else would have had a motive to kill him. Payton had appeared quite angry with Mitchell for derailing her vision for the documentary. Mitchell had treated Connor like a second-class citizen. Could one of them have reached their breaking point? And what about Lisa? Mitchell had trashed her rental property and tarnished her pristine reputation. As much as I didn't want to believe my friend and fellow business owner was a killer, she definitely had a motive. Finally there was David the producer. I hadn't had much interaction with him, but I had noticed when he and Payton had exchanged a number of agitated glances when Mitchell jumped on the bar and went off script. Had David been equally fed up with his narrator, and what was his role in the film's production? Why had everyone involved in the project seemed to let Mitchell run the show? Something didn't add up.

I was so wrapped up in the many questions assaulting my brain that I barely noticed someone join me in line.

"Hey, it's the beer lady." I heard a deep voice next to me say.

I looked over to see Connor standing a few inches away. "Oh, hi. Sorry I didn't hear you."

He blended in with the college guys in front of me. Instead of a WISH YOU WERE BEER T-shirt, he wore a pair of red and green lederhosen and a felt cap with a long black feather that looked identical to the one Mitchell had been wearing yesterday.

"I didn't mean to sneak up on you or anything, but I was wondering if maybe I could get a shot of you in line." His face was beady with sweat.

"A shot of me?"

He positioned his camera on his shoulder. "Sure. Payton told me I'm supposed to shoot everything, and I figured she might be able to cut in footage of you in line with everyone with what we shot at your pub last night. You kind of stand out, you know." He aimed the camera at the costumed crowd surrounding me.

"I guess." I shrugged. "Hey, is that Mitchell's hat?" I couldn't resist asking.

Connor's hand immediately went to his head. "Huh? This? No. I mean, I don't think so. No, I found it on the street. These things are everywhere. I'm going to tell Payton we should shoot some of the aftermath of the party. Felt hats and plastic cups on the streets—you know?" He pointed to his lederhosen. "I couldn't resist these either. Found a deal from one of the vendors. Figured I'd really get in the spirit."

I wondered how many caps the hat shop sold during the Oktoberfest. Street vendors along Front Street were making a killing on cheap German merch. Connor could be telling the truth, but the ten-inch feather looked exactly like the feather on Mitchell's cap. And Mitchell hadn't had the cap when I found his body last night. Was it merely a coincidence, or could Connor have stolen the hat as a prize for his killing? I shuddered at the thought. Suddenly I was very glad to be surrounded by hundreds of people.

Connor was oblivious to my reaction. He aimed the camera at me. "Great. That's great. Do what you're doing. Stand there and pretend like you're waiting in line." He stepped back keeping the camera focused on me.

"I *am* waiting in line." I looked in front and then behind me, where hundreds of people pressed toward the entrance gates.

"I know, but just look like it," he said, moving the camera closer.

I stared in front of me, hyper aware that Connor's lens was zoomed in on me. After I'd been standing for a few minutes and trying to keep my face neutral, Connor released his hand from the lens. "Great. I think I got it." Sweat poured from his forehead. I wanted to offer him a napkin or something to mop his brow.

He came to stand next to me again. "Thanks for letting me shoot that." There was a distinct odor about him. The poor kid was obviously super nervous. He didn't appear to be that out of shape. Maybe it was a case of unfortunate sweat glands.

"No problem, but I can't imagine that me standing in line is going to be compelling footage."

"You never know. Mitchell told me that the truth in documentary work is shooting twenty-four seven. People start to let their guard down. That's when you get the good stuff."

Since he had brought up Mitchell's name, I decided to take the opportunity to get his take on the deceased star, and see if I could get a read on him. "How long have you known Mitchell? Did you guys work on other projects together?"

Connor shook his head. "No. I met him at the start of this shoot. He had done a bunch of other work. Have you seen any of his show—*Crazy House*?"

"No. To be honest, I'd never heard of him before."

"It's a shame. He's really underrated. He wasn't exactly fun to work with, but he knew his stuff. I was really looking forward to working with him and taking away anything I could. The man was a genius. An ass, but a genius. *Crazy House* was my favorite show growing up. So many good memories. It was kind of weird to meet him in real life and have it be so different."

Connor didn't sound like he was carrying a grudge for the way that Mitchell had treated him. If anything he sounded disappointed that he wasn't going to have a chance to work with the "genius." Nothing Connor said eased my confusion about Mitchell. Had Mitchell been a master of his craft? Had he really been a talented child star? Narrating a documentary titled *Wish You Were Beer* didn't make him a genius in my book. I had to be missing something. Both Kat's and Connor's descriptions of Mitchell matched up. Maybe it was a generational thing.

"I know everyone thought the guy was an ass," Connor continued. "I mean, he was, but he kind of earned it, you know?"

"No." I shook my head. Being good at your work or craft didn't mean that you had to belittle those around you. "It seemed like he was really harsh with you in particular."

He twisted his camera lens. "That's the industry, though. My prof at film school told us we had to be tough. Mitchell was tough, and I was hoping that some of his attitude might rub off on me. I need to be tougher. You gotta be in this business. That's what David and Payton told me, too." Stains began to seep through the front of his shirt. It wasn't hot outside. I would have guessed the temperature was in the low seventies with a nice breeze. The camera Connor held probably weighed fifteen, maybe twenty pounds, but even so, it shouldn't have been causing him to sweat profusely. Was there another reason? Was it a nervous reaction?

"Is that typical?" I asked, trying to ignore the sweat plastering his shirt to his chest. "Are actors typically rude to the crew?"

He reddened. "No, I mean, no." His sheepish response was strange. "It's just that I've struggled with confidence. Mitchell didn't. He knew he was talented and demanded respect."

"But there's a difference between being awful to you and wanting respect."

"Nah. He was trying to make me stronger." His hand went to the hat again.

Connor's attitude was shocking. The exchanges that I'd witnessed between them looked more like bullying than mentoring, but maybe I had missed something.

"I see Payton," Connor said, waving wildly with one arm. "I better go. Thanks again for letting me get some shots."

"Sure," I said stepping forward with the line.

What was his story? Had he idolized Mitchell and been able to reframe Mitchell's treatment of him? Or was he lying? Did he want me to think that he'd put Mitchell on a pedestal in order to distract me from the truth? Could Mitchell have bullied him to the point of murder?

FIFTEEN

CONNOR'S GLOWING PRAISE OF THE man who had humiliated him less than twenty-four hours ago raised my suspicions. Both he and Kat had claimed that Mitchell was super talented. My brain couldn't rationalize the very different perspectives on Mitchell's personality.

"Hey, Sloan!" Kat danced through four older women who wore more modest German attire—traditional shawls, peasant skirts, and clogs. When she made it to me, she held up her hands and grinned. "Look, I'm all out of flyers."

The group of frat guys in line in front of me focused their attention on Kat. She was oblivious to the stares.

"You handed them all out already?" I asked, making eye contact with one of the guys, who blushed and whipped his head around.

"Can you believe it?" She reached into her chest and unearthed her cell phone. "You should see my profile hits. People are loving this. And don't worry, I've been telling everyone how amazing Nitro is—that it's the best beer in town. I've told them to go ahead and drink the cheap stuff in the tents, but that when they're ready for the real deal, to come to our pub."

"Our" pub? I wasn't sure that our talking point should be dissing on other breweries, and while the big guys (known in the beer world as macrobrewers) would have a few taps at the festival, none of the microbreweries represented poured "cheap" beer.

"That's great, but maybe we should tweak your pitch a little." I gave her a brief explanation about the camaraderie between brewers.

"Got it." She gave me a thumbs-up. "Should I go get more flyers from Garrett?"

I glanced at the line. In the time I had been standing here, I had only moved a block and a half. "If you're up for it? Garrett wanted to talk to you about staying in one of the rooms upstairs tonight."

"That's great. Yeah. You bet! I'll totally hand out more flyers. I'm having so much fun. This weekend is turning out to be better than I expected." She waltzed away.

Talk about a complete shift in personality. This Kat was entirely different than the Kat I had met last night. Gone were the tears and the timidity. It was as if any thought of Mitchell's murder had vanished. Bizarre behavior for someone who had fallen apart yesterday. Was something going on with Kat and Connor? I wasn't sure what was causing both of their fluctuating mood swings, but I intended to find out.

I waved to the owner of The Edelweiss as the line inched forward. The Edelweiss imported German rugs, blankets, sweaters, clocks, and chocolates. For Oktoberfest they had set up a display of Black Forest gummy bears. Her staff was handing out small plastic cups with samples to everyone within reach.

"Oh, Sloan!" I heard April's voice cut through the hum of the crowd and the music already echoing in the tents.

I tried to slide up as close as I could to the group of college students in front of me. They didn't appear to mind. One of them wrapped a beefy arm around my shoulder. "Hey, you gonna join us for a killer night?"

"No thanks." I ducked away from his grasp. "Trying to avoid someone."

"Sloan, there you are." April burst through the group of guys. "*Guten tag*, gentlemen. I must tear my friend away." She yanked me out of line.

"What are you doing, April? I've been waiting in line for a half hour."

"You have to come with me. I have something very important that I'm dying to show you." She lowered her voice and waved her hands over my outfit. "And we must do something about this."

I protested, but April latched on to me. Her manicured nails dug into my wrist as she tugged me across the street, past the Kinderplatz, and up the steps next to the gazebo.

"Where are we going?"

"My office." April plastered on a smile and greeted everyone who walked by us with her botched German. "*Guten tag. Hallo.* Velcome, Velcome to Oktoberfest."

We caught a few funny looks as people reacted to April's Americanized attempt at a German accent. Her office shared a common wall with Balmes Vacation Properties. Did this have something to do with Mitchell's murder? What did April want to show me? That reminded me that I had been wanting to ask April where she had vanished to last night.

"Hey, where did you go last night?"

"Hmm?" April replied with a breezy tone to her voice. "Last night I was at Nitro for the keg tapping, remember?"

"I know. After that. Garrett said that he sent you and Mitchell off with a growler."

April scoffed. "Don't even get me started on that stubborn boss of yours, Sloan. Did you see the shirt he's wearing today? He's trying to make a mockery of Leavenworth's most prized event."

I didn't bother to respond.

She dug her claws into my arm as we climbed the slight hill toward her office. "I don't know what happened to Mitchell. I promised him that I would find him a new rental since that incompetent Lisa put him up in a shack. I took it upon myself to invite him back to my place. It was the least I could do for someone of his caliber. We agreed to meet outside of Nitro. He went to get his things and then he never showed up."

"Did you go look for him?" I doubted that April had killed Mitchell. Wouldn't it be great, though? I could dream, couldn't I? But there was no way. She was too dazzled by having a "star" in town.

"Of course." She sighed audibly. "Sloan, need I remind you that my duties to Leavenworth are endless? Even if they involve searching every square inch of our town for a lost movie star in the middle of the night. I can't believe you would even have the audacity to ask if I went looking for him. Of course, I went looking for him, and sadly I found him—like you—lying dead in the center of the square."

"I don't remember seeing you there."

"That's because you were consoling that sniveling young girl and trying to butter up to Chief Meyers. Anyway, there are all kinds of rumors floating around about the production— internal strife, financial troubles—who knows what else? I'm beginning to wonder if we've been misled." She yanked me up the steps to her office and pushed open the front door to her real estate firm. "This way," she said, shoving me past the reception desk. The place was empty. I was sure that April's colleagues were at the festival.

When we arrived at her office, she opened the door and stepped to the side. Then she swept her arm across her body as if she were bowing in front of the queen. "Look."

My eyes landed on the far wall, where there must have been fifty framed pictures. Each photograph was displayed in a dark wooden frame with an ornate scroll. And each picture was of April. As in every single picture mounted to the wall. She had created some kind of a bizarre monument to herself.

Fifty pictures of April Ablin. April in a variety of German costumes and poses. The gallery reminded me of the kind of photo shoot new parents might do with their toddler. There was a picture of April in an orange and brown dirndl posing on top of an oversized pumpkin; a picture of April wearing a Christmas barmaid's costume of red and green plaid, sitting on Santa's lap; a picture of April wearing a spring dress and peeking out from underneath an umbrella.

"What is this?" I asked, taking a closer look at the strange shrine.

"Isn't it *vonderful*?" April's fake German accent made me want to gag. "I commissioned a very famous Seattle photographer to create the shoot."

The shoot? I stared at the photo collage. Who in the world, other than April, would commission dozens of posed photos of *themselves*?

April waved her arm across the photo display as if she were a curator at a museum. "I can't decide which is my favorite. Each of them speaks to me differently, but if I had to pick, I think this one captures my essence, don't you think?" Her hand stopped on a photo of her wearing a white fur coat and matching rabbit's fur hat with a giant pom-pom on the top. The hat was bedazzled with rhinestones in the shape of the German flag. April posed with one hand fluffing the side of the pom-pom on her hat, while standing on the summit of Leavenworth's snowcapped mountains.

"Well, isn't it stunning?" April mimicked the pose. "The artist calls it *Bavaria in Winter*."

"Original."

She flounced her garish orange curls. "Exactly. That's what he said. This collection is one of a kind. Extremely rare and priceless. I'm considering loaning it out to the Leavenworth historical society. After I enjoy it myself for a while."

I couldn't craft a response that wasn't laced with snark. "April, why am I here?" I asked, changing the subject and walking toward her desk.

"Right." She shifted her bra and squeezed her chest into her tight-laced bodice. "We have much to discuss, Sloan, and as you know, my time is in high demand right now." She gave her wall of self-portraits a parting smile and returned to the opposite side of her imposing German-gothic-style desk.

"Don't let me keep you."

"No, no. I've carved out ten minutes for you. And our first order of business is that renegade boss of yours."

"Garrett?" I picked up a glossy flyer for a home for sale at the base of Sleeping Lady. The house was modest, with a covered front porch, A-frame roof, and cozy woodstove. According to the flyer, it had two bedrooms, plus a loft, but what really caught my eye was the updated kitchen with a window facing the mountain. This was exactly the size house I needed moving forward.

"Yes, Garrett," April said with exasperation. "He simply refuses to adhere to our village's strict standards when it comes to Oktoberfest."

"I'm not sure what you mean." I folded the flyer and tucked it into my pocket.

April ran her hand across her chest. "Sloan, don't play games with me. You know exactly what I'm talking about. You and your boss like to think that you're so modern and sophisticated in your jeans and beer T-shirts, but need I remind you that you live in Leavenworth, Washington?"

"Nope." I folded my arms across my chest. "We've already covered this topic at least a million times."

"Good. Then we're agreed."

"About what?" My eyes landed on another picture of April. This time she was clad in a pair of riding boots, holding a polo stick, and posing next to a horse. The woman was insufferable. I wondered how much the photo shoot had set her back.

April scowled. "About you and Garrett Strong putting on the costumes I delivered and joining in the spirit of Oktoberfest."

"That's not going to happen."

She clenched her jaw so tight, it made my teeth ache. "Consider this your warning, then."

"Warning?"

"That's right. I've taken it upon myself to update our town bylaws. There are going to be some big changes coming, and I would suggest you and Garrett jump on board now."

The sound of voices next door gave me a momentary reprieve from April's ridiculous threats. I couldn't make out what was being said, but it sounded like someone was arguing.

"Have you talked to Lisa?" I asked, pointing to the wall that divided April's real estate office from Balmes Vacation Properties.

"No, why?"

I couldn't believe I had information that April hadn't heard. "The cabin that she rented to Mitchell was trashed."

April narrowed her eyes, causing ruts to form in the thick layer of makeup coating her brow. "Really?"

I told her about what I had seen with Lisa earlier in the day. When I finished, April stood and smoothed her ruffled skirt. "Interesting." She grabbed what looked to be a kid's listening device, went to the wall, and placed her ear against it. The voices had stopped.

I started to respond, but April placed her finger to her lips and motioned for me to stay silent. Pressing her face harder on to the wall, she strained to hear. After what felt like an eternity, she gave up and sighed.

"You know, I saw Lisa prancing around town with Mitchell," she said in a whisper.

"When?" Did April spend her days eavesdropping? I wouldn't put it past her, and the listening device had an uncanny resemblance to an old spy gear toy that Alex used to play with when he went through his spy phase.

"The first night he was in town." April adjusted one of the frames on the edge of her desk—also all pictures of her. "When was that? Tuesday or Wednesday, I think. It could have been earlier, though."

"Wait, are you sure?" I asked. "I thought Mitchell didn't arrive until later."

"I'm positive. He and Lisa were quite the cozy little couple. They had drinks at Der Keller, and she appeared to be giving him the complete Leavenworth tour. Which I reminded her was my responsibility." April rolled her eyes.

"Hmm." I didn't say more, but my mind spun as I stood and assured April that I would relay her message to Garrett.

She didn't bother to walk me to the door. And I didn't waste any time getting out of her office. Ten minutes of April Ablin was enough for me. However the meeting had been worthwhile on one account—Lisa.

Lisa had claimed that she had never met Mitchell in person until he rented her property, but April had seen them dining together and exploring our little village before the film crew arrived. That changed everything. Why had Lisa lied? And what was Mitchell doing in Leavenworth days before the rest of the crew? I wasn't sure, but I knew that I was definitely going to have another conversation with Lisa as soon as I could find her.

CHAPTER
SIXTEEN

THE LINES HAD STARTED TO die down by the time I returned to Front Street. Sounds of happy music and lively chatter floated from the outdoor tents. The air smelled of grilling sausages and kettle corn. Twilight cast a soft glow on the twinkling lights lining the street. Tourists noshed on schnitzel at bistro tables along the sidewalk. Groups gathered around gaslit fireplaces in Der Keller's outdoor patio. *Garrett needs to see this,* I thought, forgoing the entrance to the Festhalle and returning to Nitro. As expected, the pub was empty. Inside the cement floor pulsed to the beat of the drums and the pounding of hundreds of feet dancing nearby. Oktoberfest was officially in full swing, and Garrett had to be part of it.

"I'm back," I called to Garrett, who stood behind the bar nodding his head to the sound of the echoing music.

"I can't believe you can hear the music this far away," Garrett said, snapping in time with the beat.

"We're not that far away." I pointed to the east wall. "Der Keller's tent is just a few hundred feet that way." Competing bands played on five different stages every night of Oktoberfest. The headliners were showcased on the main stage in the Festhalle. There were four additional stages in each tent, where bands of every kind of style and taste would serenade happy beer drinkers.

"True," Garrett replied in agreement. "I guess I didn't realize it was going to be quite so big."

"It's a production." I moved to the bar, which had been wiped down with a mixture of vinegar and water. The tangy scent lingered in the air. "In fact that's why I'm back. You have to go check it out. I'll keep a watch over things here." I glanced to the empty bar and chuckled. "I mean, it'll be tough, but I think I can handle it."

"Are you sure?" Garrett frowned. "Is it even worth staying open? Maybe we should flip the sign to closed and go check it out together."

My heart rate spiked at the thought of spending an evening crammed into an electric tent with Garrett. "No, I don't mind."

He scowled. "Sloan, there's not a soul in here. The floor is literally vibrating from the music outside. Let's get out of here. Come have a pint with me. We can call it research."

I bit my bottom lip. "But what if someone comes by?" Even as I said it, I doubted that it would happen.

"Then they can come back tomorrow. Is it worth staying open in hopes that we get—what—one customer? Two? Even a handful. That's going to be a few pints at best. I don't know about you, but I'd rather go join the party."

"You make a compelling point." I smiled.

He came from around the bar and reached for my hand. A tingle went up my spine at his touch. "Good, let's go get our German on."

I couldn't resist and allowed him to lead me out of the pub. Garrett released my hand to lock Nitro's front door. I felt a pang of regret.

What's wrong with you, Sloan? I chided myself for acting like a teenager around Garrett. I wasn't sure if he was a distraction from my challenges with Mac or if there really was a spark between us, but I found myself constantly daydreaming about him wrapping me in his long, lanky arms and imagining his lips brushing against mine.

"Ready?" he said with a grin.

"You bet." I followed after him as we rounded the corner and headed for the Festhalle. The sinking sun reflected on the surrounding mountaintops, making them glow in vibrant reds, oranges, and purples.

"It smells amazing out here," Garrett noted as he stretched arms toward the moonlight and pretended to wave the scents toward our faces. "Should we eat our way through every tent?"

"That's what locals do," I replied, handing our tickets to a guy dressed in lederhosen manning the entrance booth.

"Whoa, where do we start?" Garrett gaped at the sheer enormity of the event. Breweries from every corner of Germany were represented. In addition to the four main tents and Festhalle, outdoor vendors snaked throughout the street. Taps flowed in every direction. Signs pointed to food, the main hall, and the sponsored tents as volunteers in red

T-shirts darted between the beer lines with loads of empty plastic glasses and flatware.

"What do you want to do first? Sample beer or grab some food?" I called over the sound of the crowd.

"Food," Garrett hollered back. "I need a bratwurst in the *worst* way."

I shook my head at his corny joke. "This way," I called, heading for the food tent. The smells from the authentic German fare made my stomach swoon. From grilled brats to whole roasted turkey legs and German potato salad served with pork schnitzel, it was a smorgasbord of flavors.

"Oh my God! This is insane." Garrett pointed to the line forty people deep queued up for a slice of apple pie à la mode.

"I told you so."

"What do you want?" Garrett asked, making room for an accordion player to pass. There were probably more accordion players per capita in Leavenworth than any other city in the world at the moment.

"I don't know. Everything smells so good."

"I'm going for a brat on a bun with a side of beans and coleslaw. What do you say?"

"Sounds good to me." We made our way to the bratwurst line. I placed my hand on my stomach in an attempt to stop it from growling. When was the last time I ate? The day had turned into such a whirlwind I couldn't remember.

"We'll take two full meals." Garrett placed our order. I offered him cash, but he waved me off. Once we had heaping plates of beer-brined beans and brats, we headed for the closest beer tent. "I kind of feel like we should try a German import. What about you?"

"Absolutely. This is Oktoberfest, after all." I studied the tap list. "The Kölsch sounds good."

"I'm going for a Dunkel," Garrett said, putting in our order and paying again.

"You don't need to pay for everything." I pointed to a couple open seats at one of the dozens of twenty-foot tables.

"It's research, remember?" Garrett balanced his plate of food and beer while following me to the table. "I've always wanted to try to brew a Dunkel."

We squeezed in between two groups of visitors decked out in German attire. From the collection of empty beer steins in front of them, it looked as if they had already put a dent in the beer supply. I sipped my pale Kölsch from the plastic souvenir pint glass after we sat down. The lager was ice cold, with a delicate fruity finish. Unlike hop-forward American IPAs, this was a light beer that could easily be sipped all day. I was impressed with the balance of the wheat and the hint of lemon in the creamy sweetness.

"How is it?" Garrett asked, biting into his brat.

"Delicious. You want to taste it?"

"Is that even a question?" There was an unspoken code amongst brewers that beer should always be shared.

I grinned and handed him my beer. He offered me his Dunkel in exchange. The color contrast between our two lagers was like night and day. While my Kölsch was the color of straw, Garrett's Dunkel was a dark reddish brown with a thick, foamy head. I knew from my years working at Der Keller that in Germany, Dunkel was the house dark beer, or any dark beer on tap.

Taking a taste, I picked up a rich malt flavor and chocolate undertones. "I like yours, too," I said, placing his stein in front of him.

"We're two for two so far. I'd say that's off to a good start."

My eyes widened. "How many are we going for?"

He glanced at the old-fashioned watch on his wrist. "The night is young, and research calls." He winked.

We devoured our dinners and sipped our beers.

Chief Meyers and two police officers weaved through the crowd in our direction. At first I thought they were extra security, but the chief headed straight for our table.

"Garrett, Sloan." She tipped her khaki hat. "Glad you're both here."

"Do you have an update on the case?" I asked, dabbing my chin with a paper napkin.

She motioned for her deputies to continue on, then she sat on the edge of the table. "We're doing some canvassing tonight. Watching a couple people of interest in the case. It's good to have eyes out there."

I thought about bumping into Connor earlier. "Have you spoken with Connor, the camera guy?" I asked.

She didn't answer, but rather gave me a stern look to let me know I should continue if I had something to share.

"Earlier he was wearing a felt cap that looked exactly like Mitchell's."

Chief Meyers pointed to the table next to us and behind us. "You mean like that hat? And that one?"

"Yeah, I know it's a stretch, but the feather on Mitchell's hat was distinctive."

"That's true," Garrett interjected. "It was longer than our brats."

"Noted." Chief Meyers said. "I'll follow up on that. Any insight on the girl?"

I shook my head. "Not really. She's been a great worker."

"Very enthusiastic," Garrett added.

"Right." I smiled. "She did tell me that she made up the story about coming here. She didn't win a trip from Mitchell. She's here trying to get a job on the production team. In fact, she told me she was going to come find you to explain her situation."

"You know, I hadn't thought of this before, but if Kat is desperate for a job in Hollywood, why has she been so enthusiastic about working for us?" Garrett asked.

Chief Meyers waited for a group loaded with beer steins to pass. "One of many questions I'll be following up on. We're looking at every angle right now. I'm waiting on financial records. Hopefully those will shed some light on a motive."

"Other than Mitchell offending everyone he met," I said.

"Other than that."

I went on to explain what April had told me about Lisa and Mitchell as well as my thoughts on Payton and David and how they both appeared relieved that the host of their documentary was dead.

Chief Meyers stood. "Keep me posted on anything new. I'm counting on you two being another set of ears and eyes for me. We are beyond short-staffed with Oktoberfest, so I can use any levelheaded help I can get. That is not to suggest that I'm swearing you in as vigilantes or anything." She gave me a stern look. "Just keep your ears open, okay? And call me first if you happen to hear any chatter about Mitchell Morgan or anything related to the case."

"Will do," I agreed.

When she left, conversation became futile because the Beer Kegs, a rock band who used old kegs for drums and percussion, took the stage. One of the groups next to us vacated their seats to go dance in the front of the tent.

"This is awesome!" Garrett shouted. "You want another?" He held up his empty stein.

I nodded.

"Same or something new?"

"Surprise me."

He left to get another round. I glanced around the merry tent. It was strange to think that a murder investigation was in process. Being around Garrett had a calming effect on me. A few hours ago I couldn't have imagined enjoying the festivities over pints. Maybe it was the Kölsch talking, but I felt relaxed and lighter.

"I give you a Helles, my lady." Garrett returned and handed me a new pint with a half bow.

"Thanks." I raised the stein in a toast. In German, "Helles" means "bright." The light lager hails from southern Germany. It's a wonderful sipping beer with sweet notes and very little bitterness. When I used to give brewery tours at Der Keller, I would often recommend our signature Helles to customers who weren't traditional beer fans. A Helles is a nice entry into beer, with subtle malty accents, a gorgeous blond color, and a low percentage of alcohol. Otto would argue that Helles is synonymous with beer and the most popular pint when in Munich.

I was about to mention how relaxed I felt when I heard

someone come up behind me. I recognized the voice immediately.

"Isn't this cozy? My wife and her boss raising a glass together," Mac said with a slight slur.

I turned to see him clutching a half empty stein. His typically ruddy cheeks were the color of strawberries. One of his suspenders had snapped and hung from his shoulder.

"Aren't you working?" I asked. Der Keller was among Oktoberfest's premier sponsors. That meant Der Keller's logo was on every piece of advertising, from the beer steins to event T-shirts and flyers, and every banner inside the festival. Their beers were on tap in each venue. Additionally, they hosted one of the tents, which meant that it was all hands on deck for the weekend. So much so that Otto and Ursula usually hired temporary help for the month leading up to Oktoberfest and kept them on through the holidays.

Mac momentarily lost his footing. He caught himself on my shoulder, sloshing beer on his arm. "Sorry about that." He wiped beer on his red checked shirt.

"Shouldn't you be in the Der Keller tent?" I repeated.

Garrett caught my eye and gave me a look to let me know he shared my concern that Mac had overindulged in the product.

Mac ignored my question and plopped down next to me. I could smell beer on his breath. "How's it going, man? I heard this was your first Oktoberfest, newbie." He rocked slightly as he addressed Garrett.

"I'm good." Garrett's tone was polite, but his lips formed into a thin, hard line.

"Mac, why aren't you at the Der Keller tent?" I said for the third time.

He turned to me. His eyes looked glassy. "Huh?"

"Der Keller." I pointed in the direction of the tent. "Should you be working?"

He picked up his stein and finished off the rest of his beer. "Nah, Hans is there. Told me I should go talk a walk."

"You mean *take* a walk?" I felt relieved that Hans was in charge. However I didn't like seeing Mac tipsy, and I certainly would never want Alex to see his dad like this. "Maybe you should drink some water," I suggested.

"Serious, Sloan. Always so serious." He reached for my hand. I ducked to avoid his grasp.

"Mac, you really need to sober up."

He threw his head back and laughed. Then he stared at Garrett. "Did you hear that? She wants me to sober up. Story of my life."

I had no idea what he meant by that. Mac had always enjoyed beer, as was evident from his expanding waistline and the constant red tone to his cheeks, but he knew his limit and how to pace himself. It wasn't like him to over-imbibe, especially at such a public event.

Garrett cleared his throat. "How's business? It looks like you're getting a steady stream into the Der Keller tent."

Mac swayed, bumping into my shoulder and off again like a pinball bouncing against the tracks in the machine. "What's that supposed to mean? If you want to say something to me, say it like a man."

"I was simply noting that you seem to have a good crowd tonight." Garrett caught my eye.

"Mac, let me walk you out." I slid my legs around to the other side of the bench and stood.

Mac sputtered something I couldn't decipher to Garrett, but let me help him stand.

"Are you coming back?" Garrett asked.

I shrugged. "Hopefully."

With that, I dragged my soon-to-be ex-husband out of the tent.

CHAPTER

SEVENTEEN

I KEPT MY COOL UNTIL we were out of earshot from Garrett. "Mac, let's go," I said with disgust, yanking him past a group of polka dancers in green-and-white-plaid skirts. "You sound like one of the frat boys. How much have you had to drink tonight?"

He stumbled over an empty plastic cup on the street. "Baby, slow down."

I firmed my grasp and pulled him by the wrist. We exited the main gate, where a volunteer asked if we needed our hands stamped to get back in. Mac started to reach out his arm, but I declined and directed him down Front Street.

"This isn't like you," I scolded. "You're sloshed."

"What? I'm fine. Just had a couple pints with the guys. That's all. Had some celebrating to do. Got some good news tonight. It's going to be good for you—for Der Keller, for everything. I'm turning my life around, Sloan. I swear."

I ignored him and made a beeline for the hotel where Mac had been staying since we had split.

"Sloan, it's you." His baby blue eyes gazed at me intently when we arrived at the lobby. The smell of flowering jasmine climbing up the hotel's stucco exterior made me want to escape to the farmhouse, pour myself a bubble bath with jasmine oil, and drown out everything else around me.

Mac's words jumbled together as he spoke. "I can't sleep. I can't eat. I can't think without you. I'm lost." His breath smelled like stale beer.

"That's the alcohol talking, Mac."

"It's not. I'm telling you I'll do anything it takes to get you back. I can't stand seeing you with that smug dude."

"Garrett?"

He nodded. "Sloan, baby, please. Give me another chance."

We arrived at the hotel's doorstep. "You know what you can do for me?" I said, holding the door open for him.

"What? Anything." He stumbled and caught himself on the door frame.

"Go sleep it off. And for the love of God, don't call Alex when you're like this."

I thought he might try to keep pleading his case, but he hung his head and tripped inside. The man was infuriating. Sometimes I felt like I had two children. I knew Mac was upset about our breakup, but could something else be going on with him? I hadn't seen him that drunk since we were in our twenties and were invited to a brewery launch in Seattle. The owners had insisted that we taste every beer they produced, to the tune of sixteen different craft beers. I sipped each sample, but Mac had downed every tasting glass and ended up with a wicked hangover the next morning. Ever since that night, I'd never seen him drink more than a few beers over the course of an evening. What did he mean he had something to celebrate? He was probably up to his old tricks. I wouldn't have put it past him to have invested in some new crazy brewing trend. Add it to the list of things that Hans and I needed to discuss.

The last thing I wanted to do was spend the rest of the night worrying about Mac. He wasn't my problem or responsibility anymore. He could take care of himself. I only hoped that he wouldn't try to contact Alex. Their relationship was on rocky ground. Having his dad call him in a state like this wouldn't do much to help stabilize things between them. Thinking about Alex made me check my phone. I wondered if he had gotten my earlier text.

I pulled out my phone to find a photo of Alex with the entire Sounders team. His smile was so wide it made my teeth hurt. "ON THE PITCH, MOM!"

Thank goodness one of us was enjoying the weekend. The next text read "10k is pretty good. Not huge. Decent. Her page is ALL Mitchell. Like every post. His page is weird. Check out this link."

I clicked on the link that Alex sent. To my surprise, Mitchell had over one hundred thousand followers. His page was filled with an assortment of old photos from his acting days on *Crazy House,* headshots, and one stock photo of Leavenworth that he posted two weeks ago with the caption "On Location Soon." I leaned against the cold stucco and scrolled through every picture. Looking through Mitchell's public persona made me feel sorry for him. There was no evidence that he had any friends. His profile consisted of him and only him—no friends. No family. Had he alienated everyone who crossed his path?

Just as I was about to put my phone away, a photo caught my eye. It was from a cast party for *Crazy House*. In the picture, Mitchell was younger than Alex. What a life for a kid. I thought about my own vagabond childhood. Was Mitchell's similar? Performing for an audience every day without a routine or friends. It could explain his behavior. Not that it excused his treatment of people, but it did give me a better understanding of why Mitchell might have needed to hide behind his outrageous persona.

I had come to understand that we couldn't escape our past. Every experience—the high points, the low points—became ingrained in our DNA. Instead of struggling to forget, I was focused on embracing the memories. Recognizing that without them I wouldn't be who I was today.

As I looked closer at the picture, I realized that there was another familiar face—David. He was younger too and appeared to be in costume. Had he been an actor on the show? Why hadn't he mentioned that fact? This photo was proof that he and Mitchell had known each other for a long time. I wasn't sure what that meant to the case, but it couldn't be a coincidence that they had ended up working together again.

I sighed and put my phone back in my pocket. Should I return to Oktoberfest with Garrett or call it a night? My brain needed a break from the constant loop of questions. Sitting alone at home would likely make me spin out of control, so I decided to head back to the Festhalle.

With a final glance at the lobby to make sure that Mac hadn't tried to sneak out, I crossed the street and headed toward the gazebo. The park was packed with kids and families. I wasn't concerned about being alone. However, my curiosity was piqued when I spotted a woman dressed in black, with a dark baseball hat concealing her face, slink from behind one of the bales of hay and glance up and down Front Street. In the hazy darkness, I couldn't make out the woman's face, but given her build and her nimble pace, I was 99 percent certain it was Lisa. I followed after her, making sure to keep enough distance between us so as not to be spotted.

She was spry. I was surprised how quickly she moved. Every few steps, she would stop and glance behind her as if she was worried that she was being followed. Did she sense that I was behind her or was there another reason she was concerned that she might have a tail? Twice I had to duck behind buildings to stay out of sight. The tiny dark hairs on my forearms stood at attention as I watched her sprint across the street. We were getting far enough away from the activity that I could barely hear the accordions or kids' laughter.

Cool night air assaulted my lungs. Maybe this wasn't a good idea. Darkness seemed to close in with every step. The streetlights on this stretch of road were spaced a good thirty to fifty feet apart, which meant that the only light to guide me was from the moon above.

When Lisa arrived at Mitchell's cabin, she came to an abrupt halt and checked to make sure the coast was clear. Then she removed something from her back pocket. I hurried and hid behind a sturdy oak tree. In a flash, she unlocked the front door, slipped in, and pulled it shut.

I inched closer. It had to be Lisa. Who else would have a key to Mitchell's rental? But then why would Lisa be sneaking around in the dark?

Each balcony on the cabin contained built-in flower boxes. I could smell the fragrant flowers, but couldn't see them in the dark. I made it to the base of the porch and saw a flash of light stream across the front window. My heart lurched. I dropped to my knees and made my way around to the back deck.

I crouched behind a long picnic table and stared into the windows. Lisa had a flashlight. She was running it in a zig-zagging pattern throughout the living room. This was getting stranger by the minute. Why the secrecy? I needed to get closer.

I crawled toward the sliding glass doors that opened to the deck. My knee hit a loose board. A high-pitched creaking sound erupted from beneath me. I froze.

The squeaky board sounded like a squeal to my alert ears. Blood rushed through my head. What was I doing? Hadn't Chief Meyers warned me to be careful? Here I was traipsing after a potential murderer in the pitch-dark.

I took another timid move forward, keeping my eyes focused on the front window. The flashlight had disappeared. Lisa must have ventured farther into the cabin. I let out a long breath and carefully crept on. I made it all the way to the sliding door. Then I pressed my face to the icy glass and tried to see inside. It was too dark to make out anything.

Now what, Sloan?

I hadn't exactly formulated a plan. Chasing after Lisa had been a spur-of-the-moment decision. Could she be Mitchell's killer? I quickly tried to craft an excuse as to why I had followed her. I could knock and say that I'd seen a strange light and called the police. That would deter Lisa from hurting me, right?

Or you could turn around and run, my rational brain cautioned.

I ignored that voice, stood, and tiptoed around the side of the cabin to the front door. Chief Meyers had just asked us to be her extra set of ears and eyes. I was doing my civic duty to follow her, or so I tried to tell myself.

It's now or never, I thought. My mouth went dry as I reached my hand to the door and knocked timidly.

In response, the glow of the flashlight swept across the front window. I could feel my heart pounding in my chest.

Was this stupid?

I was a grown woman. I was strong and confident, and after all, this was Leavenworth, Washington. The only place I had ever known as home. If Lisa had killed Mitchell, then she deserved to be confronted. Plus I was taller than her and used to carrying heavy kegs and bags of grain around the brewery. If she put up a fight, I could hold my own.

I knocked again, this time louder and harder.

The flashlight clicked off.

What if it wasn't Lisa?

A mosquito buzzed past my ear. I flinched. Then I held my breath for a second. The door handle made a clicking sound, and the next thing I knew, a shadowy figure appeared in the door frame.

My mouth went dry. "Is everything okay in there?" I asked, trying to sound composed.

"Sloan?" Lisa's face glowed with a ghostlike aura from the flashlight.

"I was out walking and saw a light flicking on and off inside. I thought maybe the killer had come back." I figured it was best to leave out that I thought there was a good chance that she was the killer. The smell of garbage and filth was even stronger than it had been earlier. My stomach recoiled at the rotting scent. How could Lisa stand to be in there?

She placed her free hand on her heart. "Geez, you scared me."

"What are you doing here?" I tried to block the scent by covering my nose.

Lisa didn't answer right away. She propped the flashlight on her shoulder and shined it down Front Street. Then she sighed. "You better come inside."

I hesitated. Lisa couldn't harm me on the porch, and I could make a break for it if she tried anything.

She stared at me. "Sloan, come inside."

"I'm supposed to be back at the festival," I said. "And, wow—that smell is intense."

"I know. I'm trying not to puke." Lisa's eyes looked like two tiny black spots. "Listen, I know this looks weird, but it's not what you think."

"What do you mean?" I played dumb and kept my feet firmly planted on the porch.

"Sneaking around the cabin." She held the flashlight out, making bright yellow and white spots dance in front of my eyes. "Chief Meyers hasn't cleared us to come inside, but I had to get in here tonight."

"Why?" Seriously, had something else died in the cabin? The stench was unbearable.

"You saw it earlier. Mitchell trashed the place." Motioning the flashlight behind her sent a strobe of light over the debris. I noticed police caution tape stretched between the kitchen and living room. Had Chief Meyers found something incriminating? She didn't mention anything. Not that she would necessarily divulge classified information to Garrett and me, but she had said that they were exploring every angle.

"Yeah, but I don't understand. Why do you need to get inside?"

She reached into her jacket pocket and pulled out her cell phone. Then she positioned the flashlight under her other arm and proceeded to show me a dozen photos of the damaged property. "I had to take pictures. Mitchell single-handedly destroyed our reputation."

That seemed like a bit of an exaggeration, but I let her continue.

"He tried to ruin me. I'm fighting back. I needed concrete proof of the destruction. How am I ever going to get this smell out?" She pressed her fingers underneath her nose. "Chief Meyers wouldn't let me stay this morning. I begged her. I promised I wouldn't touch a thing, but she claimed that it was police protocol. Something about contaminating a crime scene."

That sounded legitimate to me.

Lisa focused the light on the shredded couch. "What the chief doesn't understand is that our business relies on guest reviews. Not only will Mitchell's review taint our perfect record, but cleaning and replacing the furniture is going to cost me thousands."

I wanted to interject that, given the lack of housing during Oktoberfest, I doubted Lisa and her mom would have any trouble renting out their properties. And wouldn't their insurance cover any damage caused by a guest?

"I have to have proof." Her voice cracked. "That's how the internet works these days. With Mitchell dead, what if his review ended up going viral? Or worse, what if some crazy rumor started, like he was killed in filth? No way. I'm not risking that. I'm posting these pictures tonight to show the world what he did to us."

"Is that even legal?"

Lisa flipped her head around and held the flashlight like a spotlight. "Of course it's legal. Look at this place. I manage this property. It's my responsibility. The owners entrusted me with taking care of their cabin. I convinced them to get out of town for a weekend. They're going to come home to this." She sounded like she was going to have a breakdown.

"No, I mean in terms of the investigation. What if Chief Meyers didn't want you to take pictures because it might impact her work?"

"How?" Lisa frowned. "Why would taking a few pictures matter? I haven't touched anything." She turned on her phone again and held it out to show me a picture. The photo was pretty grainy, thanks to the fact that Lisa had taken it in the dark with a flashlight. Even with the poor quality, the damage done to the luxury cabin was clearly evident.

"I don't know. What if Mitchell didn't do the damage?" I suggested. "Or there could be critical evidence inside."

"What do you mean?" she snapped.

"Chief Meyers and her team have to follow protocol. Maybe they're trying to preserve the scene. Maybe Mitchell's killer rifled through his things in search of a clue or something they left behind."

Lisa considered this for a moment, but then shook her head. "How do you explain the rotting food? This horrific smell? Why would his killer bring garbage and dump it? That doesn't make any sense. No. I know he did this, and I'm not going to allow him to ruin our reputation. I'm posting these pictures the second I get back to my office, and if Chief Meyers gets mad about it, I'll deal with it."

I stepped away from the doorway. The smell was making me nauseous. "Lisa, she could do more than just get mad at you. She could arrest you."

"Put yourself in my position, Sloan. Imagine someone wrote a scathing review about Nitro or Der Keller? What would you do?"

I thought about it for a second.

"Then imagine they went one step further. Maybe they intentionally drop a bug or a spider or a piece of glass into one of your pint glasses, snap a picture, and set out to destroy you online. Wouldn't you do whatever it took to protect your reputation?"

She had a valid point, but there was still the sticky issue of her breaking into a crime scene.

"I do understand," I said with genuine feeling. "But I

think you should talk to Chief Meyers before you post your retort. She's reasonable. I'm sure if you tell her what you just said to me, she'll work with you."

Lisa was undeterred. "I really don't see what relevance posting a few pictures has to a murder case."

I didn't want to debate the topic, but her response made me wonder if she was being entirely truthful. I wanted to ask her about what April had told me earlier. However, I had pressed her enough for one night. And if I was being honest with myself, I didn't want to press my luck. We were alone and at least a half mile away from the party down the street. The safe route would be to stop by Lisa's office in broad daylight tomorrow and see if I could find out if there was some other reason that Mitchell had been motivated to post a nasty review.

CHAPTER

EIGHTEEN

BY THE TIME I LEFT Lisa, I wondered if Garrett had given up on me. I returned to the Festhalle where partygoers had formed a conga line and were dancing their way through the rows of picnic tables. Knee-high socks bunched around ankles, suspenders fell loose, and the noise level had risen substantially. We had reached the witching hour. This was the point of no return. I felt sorry for the inebriated partygoers, knowing that they would live it up for another few hours and pay with pounding headaches in the morning.

I checked the first tent, where Garrett and I had had dinner. He wasn't there. An older couple slow-danced in front of an empty stage. Or at least it looked like they were dancing. It might have been that they were trying to hold each other upright.

Next I tried the Der Keller tent. It was on the farthest edge of the festival grounds. While the other tents were bright white, Der Keller's was deep red, so dark that it blended in with the night sky. Fifty-foot banners with the brewery crest (two lions waving German flags) flanked each side of the tent. Inside, staff and temporary workers circulated the busy space wearing red checkered *Trachten* shirts and black suspenders. The Krause family had spared no expense in creating an authentic Bavarian vibe within the tent. Black, red, and yellow swaths of fabric had been draped across the ceiling, like billowing sails. Candelabras with real tapered candles and greenery gave the ceiling an ethereal glow. Sturdy wooden tables, carved by Hans, sat in neat rows. The wall behind the stage had been painted with a mural featuring a pastoral German village. It was no surprise that there were still people in line for pints at the elaborate bar. Der Keller had won the Oktoberfest design award for as long as I could remember. I was fairly confident that they would take home the trophy again.

I squeezed up to the bar. Hans was pulling a pint from the row of fifteen tap handles. I knew that Der Keller's brewers had been preparing for months to stockpile enough kegs to meet the Oktoberfest demands.

"Sloan," Hans shouted hello, and handed a beer stein to a customer waiting nearby. He leaned across the bar and kissed my cheek. "Were your ears burning? Garrett and I were just talking about you."

"That's right." Garrett's voice made me turn to my left. He had one elbow propped against the bar.

I could feel a blush creep up my cheeks. "You were?"

Hans wiped his hands on a bar towel. I wasn't used to seeing him in Der Keller gear. Usually he wore flannel shirts, boots, and carpenter's pants. Tonight, he had put aside his tool belt and had on a classic red-and-white-checkered German shirt with Der Keller's crest embroidered on the breast pocket and a pair of jeans. Unlike Mac, he had forgone the suspenders and lederhosen. And unlike his brother, he didn't appear to take notice of the fact that at least ten young women had gathered near the bar and were staring at him with dreamy eyes.

"You look good. Like a tourist," I teased.

"Don't go there. That's one of the things Garrett and I were talking about." Hans motioned to a barmaid who balanced four steins in each arm. A German band had the crowd clapping along to the beat at the far end of the tent, and taps flowed behind us. "It's going to be like this for weeks to come, and since I'm the good son, I couldn't refuse wearing the company uniform. You know how my parents are, Sloan. They ratchet up their broken German and look at you with their endearing eyes. How could I say no?"

"You couldn't." I shook my head and laughed. Any request from Otto or Ursula had me saying yes.

Hans nodded to the bar. "Can I get you a pint?"

"No thanks. After seeing your brother making an ass out of himself, I'm cutting myself off for the night."

"Don't let him ruin your fun. He's a genius at making an ass of himself," Hans said, grabbing Garrett's pint glass to refill it. He poured a half glass for me. "You have to try this, though—it's our Apple Weizen. You're going to love how it turned out."

I acquiesced and tasted Hans's offering. The apple beer was slightly tart, with a sweet finish. It shared similar notes with our Cherry Weizen, but I could tell the brewing team at Der Keller had used a different proportion of wheat and malt.

"This is great," I said to Hans. "Did they ferment this in the freezer?"

Hans slapped his hand on the bar. "See? I told you she would pick up on that," he said to Garrett.

Garrett let out a low whistle. "The woman has a talent. I never would have picked up on that." He took a taste of his beer and then turned to me. "Come to think of it, how in the hell did you pick up on that?"

I shrugged. "Lucky guess."

Hans tossed a bar towel at me. "Liar."

"No, really. It's common practice, especially with Belgian beers. You have to tame the yeast with cold temps in order to ensure the right flavor profile."

Hans leaned his elbows on the bar. "This isn't a Belgian beer."

"I know, but there's a tiny hint of that banana flavor that comes through when fermenting in a cold chamber and Weizens share some of the same qualities with Belgian beers."

"Are you getting any of this?" Hans asked Garrett. "She lost me at banana."

Garrett stared at his glass as if he was seeing beer for the first time. "Nope. I pride myself on my chemistry background, and I promise you I completely missed anything remotely near bananas."

"Try it again," I urged. "Swish the beer around for a minute and let it sit on your tongue."

"Hang on." Hans pushed away from the bar. "Let me get in on this." He poured himself a small taste of the Apple Weizen.

I watched as they both swirled the beer and allowed their palates to absorb the many layers of complexity.

"She's right," Garrett said after a minute. "I'm either very open to suggestions or there is a touch of banana."

Hans agreed. "It's true. I'm getting it now. It plays off the apple well, doesn't it?"

I smiled broadly. "I'm sure that was the intention. You get the tang and crispness of the apple paired with that subtle banana sweetness. It's a great beer. Who brewed this?"

Hans's cheeks burned red. Seeing him flustered surprised me. "Who? Did you brew it?"

He shook his head. "You know me. I just fix things around the pub." As if to emphasize his point, he removed a Swiss army knife from his pocket and flipped it open.

"Then who? Your dad? I thought you said he was scaling back." I studied the pint. The beer had been filtered perfectly. I could see my reflection through the glass.

"He is." Hans stabbed the tip of his finger with his knife. I looked to Garrett for support. "What, did you brew this?"

"Not me." Garrett held his hands up. "Although I wish I could claim it. It's a great beer."

"Who, then?" I stared at Hans, who turned even redder. His cheeks matched his shirt. A sinking feeling hit my stomach. "No. No way. Not Mac?"

Hans frowned and nodded. "Can you believe it? He said that losing you has reignited his passion for beer. He brewed it special, just for you."

I thought about dumping out the rest of my pint on the floor.

Garrett placed his arm around my shoulder, making my spine stiffen. "You have to give the guy credit, this is a tasty beer." He gave me a squeeze and then removed his arm.

"I guess." I changed the subject. Mac could spend the next ten years brewing the perfect beer. It wouldn't change the fact that he had betrayed me. You'll never guess who I just caught sneaking around Mitchell Morgan's place."

"Not my brother?" Hans said with a frown. "I thought you made sure he got to the hotel."

"I did." I pushed aside the beer and explained how I'd seen Lisa dressed in black and sneaking down Front Street.

"Wait, you followed her?" Garrett interrupted.

I gave him a sheepish smile. "Technically yes, but I was careful. I didn't go inside the rental."

Hans shot Garrett a look of exasperation. "In that case, what are we worried about?"

"Honestly, you guys, I can take care of myself, and trust me, I could have taken Lisa if it came to it."

"That, I don't doubt," Garrett said.

"She's obsessed with the negative review that Mitchell wrote." I went on to tell them about Lisa's claim that she had come back to take pictures, and that April had spotted Lisa and Mitchell around town.

Hans waited for a barmaid balancing heavy steins to pass by before speaking. "You think Lisa killed him over a bad review?"

"I don't know. Maybe it wasn't just the review. Maybe there was more between them. That would explain Mitchell destroying the cabin."

"Or the killer left something incriminating there," Garrett added.

"Right. That's definitely a possibility," I agreed. "I can't imagine Lisa killing him, but then again, she's acting like a woman scorned over the review. Maybe she's a good liar. She could have gone back to get whatever evidence she left behind when she killed him."

We were interrupted by someone bumping into Garrett. Tiny droplets of beer splattered on my shoulder.

"Oh, sorry. Did I spill on you?" It was Payton. She swayed, sloshing her half empty beer more. David came from behind to help steady her. I wondered how much they had had to drink. Both of their cheeks were bright with color and glistened with sweat. If they were filming a documentary, it didn't seem very professional to get drunk. But then again, I wasn't a filmmaker. Her body language also made me wonder about the pills she had taken last night.

"How's the headache?" I asked.

She raised her pint glass. "Headache? What headache?"

"Didn't you have a headache last night?"

"Oh yeah, that's right. It's all good. We just learned how to do 'The Chicken Dance,'" Payton said, trying to catch her breath. Her WISH YOU WERE BEER T-shirt was damp with sweat or beer stains. Or maybe both.

"Leavenworth sure knows how to party," David said, wiping his brow. "And look, my favorite brewers congregated together. Where's Connor? We should be shooting this."

Payton nodded. "Yeah. What are you all talking about? Assessing the competition or mapping out strategy?"

"We're friends. We're just talking." I exchanged a look with Garrett and Hans. We'd already been over this with Payton and David. Had either of them done any research into the craft beer industry? Doubtful, if they were constantly shocked that we hung out together.

"Oh my God! That's brilliant. Did you hear that, David? They're friends, and they're talking. Why aren't we getting this? This is exactly what I was trying to explain to Mitchell." Payton punched David's shoulder.

"You were trying to explain that brewers are friends?" I asked.

David slapped a twenty-dollar bill onto the bar. "Two pints of whatever you recommend," he said to Hans. "You were right, Payton. This is the best. We need to hang out with this group every night."

She glanced at me and must have noticed my confusion. "Sorry, we just love your candor and openness. People tend to clam up when the cameras start rolling. This kind of everyday conversation is exactly what we're going for in the film. We want to give viewers a taste of how things really go down in the world of craft beer. That's what will resonate with viewers and—hopefully—the critics. I want glowing reviews in *Rolling Stone* and *Vanity Fair*. We land a few coveted publications, and suddenly we'll have a line out the door for foreign rights." Her words mumbled together a bit as she spoke. "My team spent weeks putting together an overarching script to get conversations like this rolling. Mitchell refused to follow it. He seemed to be under the impression that as the host he had creative license over the production." She rolled her eyes. "He didn't."

"No, he didn't," David added with a curl of his top lip. "Talk about ego. Payton and I had been talking about replacing him, but fate stepped in. We need a new host, and you can bet that whomever we hire to take Mitchell's spot is going to know their place in this production from day one."

Garrett kicked me. Had David just admitted that they were going to fire Mitchell?

"Do you have anyone in mind?" I asked.

Payton gave me a coy smile. "We've been running some film the last couple of days. Nothing is final yet, but I think there's a pretty good chance our new host is going to be someone I'm sure you all know. Someone who has a much better grasp on craft beer culture."

"And hopefully someone who will be easier on the budget," David added.

"Really?" Hans raised his brow. "You mean you're hiring someone from Leavenworth? I thought that Mitchell was a big Hollywood star."

David, who had just lifted his stein to his lips, spit out the sip. "A big Hollywood star? Mitchell?"

Garrett nodded. "Yeah, that's what we were told."

Payton stared at her manicured nails. "Please! Didn't he wish? Mitchell had a decent and somewhat obscure following thanks to a recurring role he had two decades ago. Did you ever see the show *Crazy House*?"

"*Crazy House*?" I repeated, pretending like I'd never heard of it. I wanted to see what Payton—and more importantly, David—said about the show and their relationship with Mitchell.

"Yeah. It was on the Disney Channel twenty years ago. Mitchell was a child star. His career tanked once he hit puberty. He's been living off royalties from syndication. Netflix picked the series up, so it's had a new round of viewers, and of course he has a following from his glory days, but otherwise no one in Hollywood could pick him out of a police lineup." Payton stopped to chug her beer.

"I don't understand. Then why didn't you fire him? When he was at Nitro the other night, he was making demands like an A-lister."

David took another sip of the beer. "Contracts. We had signed a contract with him to host three upcoming documentaries—*Wish You Were Beer, Time to Wine Down*, and *Whiskey Business*. We had no idea he had such an inflated ego when we hired him. Child actors." He scoffed. "I'd been on the phone with our legal team back in LA, trying to figure out what our options were. Mitchell technically wasn't in breach of his contract. He showed up on time and all that good stuff, but his attitude was out of control. In hindsight, we should have signed him for one project at a time, but we cut him a dirt-cheap deal on the three productions. He was hungry for the work so we thought it was going to be a good match."

"And then everything went south," Payton said, her voice thick with bitterness.

"How long have you guys known Mitchell?" I asked.

"David's known him for years, right?" Payton and David shared another veiled look. "David's been in the business forever. I like to tease him about his early acting days."

"I like to pretend those years don't exist," David retorted.

His thinning gray hair and sagging jowls made him look more like a retired professor or lawyer than an actor.

"Yeah, but you never would have made all that cash, had it not been for residuals," Payton said. She swayed to the music as she spoke. Like Kat, she had certainly had a shift in personality compared to last night when she had stormed out. "Making a film costs money. It's not just the shoot here, it's everything after. We have to pay to submit it to film fests, and then cover the cost of travel and touring."

David reached for his pint glass. He took a long drink. "You can say that again."

The mood had changed. His exuberance had vanished the minute Mitchell's name came up.

"You were an actor?" Garrett asked. I had forgotten to tell him about the photo I'd seen earlier, thanks to Alex.

Payton jumped in. "Oh yeah, you didn't know that? David had quite the run back in the day. How many sitcoms were you on? Three?"

"Four." David didn't look up from his pint.

"Four." Payton took a swig of her beer. If David was uncomfortable talking about his past, Payton didn't notice. "Yeah, he was the man for a while. Then he did the smart thing and made the transition into directing and producing. So many childhood stars blow their money, but not David—he invested wisely, right? Everyone knows that the real money is in production."

David gave her a half smile. "Excuse me, I need to use the bathroom," he said, leaving his nearly full pint glass and making his exit.

Why did talking about his past make David bolt?

"Were he and Mitchell on *Crazy House* together?" I asked Payton, after David left.

She gave me a sharp look. "Yeah. How did you know that?"

"Lucky guess. You said he was on a few sitcoms." Garrett caught my eye and raised his hands as if to say, *What are you doing?*

Payton's stein was nearly empty. She held it to her lips and tipped it back in an attempt to drink the very last drop. "He doesn't like to talk about it. I think it's kind of like girls who used to be cheerleaders in high school. They want to leave the past in the past."

"But he hired Mitchell?" I said, trying to understand the connection.

"True." She motioned to Hans for a refill. "Don't bring it up to David, though. He made a mistake. I think he felt sorry for Mitchell. That whole child actor thing, you know. And we got Mitchell at a great deal. The budget on this film is tight, so David figured he could save a penny or two and help an old friend out. That backfired. I don't think David had any idea what a nightmare Mitchell was going to be."

Hans wasn't moving fast enough for Payton. She grabbed her stein. "Time for another." She pushed her way through the throng of young girls who had been vying for Hans's attention.

"Hmm." Garrett stared at her. "The plot thickens."

"You can say that again," I replied.

Each new piece of information led to more questions. If David and Payton were frustrated with Mitchell and trying to figure out a way to fire him, could one of them have taken matters into their own hands and killed him? And if David and Mitchell had worked together years ago, was there another reason that he had hired the washed-up star? Could Mitchell have known something about David's past? Something worth killing for?

CHAPTER
NINETEEN

I DIDN'T STAY MUCH LONGER. My body needed sleep, and my mind needed rest. The minute my head hit the pillow, I was asleep. It wasn't until I heard the sound of Alex's alarm clock buzzing in his room that I realized I had crashed. I hurried across the hallway to silence his alarm. A pang of sadness hit me as I surveyed his room. Posters of the Seattle Seahawks and Sounders plastered the neon blue walls. Stacks of books and notes were piled on his desk. A bunch of his dirty clothes had been stuffed at the foot of the bed, along with a handful of dirty dishes. Probably from late-night snacks, I thought to myself, picking up the dishes.

My eyes landed on a framed photo resting next to his bed. It was of the six of us—Mac, Hans, Otto, Ursula, Alex, and me. We had taken the photo to commemorate the forty-year anniversary of Der Keller. It had been quite a party. The Krause family had opened the doors to the pub and tasting room and invited everyone in town to raise a pint. There had been authentic German food, music, and plenty of frothy beer. I stared at the woman in the picture, barely recognizing myself. My hips were fuller, and my eyes held a twinkle that had vanished the day I discovered Mac shagging the beer wench.

As I studied the picture, I realized there was something behind my smile that I hadn't noticed before. Loneliness. Despite the fact that I was surrounded by family, my eyes revealed my unhappiness. How long had I been unhappy with Mac? And worse, why hadn't I done something about it sooner? I didn't want Alex to see the mom in the picture. I wanted more for him. I wanted to model confidence and inner strength.

I placed the photo back on his nightstand and left his room. The rambling farmhouse felt cold and oppressive without him. On instinct, I returned to my bedroom and found the flyer I had taken from April's office of the cabin for sale at the base of the mountains. Then I made my way to the kitchen to start a pot of coffee. While I savored my coffee, I looked over the flyer. The cabin was the perfect size, less than fifteen hundred square feet, with a cathedral ceiling and two wood-burning fireplaces. With its location on the edge of the forest, I wouldn't have to maintain a massive garden or hop vines, and on days like this, when Alex was gone, I didn't think I would feel quite so isolated or alone in the cozy A-frame.

April had been bugging me about putting the farmhouse on the market. Thus far, I had held off on making any major moves. Everyone had told me not to do anything radical, but the more I thought about it, the more I wanted a change in scenery, and a new place, like the cabin. Maybe it was time to have April run some numbers and have a deeper conversation with Mac about our future.

I folded the flyer up again and tucked it in a drawer with take-out menus and Alex's old Crayola pencils. As much as the idea of downsizing excited me, the idea of talking to Mac—really talking—was terrifying. I already knew every argument he would make. I could hear him pleading and calling me "baby," which made my skin crawl. There was no chance that we were getting back together. Sometimes infidelity made couples stronger. But not with Mac and me. Our problems began years before he strayed. He had made a huge mistake in cheating, but I wasn't blameless either. The photo on Alex's nightstand was proof. I had stayed in an unhappy marriage for the sake of my son. Now I was done. I was done with Mac, and I was done with worry. My choices were my own. I was going to show Alex what putting yourself back together and starting over looked like. Hopefully I would stay upright in the process, but even if I had to risk falling down, it was worth it. He deserved a mother who was fully present. I was going to show him that I could start over and create a new, wonderful life for the two of us.

With my internal pep talk complete, I finished my coffee, took a quick shower, and headed for Nitro.

Volunteer crews were already hard at work in the town square, cleaning up the aftermath of last night's festivities. Two workers on opposite sides of the street blew leaves into piles. Another group swept the sidewalk in front of the gazebo and gathered deflated balloons and soda cans. Plastic cups, soggy felt hats, and crumpled up tickets and flyers littered Front Street. Yet another reason that villagers had a love/hate relationship with Oktoberfest. I wondered how late the party had gone last night.

When I rounded the corner toward Nitro, I was pleased to see that we had been spared. Our window boxes and patio had been untouched by the crowds. I unlocked the front door and went straight to work organizing supplies and mapping out a brewing plan and food for the pub for the next few days. Assuming the rest of the weekend went like last night, we shouldn't be busy in the evening, but there was a good chance we might get an early afternoon rush before people headed into the festival.

I made sure to work quietly, not wanting to wake Garrett or Kat. Come to think of it—had Kat stayed? I never saw her in the madness of the festival. Had she ended up back here or crashed somewhere else?

I didn't have to wait long to find out, because about twenty minutes after I arrived, she tiptoed down the back stairs and into the kitchen, where I was taking stock of our supplies in the fridge.

"Morning," she said in a timid voice.

I dropped a box of butter on the floor.

"Sorry. I didn't mean to sneak up on you." Kat's face was puffy, and her eyes half open.

Returning the butter to the fridge, I turned to face her. "No worries. I didn't know if you were here and if either you or Garrett were up."

"Yeah. It was so nice of him to offer me one of the upstairs guest rooms. Have you been up there? This place is like a museum. You should see the wallpaper in the room I'm staying in."

I shook my head. I'd eaten at Garrett's aunt's restaurant on a few occasions, but never ventured upstairs in the bed-and-breakfast. I knew that there was no shortage of space in the old building. Garrett had been brainstorming what to do with the second floor. For the moment, the six guest rooms were empty, except for Garrett's bedroom.

"Can I tell you something?" Kat said, rubbing the edge of her eye. "The bedroom kind of gave me the creeps. There are a bunch of old photos in it, and I swear everyone in the photos is staring right at me."

My mind flashed to my conversation with Garrett yesterday. He had mentioned that a woman had called asking for me. Had she stopped by after we closed? Was she here in Leavenworth right now? I couldn't quell the nerves in my stomach at the thought.

"Are you okay?" Kat blinked and then massaged the corner of her eye.

"What? Oh, yeah, just lost in thought for a moment."

She gazed longingly at the vintage coffee maker on the countertop. "Would it be too much to ask to make a pot of coffee? It was a late night."

"Sure." Happy for the distraction, I moved to find a canister of beans in the cupboard. I dumped them in the grinder and pulsed them into a fine powder.

"The smell alone is waking me up." Kat walked closer. "Can I help?"

"Do you want something to eat?" I offered.

Her neck splotched with bright spots. "No, no. You and Garrett have been so nice to me. You don't have to feed me."

"You're working in exchange for your room and board, remember?"

She gave a half nod.

"Good, then let's see what we can pull together." I poured cold, filtered water into the coffeepot and returned to the fridge. Kat's lack of funds took me back to my days of working any odd job I could to pay my way through school. Growing up in foster care had cemented my need for independence. I didn't want her to worry about where or how she was going to get her next meal.

"How about a cheesy egg, potato, and sausage scramble?" I asked, taking eggs, sharp cheddar, and German sausages out of the fridge.

Kat grinned. "That sounds amazing. Put me to work."

I had her crack and whisk the eggs while I grilled the sausages. "Kat, I want to ask you about Mitchell again," I said, drizzling olive oil on the griddle. The spicy sausages filled with pork, fennel, sage, garlic, and onion were a staple in the Krause dining room. Ursula often served *Bauernfrühstück* (German famer's breakfast), a hearty potato and egg scramble made with leftover sausage or bacon and brimming with veggies and melted cheese. On a cold winter morning, nothing was better than a sizzling skillet of Ursula's home-cooked farm-style breakfast. Sometimes she would even swap in bratwursts that she had marinated in beer, onion, and butter for hours. My mouth watered at the memory and the scent of the sausages beginning to brown.

"Is this right?" Kat asked, showing me the frothy eggs.

"Yep. Now you can add salt and pepper and grate in a half cup or so of the cheddar." I pointed to the block of cheese on the counter.

"Got it." She pushed up the sleeves of her baggy sweatshirt. "What do you want to know about Mitchell?"

I flipped the sausages with a pair of tongs. "You mentioned that he arrived on the same day as you, but someone else mentioned that they had seen him around town a few days prior to that. I know you said you were following his every move. Do you think there's a chance he arrived in Leavenworth early?"

Kat shredded the cheddar with such force I was worried that she might slice her finger. "Yeah. I do. I got a text last night from one of my followers. Hang on. I'll show you." She set the cheese on the counter and grabbed her phone out of her pocket.

I turned the griddle to low and moved the sausages off to one side.

"Look at this," Kat said, expanding the picture on her phone. "That's Mitchell, and that looks like Front Street, right?"

I wiped my hands on a towel. She was right. In the picture Mitchell was standing in the middle of Front Street wearing a green felt hat and pointing toward the Festhalle. The photo had to have been taken days before Oktoberfest, because when Kat zoomed in closer, it was apparent that the tents were still being set up.

"Isn't that weird?" Kat asked.

"Yeah." I took a final look at the photo to see if I could make out any other details, but nothing jumped out at me. "Where did your friend get the picture?"

Kat shoved her phone back into her pocket. "She saw it on someone else's Instagram page. They tagged Mitchell in it."

"Do you know who posted the picture?" I could feel eager energy pulse through my body. If Mitchell arrived in Leavenworth early, had he come to meet Lisa? Or someone else? Could he have been having a secret affair?

"I don't know." Kat shrugged. "It's super weird that he didn't post anything on his page about being in Leavenworth. He posted at least three times a day. People called him an 'oversharer.' You know, like, constantly sharing every minute of his life. He did a teaser post a couple weeks ago about being on location soon. That's it, though. Nothing from here."

"He didn't mention anything about being here? That is odd." I left the beautifully charred sausages to grab a bag of hash browns from the freezer. It was possible that Mitchell showed up in advance of the crew to do research, scout out the beer scene, or maybe even add a few days of vacation to his filming schedule, but I was more inclined to believe April. Had Mitchell come to meet Lisa? If so, why the secrecy? I certainly hadn't seen him around the village. "Could you ask your friend where she found the picture?" I asked Kat, as I tossed hash browns onto the griddle.

"No problem. She's probably not awake yet, but I'll text her later."

I dropped it, but couldn't help wondering if Kat was

stalling. As much as I wanted to trust her, I had to keep my guard up.

"Hey, what smells so good?" Garrett interrupted my thoughts. If possible, he looked even more bleary-eyed than Kat. "Are we serving breakfast for the hangover crowd?" He wore a pair of baggy pajama pants with silhouettes of beer bottles and a thin sweatshirt with his old company logo. I had to place my hand on my stomach to stop it from flopping. I wasn't used to having such a visceral reaction to someone. Garrett was attractive, but it was more than that. He was so comfortable in his own skin that he naturally exuded an inner calmness. I envied his casual attitude.

I gave the hash browns a healthy shake of salt and pepper. "That's not a bad idea, actually. Although that crowd won't be awake until long after noon."

Garrett helped himself to coffee. "You're making breakfast for us?" He sounded like Alex.

"Yep. A traditional German farmer's breakfast. Hans calls it a 'stick to your ribs' meal."

Pinching his well-toned waist, Garrett grinned. "I could use a rib-sticking breakfast, especially if we're going to brew today."

The hash browns had crisped and turned golden. I sliced the sausages and added them to Kat's eggs and cheese mixture. Then I tossed in fresh garlic and peppers. Scrambling the eggs in with the hash browns only took a few minutes. I finished it with a touch of parsley and scooped healthy servings into three bowls. We gathered around the countertop with steaming mugs of coffee.

Garrett dug into his scramble. A long string of melted

cheese stretched from the bowl to his lips. "I don't know what I did in a past life to deserve this, but I'm telling you right now, you make breakfast like this every day, and I'll give you half my shares in Nitro."

I chuckled. "I'll make breakfast anytime. No need for shares." Nothing could be truer. The last thing I wanted was stock in another brewery.

Kat devoured her bowl. "Can you teach me to cook like this?" she said with a full mouth.

"You bet." I took a bite, making sure to get a piece of sausage and peppers. The *Bauernfrühstück* had turned out well. I thought Ursula would be pleased with my attempt at recreating her traditional breakfast.

After we finished our meal, we mapped out a game plan for the day. Garrett and I would open early—at 1:00 after the parade. Every Saturday the Muenchner Kindl led a procession down Front Street. Everyone in the village participated, waving flags and dancing along with Leavenworth's Musikkapelle (a traditional Bavarian band that played marches and polkas from the Old World). The star of the parade was the official Oktoberfest keg, driven to the Festhalle in a *Bier* wagon, where it would be tapped, signaling the start of the festivities.

We figured the vast majority of tourists who came to see the parade would likely follow the *Bier* wagon into the tents, but locals might want to take brief respite inside Nitro's non-Germanified walls. Plus there was a chance that adventurous beer lovers would stray from the masses to get a taste of what else Leavenworth had to offer, especially since Kat had handed out hundreds of tasting coupons. Hopefully at least a few tourists would take us up on a free tasting.

If yesterday was any indication, we would close in the early evening again. While Garrett and I prepared for the day, we sent Kat back to the printer for more marketing materials, which she could hand out along the parade route and at the Festhalle later.

"Thanks again for breakfast," Kat said, scraping her bowl. "I'll do the dishes and then go put my dress on for the parade."

Garrett handed her his bowl. "Thanks." Then he motioned to the office. "Sloan, I want to show you a new recipe I sketched out last night."

I followed him into the office that we shared. It was a small room with two desks and a filing cabinet. The walls were made of whiteboard and covered with Garrett's notes and formulas. "Please don't tell me that you're going to try and clone Mac's Apple Weizen," I said, taking a seat at my desk.

"If brewing a perfect beer is the key to your heart, I just might have to give it a try." He winked. "That would really get under his skin, wouldn't it?"

"Yep."

Garrett took the cap off a red dry-erase pen and tapped a recipe he had written in blue ink on the wall. "You're going to think I'm crazy, but after we were talking the other day about late fall beers and the holidays coming up, I've been toying with some new ideas. It stemmed from the cranberries and I hate to admit this, but . . . my convo with April."

"April is influencing your beer choices?" I could hear the disbelief in my voice.

"Hear me out." Garrett held out both hands. "Don't panic. I'm not thinking about tossing out our T-shirts for lederhosen, but what do you think about doing a rogue holiday line of beers?"

"Like what?"

He walked to the whiteboard and erased a corner. Then he began sketching a Christmas tree. "Think of all things Christmas. I mean German Christmas, but with our Northwest slant—pine needles, cranberry and popcorn strings, mulled wine, Christmas stollen, chocolate, and nuts."

I appreciated that Garrett liked to push the envelope when it came to beer, but I wasn't sure I wanted popcorn and pine needles in my pint glass.

"You're not into it?" Garrett's smile sagged. He held a green dry-erase pen to the board and made a doodle of a beer stein.

"No, it's not that. It's just how we execute creating rogue flavors. Can I look at your notes?" I took the papers from his hands. The smell from the dry-erase pen was potent.

He ran his hands through his hair. "I guess I had a bit of a revelation last night. I've wanted to do something totally different here, and we are. I don't want to add a bunch of German décor in here or start wearing lederhosen. April's been on my back since we opened, and trust me, I'm not going to let her dictate what we do, but Hans and I stayed up until two last night talking about his childhood in Leavenworth and his impressions as an adult. I was watching the crowd dancing and drinking. People really love the German vibe. They embrace it like nothing I ever experienced in Seattle. Which is how I got on this loop about figuring out a way to bring a piece of that to Nitro, but still stay true to my vision."

"That makes sense." I focused in on his meticulous handwriting. He had roughed out a recipe for a chocolate hazelnut imperial stout brewed with roasted nuts, cocoa nibs, and vanilla bean. That could work. His idea for cranberries involved a Gose (an old German wheat beer that originated from Goslar). Gose beers are low in hops, and Garrett's vision included hints of sea salt, buttered popcorn, and pressed cranberries. As I reviewed his recipe, I became more excited. The salt would bring out the tanginess of the berries, which would complement the creamy, buttery undertones of the popcorn. Maybe he was onto something, after all.

"Well?" He winced, as if anticipating that I would shoot his idea down.

"You know what? I love this. This is fantastic. A hoppy pine IPA and a strong ale aged in wine barrels. You're a genius."

"Yeah?" Garrett bit his bottom lip. "Is it too out-there?" He tapped the tip of the pen to the whiteboard.

"No. It's smart. You're right, weaving in a nod to Germany while maintaining your Northwest style is a great idea." I pointed to a drawing he had done of a Christmas tree next to his notes on a pine IPA. "This might get April off our backs, too."

Garrett's eyes brightened. "Can you imagine?"

"A girl can dream." I grinned.

He clicked the cap back onto the pen. "If you think it's a

good idea, we can get started on some experimental batches in the next few days."

"Count me in." I was about to ask Garrett about Kat when a timid knock sounded on the office door.

Kat peered inside. She was holding a stack of flyers that she must have picked up from the printer. "Sloan, there's a woman up front who asked to see you."

My knees buckled. Garrett reached out to steady me. I gave him a weak smile in return. "I'm fine," I lied. Was I about to meet my mother?

CHAPTER

TWENTY

I'M NOT SURE WHAT GARRETT said to Kat. Sounds became fuzzy around me. A bitter taste formed in my mouth. My breathing felt labored as I took heavy steps toward the front. Kat didn't follow after me. Nor did Garrett. This was something I had to face on my own.

Time seemed to slow. Part of me wanted to bolt. What if I didn't like her? What if she didn't like me? And what could she possibly say to me about giving me up? Leaving me to float from house to house for my entire childhood without ever checking in. Had she wondered about me?

I tried to swallow, but my throat constricted. Maybe I wasn't ready for this.

Sloan, you're a grown woman. You can do this. I sucked air through my nostrils, squared my shoulders, and hurried to the bar before I had a chance to change my mind.

To my surprise, I recognized the woman waiting for me, but not because I'd seen her in a photograph. I knew her.

"Sally?" I said, unable to keep my voice from quivering.

"Sloan!" Sally slid off a barstool and came to hug me.

She had aged in the years since I had seen her, but I would have recognized her face anywhere.

"You look amazing." She released me, but grabbed my hand and clutched it tightly. "You've grown more lovely with time, if that's even possible."

"I can't believe you're here." I squeezed her hand as memories of my time with her flooded my body. Sally had been my social worker and the one constant in my childhood. I had often fantasized that instead of placing me in a new home, Sally would adopt me herself. She was short and sturdy, with wiry gray curls and thick black glasses. Freckles and age spots dotted her fair skin. Her blue eyes held a familiar kindness. Sally had been a grounding force in an otherwise chaotic lifestyle. I remember the calming sound of classical music playing in her office and how she had gone to the principal and school board to ensure that I got scholarship money for community college.

Tears spilled from my eyes.

"Sloan." Sally squeezed my hand tighter. "Shall we sit?"

I didn't trust myself to speak, so I nodded and brushed away the salty tears with my finger. "Sorry, I don't usually get emotional," I said, after we sat at the high-top table.

Sally reached into her simple black clutch and removed a package of tissue. "This reunion calls for tears." She opened the package, handing me a tissue and then taking one to dab her own eyes. "You have no idea how I wish I could have gotten you to shed a tear or two when you were young. You never did. You were so strong. I've never met another child quite like you."

"I don't know if I was strong. Maybe stoic," I said, wiping my eyes.

"No, you were strong." Sally held my gaze. "I've thought about you so often over the years. I've watched your career grow and cut out a number of newspaper clippings about the up-and-coming female brewmaster who has been taking the brewing world by storm." She patted a file folder resting on the table. "I've saved every article. I hope you don't mind, but I feel a touch of pride every time I read your name in the paper."

I laughed. "I don't know about taking the world by storm, but I do love to brew."

Sally placed her hand over mine. "I always knew that you were going to make it. Sadly, in my line of work, I couldn't say that about many kids. But you, you had this spark and inner confidence that couldn't be shaken."

"Thanks." I felt a new batch of tears starting to form. "You helped. If it hadn't been for my weekly visits in your office, I might not have survived."

Her hand was warm and comforting. "You would have survived with or without me." She sighed. "Do you know that I tried on many occasions to become your guardian?"

"You did?" I gasped. "I used to daydream about our weekly check-ins. I imagined walking into your office and you telling me that I never would have to go to another foster home again."

"Me too." Her face clouded. "Things were different back then. The state didn't feel like a 'spinster' in her midforties was an appropriate match for adoption. I'm happy to say that over the years we've loosened our ideas about what constitutes a family."

"Right." I nodded.

A look of sadness washed over her, but she recovered. "You have a family, I hear."

"Yeah." I hesitated. Should I tell her about Mac?

"Tell me about them," she nudged.

Everything spilled out. I told her the story of meeting Otto and Ursula and how they had made me a part of their family. I beamed when I showed her pictures of Alex and then shed a few more tears when I explained how Mac had cheated and I felt like I was not only losing him but losing the entire Krause family.

After I finished, she removed her glasses and placed them on top of the file folder. "Sloan, listen to everything you've just told me." Her eyes were firm and knowing. "You are part of the Krause family. Regardless of what you decide to do about your relationship with Mac, you are family. You're parents together—that's forever. And from the way you speak of Otto and Ursula, I'm confident that you've forged a bond with them that can't be broken."

I had forgotten how comforting it was to be in Sally's presence.

"If it wouldn't be too much to ask, I would love to meet Alex," she continued. "It's unwarranted and selfish of me, but I've always felt such a connection when reading about your accomplishments. You've earned every accolade that you've received, but I can't help feeling like a proud . . ." She trailed off. "Aunt."

"Of course! You have to meet Alex." I glanced outside where people passed the window waving German flags. The parade crowd must be beginning to gather. "How long are you in town?"

Her eyes darted to the file folder and then back to me. "Unfortunately, not long. I'm leaving for an Alaskan cruise later tonight. I have to get back to Seattle immediately, but I've been waiting for some information to come in. It arrived yesterday, and I wanted to come share my news with you in person."

My throat tightened. The way she said "share my news" didn't sound positive.

She placed her glasses on the tip of her nose and opened the file folder. "When I got your email, I was so thrilled to hear from you. I don't know if the agency told you that I retired?"

I nodded. "They did. In fact they wouldn't give me your personal email, so I had to beg them to pass on my message."

"State bureaucracy." She rolled her eyes. "To be honest, I was surprised to receive your request. I thought that you weren't interested in finding your birth parents."

"I wasn't." I told her about the photo that Garrett had found and how seeing it had made me reconsider.

She flipped through newspaper clippings. "The minute I got your email, I sent a request for access to your file. I have to tell you, your case was always a bit of a conundrum."

"How?" I leaned on the table.

"You were left in the children's ward at Wenatchee Hospital. Unlike most children placed in the care of the state, you were well clothed, nourished, and obviously had been well loved."

I forced the soles of my tennis shoes onto the bottom rung of the barstool in an attempt to maintain my balance. A wave of dizziness assaulted my body. The spotty memories I had from my early years never felt solid. Sally had once assured me that it was a normal coping strategy from the trauma of moving so often and being abandoned.

"Should I continue?" Sally's voice was soft. It almost sounded like it was far away.

"Please." I nodded.

"You were six years old, almost seven. Again not unheard of, but given your health and well-being—there were no signs of physical or mental abuse, no indication of exposure to drugs, your hair was braided with two pink bows, and your shoes were brand-new. Whoever left you loved you." She removed a photo from the file folder and slid it across the table toward me. "This was taken on the day you were found at the hospital."

This time I couldn't contain my emotions. Fat tears swelled. My nose began to drip and my shoulders quaked as I stared at the little girl in the picture. She looked happy. Perhaps slightly confused, but the young child staring back at me could have been on her way to dance lessons, not being deserted at a hospital never to see her family again.

Sally gently pressed three tissues into my hand. "Take your time, let the emotions out."

Once I had regained my composure and dried my tears, I met Sally's eyes. "I'm okay. I'm ready to hear more."

She frowned. "I wish I had more to share."

"I don't understand."

"Neither do I." She pulled out five sheets of paper and handed them to me. "Your case bothered me. I went to my boss on a number of occasions to try and find out more. Your file only contained this photo. I asked him for more details, what they were doing to try and find your birth parents. Typically in cases like yours, there's media outreach. There was never any for you, and when I pressed him on why, he told me it was a lost cause. I spent eleven years trying to gently extract any details about your past in our meetings."

"You did?" I didn't recall that.

She shook her head from side to side. "In a child-centered way. You came to trust me, and over time, you divulged small details about your early life. When I would share what I had learned with my boss, he would tell me it was insignificant, and then he would move you. I didn't realize it at the time, but I think he intentionally moved you from foster home to foster home to break our bond. It eroded your trust in me. I promised not to move you, but it wasn't up to me."

"What?"

The soft features in her face hardened. "I should have realized it sooner. I'm so sorry."

"It's not your fault." I reached out to comfort her. "But why? Why would he want to break up our connection?"

She shrugged. "The only thing I can think of is that it had to do with your birth parents. It was as if he didn't want me—or you—to find them."

My head throbbed. None of what Sally was saying made sense.

"He told me that I had grown too attached, that I needed

to maintain a clinical approach. Part of me wondered if he was right. You captured my heart the minute I met you, and your story was so heartbreaking and such a mystery. Maybe I had crossed a line." Her fingers were pressed together so tightly that the tips of each finger turned white.

"You were looking out for me, Sally." I fought back tears.

She forced a smile. "I know that now." Pausing for a moment, she unclenched her hands. "And now I know for sure that I wasn't wrong."

"Why?"

She handed me the papers. "This is it. This is all that's in your file. A page of notes from each of the foster homes you were placed in. None of my chart notes are here. They're all missing. Years and years of therapy sessions are missing. When I asked for your file, this is what was left. The photo and five pages of basic notes about placement dates." Her voice was laced with anger.

"I don't understand."

Sally's eyes were like daggers. "Sloan, I should have come to you earlier. I thought about it. When you got that scholarship, I knew you were on your way. I knew you were going to be fine. I almost reached out to you, but I figured it was better to leave it alone. You didn't need me adding angst and questions as you were about to launch into adulthood." She exhaled. "I'll never forgive myself. I should have trusted my instincts. But the state made me believe that I wasn't acting professionally and was even creating imaginary scenarios in my mind. Now I have no doubt. Someone doesn't want you to find out about your past. And they've gone through a lot of work to destroy anything that might lead you to your birth parents."

CHAPTER

TWENTY-ONE

"I'M SORRY," I SAID, TWISTING my ponytail so tight I thought it might cut off circulation to my head. Why would someone want to keep my birth parents' identity secret? For as long as I could remember, I had believed that I had been unwanted. Abandoned. But now Sally's revelation made me question that. She was convinced that I had been well loved. What could have possibly transpired to make my parents leave me at a hospital?

For the moment I let the thought creep in. It was almost worse to imagine my parents struggling with their decision. Or even agonizing over it.

My heart ached for Alex. I wished he were here. Nothing, no amount of stress or financial worry, could keep me from him. What could have happened to cause my parents' retreat?

"Sloan?" Sally's somber voice shook me from my thoughts.

"I'm okay." I gave her a half nod. "I'm just trying to make sense of everything you told me."

"Me too." She reached for my hand again. "Please accept my apology."

"Your apology? This isn't your fault."

Her hand was cold to the touch. "I should have advocated more. I should have pressed and asked more questions. I knew all those years ago that something wasn't right about your case, but I chalked it up to being too attached to you."

"Sally, listen." I sat up and squeezed her hand. "I don't have any idea why your boss—or maybe my parents—wanted to conceal their identity, but I do know that without you in my life, I never would have ended up here. I would have been one of the statistics. You helped give me normalcy."

She drew her hand away. "Thank you, Sloan. I just wish I would have listened to my instinct."

"It's okay. The question is what do I do now?"

"For starters, this is for you." She slid the entire folder toward me. "If you'll let me, I'd like to help. I have contacts in the field. I can put out some feelers, but I haven't done that yet. I wanted to talk to you face-to-face. If you want to leave it here, I'll support you in that, and if you want to pursue this, I'll spend every waking minute working with you."

"You don't need to spend every waking minute on this," I said with a smile. Staring at the file, I considered my options. The easiest route would be to drop it. I could tuck the file in the back of my closet and go on with my life as if Sally and I had never had this conversation. I had mastered the art of detachment. I could return to brewing, immerse myself in steeping grains and boiling hops. But that was the old Sloan. That was the Sloan who suffered through a failing marriage because she was too scared to want more for herself. The new me wouldn't turn her back on her past. She would go to any length to reconcile her tumultuous childhood with her desperate need for stability. I had to pursue this.

Sally removed her glasses and placed them in a case in her purse.

"Thank you for sharing this with me." I sat up and breathed in the scent of nutty grains. Garrett was probably testing another batch. "I want to learn more, and I would love your help."

Her face relaxed. "Oh, I'm so glad to hear that. I have an email drafted and ready to send to a few of my colleagues. I almost hit send before I left to come here, but decided against it. I'm not sure if it's safe. That's one of the reasons I just got in the car and drove here. I've tried calling you a few times, but then I started wondering if someone could be monitoring my calls or email."

"Really?"

Sally's eyes clouded. "I don't want to sound overly dramatic, but I'm not sure what we might be getting ourselves into. If the state is involved in some way—" She paused. "Well, there could be risk involved."

"I'm sure it's fine." I picked up the file folder. It felt like dead weight in my hands. "Do your colleagues still work for the state?"

"Yes." Sally nodded. "Two of them are still employed by Child Protective Services, but they're both people I trust. Otherwise, I think it might be best to keep this between the two of us for the time being."

"Okay."

She glanced at the clock on the far wall. "If I'm going to make my boat, I should probably head to Seattle soon. I wish that my timing were better. My sister and I have saved for the last two years to go on this trip together. I thought about postponing. I told her that you were my priority."

"No. Absolutely not. I've been parentless for over three decades. Another few weeks isn't going to make a difference." I lowered my voice, even though it was just the two of us in the bar. "And I really think we should be strategic about how we proceed."

"Agreed. I don't want to put you in any danger."

"Danger?"

"Sloan, if someone has kept your parents' identity secret for over thirty years, what length might they go to to ensure it stays secret? I made one inquiry, and hundreds of pages of therapy notes are missing. That can't be a coincidence."

She was right. "I don't want you in the middle of this."

She brushed me off. "That's nonnegotiable. I'm already invested, and this is personal. Why would the department lie to me? I feel like I've been used. I was nothing more than a pawn for them. And then of course, I would do anything for you. Anything." Her eyes misted again.

"Thank you. You've already done enough. And you need to get going." I pointed to the clock. "You don't want to miss your ship."

She sighed. "I feel terrible dumping this on you and then leaving."

I stood. "No, it's good. It will give me some time to think and formulate a plan. Let's get together when you return from the cruise and map out a strategy then."

"If you're sure?" She hesitated.

I pulled her to standing. "I'm positive. Plus, that way when you're here next, you can meet Alex."

"I would love that." She wrapped me in a final hug. "Sloan, I am sorry."

"Sally, don't be. I'm relieved that you shared everything with me." I walked her to the door. "Now, go have fun in Alaska. Take a thousand pictures and don't get eaten by a bear."

My attempt at humor fell flat. Sally nodded, but then gave me a one parting frown. "I promise that I'll be with you every step of the way until we figure this out."

"I know." I held the door open for her and watched her go. "Good luck getting out of the madness," I called after her. Front Street was jammed with people lining the parade route. Organ music echoed in the distance. Like yesterday, the atmosphere was jubilant, although tinged with a hint of hangover, as was common the morning after the first night. Nearly everyone smashed together on the sidewalk was sporting a pair of sunglasses and nursing a bottle of water or Gatorade.

Talk about a strange turn of events. I had thought that today might have been the day I would meet my birth mother, but instead Sally's visit had opened a new mystery. What could possibly be so important about the identity of my parents? Sally had made it sound as if I was part of a major conspiracy. Could my parents be famous? Or master criminals?

Sally had been trustworthy, but could she be right about being too attached to me? Maybe this was a figment of her imagination. Maybe the case notes accidentally got shredded. After all, I'd been out of the system for over twenty years.

"Sloan, you up here?" Garrett's deep voice echoed in the empty bar.

"Yeah." I inhaled and plastered on a neutral smile. In times like this I was glad that I had developed a steely exterior.

"How did that go? Was that . . ." He trailed off.

"My birth mother?" I offered, then shook my head. "No. That was my social worker."

"Your social worker?" He raised his brow.

"From childhood. She was my case worker." I wasn't sure how much more I was ready to share. I needed some time to process what I had learned. "She brought me my file and has started some inquiries for me."

If Garrett was unsatisfied, he didn't give any indication. "That's good."

"Yeah. It's good," I agreed, tucking the folder under my arm. "It was nice of her to stop by. I haven't seen her in years. Let me go put this away." I left for the office before he had a chance to ask any more questions. My hands trembled as I shoved the file folder in my bag. Later tonight, when I was back at the farmhouse, I would give it a closer look, but for the moment I had to focus on Nitro.

Kat danced by me in her barmaid costume. "I'm off to the parade. Don't worry, I won't let a single person past me without giving them a Nitro flyer."

"I'm sure you won't." I waved, wishing that I shared her carefree spirit. I took a minute to compose myself before returning to the bar.

Garrett had the front door propped open, sending in a

rush of cool fall air. The smell of kettle corn and horses wafted inside. "There are people everywhere," he said as I approached the patio.

"Yep. It'll be like this every Saturday for the next three weeks," I replied, noting the masses who had squeezed along the sidewalk to catch a glimpse of the procession.

At that moment, the alpenhorn sounded, signaling the start of the parade. Garrett hopped onto the top of one of the wrought-iron tables to get a better view. He reached his hand out to me. "Come up. You can see everything."

I didn't want to tell him that I'd seen (and participated in) the parade every year for the last two decades. Instead I took his extended hand and joined him on a nearby table. It was a good vantage point. I could see over the top of the crowd that had swelled and now lined the street and sidewalk down Second Street. The pulsing sound of the polka made the crowd shriek with excitement. I watched as familiar faces and friends skipped along the route in pink and green ruffled dresses and forest green lederhosen, waving flags and tossing candy to children. No surprise, April Ablin pranced in the front, bowing to spectators and embodying her self-professed role as Leavenworth's ambassador. For the first time, I saw her in a new light. April had no family to speak of. Her entire world revolved around our town. Maybe we had more in common than I had realized. Suddenly her photo display made me feel sad for her.

The sound of accordion music and children's happy laughter faded as I got lost in my memories. Had I been loved? What did I remember about my life before I had entered the foster care system? There were a few fleeting memories, but they felt like clouds bouncing along a stretch of open blue sky, and the harder I tried to force the memory, the faster they vanished, evaporating into the heavens.

There was a flicker of a dinner table with a huge family gathered around it. It might have been someone's birthday. A hazy picture of candles and a pink cake faded in and out, like a camera lens trying to focus. Was it my birthday?

As quickly as the picture entered my mind, it disappeared, replaced by a hospital and a woman holding my hand. Her grasp made my fingers feel numb. She didn't want to let me go.

I nearly lost my balance on the table. Garrett caught me and stared at me with concern. "You okay, Sloan?"

"Fine. Just trying to get a better view of the keg," I lied, and stood on my tiptoes. The memory was lost. Had that been my mother? Were my memories even trustworthy? It was entirely possible that I was creating images I wanted to remember from my adult brain.

I could feel Garrett's eyes on me, so I clapped along to the beat of the marching band and forced the thoughts away. My gaze landed on the corner of Front and Second Street. David leaned against an antique lamppost as Connor filmed the procession. I wasn't surprised that they were documenting the parade. It would make for colorful entertainment in their documentary, and many visitors reported that the parade was the highlight of their trip to Leavenworth. However, what did surprise me was seeing David chatting amicably with none other than Mac. What was my soon-to-be ex up to now?

CHAPTER TWENTY-TWO

I STARED AT THEM AS David leaned close to Mac and said something in his ear. Then Mac pointed out the traditional Bavarian dancers who twirled down the street. I could feel my heart rate quicken as the parade ended with the keg rolling toward the Festhalle and Connor turned his camera from the back of the wagon and focused it on my ex-husband. The crowd funneled after the keg. Mac stood on the corner gesturing with his hands.

Garrett turned to me. "That was cool." He paused and followed my eyes. "Looks like Mac is hamming it up for the camera. I can't blame him. From this vantage point, he could easily pass for a German."

"He is German," I muttered.

"Right." Garrett chuckled. "I meant that it looks like we're in the heart of Germany. No wonder they wanted to film during Oktoberfest."

I hopped off the table. I didn't need to see more of Mac to make the morning worse.

Garrett followed suit. "Well, should we go ahead and keep the doors open?" He glanced at the emptying streets. "Kind of looks like everyone is heading for the tents."

"That's for the tapping ceremony, but I'm sure people will trickle back out." I brushed a handful of leaves from the tabletop. "We've got nothing to lose, right?"

"Only money." Garrett winked. "If you don't mind keeping watch up front, I thought I might start a test batch."

"Go for it." I kept the door propped open and placed a sandwich board in front of the patio.

"Holler if you need me," Garrett said, making his way to the brewery.

I didn't tell him that it was highly doubtful that we would see an afternoon rush, but stranger things could happen. With the door open, I could hear the booming sounds of the keg tapping in the distance. I knew the beer was flowing when a huge round of applause broke out. A few people trickled in over the next hour, cashing in the flyers that Kat had handed out. I was happy to pour pints and chat about our unique slant on craft brewing. As expected, most people stopped in for a taste and then continued on to the main party. I didn't mind the slower rhythm to the day. It gave me a chance to let my thoughts simmer.

Sometime after two, Lisa came up to the bar. "Hey, Sloan," she said in a hushed tone. "Do you have a minute?" Her bulky key ring weighed down her narrow wrist.

I looked up to survey the pub. There was a party of six outside on the patio sharing two pitchers of our Cherry

Weizen. Inside, two couples sat at bar tables, tasting flights. "Sure, what's up?" I replied. "Do you want a beer?"

She shook her head. "No, no. It's too early for that."

I almost laughed. In the world of brewing, *anytime* was beer time.

"I want to talk about last night," she said, leaning over the bar.

"What about?"

"You know what about," she said in a low voice. Then she glanced behind us. "Sorry. I didn't mean to snap. I'm on edge."

I rinsed a pint glass and waited for her to continue.

"Look, I know I shouldn't have gone back to the property, but like I told you last night, I had to respond to that review." She tugged the key ring off her wrist and set it on the top of the bar.

"That's what you said, but I don't understand why you had to go back to the property."

She ignored my comment. "Have you talked to Chief Meyers?"

I shook my head.

"Okay, good. Good." Her tone was almost manic. "Okay, really, that's so good."

"I didn't say I wasn't going to talk to her. I haven't had a chance yet."

Lisa scowled. "Please don't, Sloan. I'm begging you. If you tell her that I broke in last night, she's probably going to arrest me."

I stared at her. "Lisa, this is a murder investigation. Chief Meyers needs to know. Last night you told me you have a key, right?"

She picked up a coaster and tapped it on the top of the bar. "Of course I have a key. I manage the property, but you know what I mean, breaking into a crime scene. She's going to arrest me. I know it. Everyone thinks I killed him." Her voice rose. "I can't believe it. Why would I kill the guy? I didn't even know him."

This was my opportunity. She'd brought the subject up, so I decided there was no time like the present to ask her about what April had said. "Lisa, are you sure about that?"

"Sure about what?" Her eyes narrowed.

"I've heard from a few people that you and Mitchell were seen all around town." That was a slight exaggeration, but I wanted to see how Lisa would react.

Lisa's face blanched. "What? Where did you hear that?" She clutched the bar. "No, no, no, no. That can't have gotten out. We were so careful."

"What?" I stared at her.

She pounded the coaster. "Sloan, this is a disaster. I hate living in such a small town sometimes. How does everyone know my every move?"

I returned the pint glass to the shelf. "Lisa, I'm not sure what to believe right now. First you claim not to have ever met Mitchell, then you sneak into his rental, and then you lie about knowing him. What's going on? I'm worried about you."

"You believe me, though, right? You know I didn't kill him."

"I don't know anything."

"Sloan, you have to trust me."

"You have to explain what's going on, Lisa."

She folded the cardboard coaster in half. "Okay, I did meet Mitchell earlier. He came to Leavenworth three days ahead of the crew. When I arranged their stays, I sent each member a confirmation email about their rentals—key codes, directions, links to activities around the area—that sort of thing."

I nodded.

"Mitchell emailed me directly and asked if he could come early. He said that he was interested in investing in property but wanted to keep it under wraps. I agreed. He had strict parameters. He didn't want anyone to know that he was in town. He was going 'incognito' until the rest of the crew arrived. And I couldn't tell anyone who he really was."

"Okay." I could hear the confusion in my voice. "Would anyone in Leavenworth recognize him?"

Lisa rolled her eyes. "No. I tried to tell him that—tactfully— but it didn't go over well."

"Why were you showing him property? I thought you and your mom managed vacation rentals. I didn't know you sold them too."

She put her finger to her lips and shot her head to the left and right. "That's also under wraps right now."

"I don't understand."

"April Ablin," she whispered. "She's going to be fuming when she learns that I obtained my real estate license."

"You're going into the real estate business?"

"Not officially, but when it comes to the properties we manage, we decided it would be a strategic idea for Balmes Vacation Properties to list and sell any vacation homes in our portfolio."

No wonder she wanted to keep that quiet. April had been Leavenworth's top-selling real estate agent for the past ten years. In part because April undercut her commission and used less-than-moral techniques to steal away her competition's clients.

"The vacation home market is different than traditional home buying. April knows that, and many of our clients have requested our services in the past. We had ventured into it while I was learning the business, but now that I have a good handle on the market, it's time to expand. My mom would like to retire in the next few years, and this seemed like the right time."

"It's a good idea," I said.

Lisa gave me a small smile. "Thanks. I'm sure you can imagine how April is going to respond when she hears."

"Can I be there for that conversation?" I joked.

"Please. I might need to bring a team of bodyguards with me."

"How does this relate to Mitchell, though?"

"He was going to be my first client. I have seven properties with owners who are open to sell if the right offer comes along. Nothing is up on the market yet. I explained that to Mitchell. I also told him that if he was serious about touring any of the properties, he would have to come a few days early. As you know, we're completely booked. I couldn't very well bring Mitchell through the houses with guests inside." She stopped speaking when one of the couples approached the bar. They had finished their tasting flight and decided to stay for a full pint of Cherry Weizen.

Lisa banged the broken coaster on the bar while I poured

two ruby red pints of the Weizen. Once they returned to their table, Lisa continued. "I thought things were going really well. Mitchell arrived on Monday night. Per his request, I had his cabin stocked with groceries and set up local food delivery so that he wouldn't be seen. I showed him properties on Tuesday and Wednesday. You met him, so you know what his personality was like. He had a complaint about every property. The ceiling was too high, or there was too much carpet or too much hardwood. He was hard to please."

"That was my impression of him, too," I agreed.

"Right? But I could deal with that. Some of my clients are demanding, and I'm a professional. That changed on Wednesday night. The rest of the crew was arriving Thursday morning, so Mitchell invited me to have dinner with him at his cabin to go over an offer. I thought he was ready to make an offer, but it turns out he had another kind of offer in mind." She stuck out her tongue.

"He hit on you?"

"More than that. He basically attacked me. I told him I wasn't interested, and he wouldn't take no for an answer. Fortunately I had a pen in my hand because I was dumb enough to think I was about to make a sale. When he lunged at me, I stabbed him in the arm and then got the hell out of there." She twisted a thin silk scarf around her neck. It was ivory in color and brought out the highlights in her hair.

"Why didn't you tell anyone?" I thought back to the wound that I had seen on Mitchell's arm the first day I met him.

She sighed. "I don't know. It freaked me out. I've been

rattled ever since, and I know *for sure* that's why he posted the nasty review and trashed my rental. He wanted to get back at me for turning him down."

Lisa flicked the coaster. It landed on the far end of the bar. "I know I should have said something earlier. That's why I didn't want you to go to Chief Meyers about last night."

"I get it, but, Lisa, you have to tell her this. I know you're worried about getting in trouble, but if you don't tell her, that will look even worse. She needs to know that he attacked you and that he was in Leavenworth days earlier than anyone knew."

She nodded. Then she picked up her key ring and slid it over her wrist. "Okay. I will. Please don't say anything to anyone else, though."

"You have my word," I assured her.

She stood, walked to the end of the bar, and picked up the coaster. "Sorry about this," she said, handing it to me.

"I've seen worse. Being on this side of the bar means people tend to talk." I bent over and pulled out a box of coasters. "We keep a lot of these and napkins on hand."

"Thanks, Sloan. I feel better talking about what happened."

"Anytime."

"You know the person you should keep an eye out for, though?" Her tone shifted.

"Who?"

She cupped her hand over her mouth, making her keys dangle against her cheek. "David, the movie producer."

I tried to keep my expression passive. "Why?"

"Mitchell was convinced that David was up to something shady."

"Shady?"

She shrugged. "His words. Not mine. He could have been paranoid, but he brought it up three times. He kept asking about what property I was going to put David up in and whether we could take a look. It was weird."

I wondered why she was telling me this now. Was she trying to deflect attention from herself?

"He must have said that David was 'out to get' him a dozen times. When I asked him what he meant, he would change the subject."

"You should probably tell Chief Meyers that."

She nodded. "Yeah, good point. I'm going to see if I can go find her now."

I handed her a new coaster as a parting gift.

With that, she left the pub. I believed her story. Did that mean that the cabin's state of disarray had nothing to do with Mitchell's murder? It made much more sense that he had retaliated by trashing her property and her online reputation. However I couldn't completely write her off. He had tarnished her business and attacked her. If anything, that gave her even more motive to kill him. But now I had a new focus—David. Why had Mitchell claimed that David was out to get him? Or the better question was, had David followed through with that threat?

CHAPTER

TWENTY-THREE

MAC SAUNTERED IN NOT LONG after Lisa left. "Sloan, hey, hey. Pour me a celebratory pint."

"You're pretty chipper today," I said. "I thought you would be sleeping one off, given how much you had to drink last night."

"It's Oktoberfest, cut me some slack." His eyes were glossy and lacked their usual glint.

"I'm not your keeper. Do whatever you want—it's your liver." I poured him a pint, not bothering to let the frothy head settle.

"A toast." He held up his pint.

"To what?"

"Can't say yet, but it's going to be great." He took a sip of the Cherry Weizen and studied my reaction.

I wasn't about to get sucked into his games.

"Aren't you going to ask me more?" He sounded like a wounded child.

"Nope." I rearranged bowls of nuts and Doritos on the bar. His heavy sigh made me smirk. "Fine, I'll tell you, then."

"Mac, you don't have to tell me anything. Like I said before, what you do is your business completely. It doesn't have anything to do with me." I crunched a Dorito to emphasize my point. "This isn't the time or place, but we're going to need to sit down soon and talk about what's next. Dividing things up, selling the house, Alex, Der Keller—everything."

He took a swig of his beer. "You are my life, Sloan. Don't say things like that. Are you trying to torture me?"

The man was infuriating. He had cheated on me and ruined our marriage, and yet had the audacity to try and blame me? I ignored him by opening another bag of Doritos.

"Sloan, listen, this is pretty big news. Like big, big news. It might change what you're thinking about our future. You have to give me another chance. I'll do anything, baby." He darted his eyes around the bar. "Look, I'm not supposed to talk about this to anyone yet, but I know you can keep a secret. I've been asked to take over as host for *Wish You Were Beer.*" He looked at me with an expectant grin.

"What?" Chips spilled on the distressed wood bar. "What are you talking about?"

He sat taller on his barstool. "David told me at the parade this morning. They need a new host, and they want someone who knows craft beer and all the players, and after a few pints last night, he decided that I'm the perfect guy for the gig." Pausing to gulp down another drink of the Cherry Weizen, he pounded the Der Keller logo on his chest. "Won't it be great publicity for the brewery? I mean, this is an international production. This will be good for us, too. I know you don't believe me, but I'm a changed man. I've been brewing again. I'm going to host the film. I'm revamping my entire life. For you."

"Why did David approach you?"

He looked injured. "What? You don't think I'm documentary material?"

I had to bite my lip to stop myself from shooting back a snarky reply. "I didn't say that. I'm just curious how you two connected."

"We've been talking for a while. No one knew this, but David wanted Mitchell out. He told me that he'd been trying to find a way to fire Mitchell, basically from the moment the ink dried on his contract."

"Really?"

He nodded rapidly. "The guy was a loser. I guess he had a mega ego. I heard that he was a child star. Had some show back in the nineties? Apparently he was under the delusion that he was some kind of star."

Mac would know something about being delusional.

"David and Payton have been working on an exit strategy for weeks. Long before they arrived in the village. I guess they realized in the first few meetings that Mitchell was going to be a nightmare to work with, but they had to figure out a way to get out of their contract without owing him a gob of cash."

How convenient that he ended up dead, I thought. Mac's information matched what David had told me earlier.

"I showed them around Der Keller that first night, and David took me aside and said that he liked my energy. He thought I would do well on camera and told me that nothing was solid yet, but that I could pretty much count on getting the job. He had a few loose ends to finish up with his lawyers."

Did loose ends involve killing Mitchell? I couldn't believe that David had offered Mac the job before Mitchell was murdered. What if he had learned that he couldn't break the contract he'd made with Mitchell? Had he decided to find another way—a more permanent way—to ensure that Mitchell wasn't the host of *Wish You Were Beer*?

"Can you believe that yours truly is going to be in a movie?" Mac thumped his chest.

"No, I can't."

"Don't sound so enthusiastic. This is going to be great, for both of us."

"How?"

He sighed. "Like I said, think of the publicity we're going to get for Der Keller. That alone was worth the investment."

"Investment?" My senses went into high alert. Here it was. I knew there had to be an angle. Mac always had an angle.

His cheeks matched the Cherry Weizen. "It's nothing. They offered us an exclusive role in the film. Payton and I just met. She's going to set up some official paperwork for me to sign later. Der Keller will be the signature advertiser. That means that our logo and branding will be shown throughout the documentary."

"Wait a minute." I wiped dust from the Doritos on a hand towel. "What kind of investment did you have to make?" Mac was notorious for leaping into new business "opportunities" without giving them any thought or doing the necessary due diligence.

"I didn't have to make an investment. I wanted to." He sounded defensive. "It's a great opportunity. Sponsoring a beer documentary set here in Leavenworth is definitely in line with our marketing plan."

"But we already went through this. You can't make any major purchases for the brewery without involving me and Hans."

Mac folded his arms across his chest. "It's not a major investment, Sloan. Relax. It's a few thousand bucks in exchange for advertising that hits our key demographic, raises Der Keller's profile, and puts us in the spotlight as the place to be for Oktoberfest."

"Have you talked to Hans?"

He gulped down another sip of beer. "No. I don't need my kid brother's permission to spend a small amount of our ad budget."

"Actually, you do. That's why your parents restructured the company the way they did."

Mac's eye began to twitch. He pushed away from the bar. "Look, I don't know why you're making such an issue out of this. I thought you would be happy for me—for us."

"This doesn't have anything to do with being happy for you, it's about how we're managing Der Keller moving forward. And to be honest with you, I don't have much faith in the documentary. Payton and David haven't been very professional. They claim to have done research into the industry, but know nothing about craft beer. Their camera guy is green to say the least—I would put good money on the fact that this is his first job, and unless I'm mistaken, usually the host gets paid for hosting duties. Not the other way around."

"Fine. I get it. You and Hans want to treat me like a child and make me come to you with every single penny I spend. If that's the way you want it to be, fine. I told you that I'll do anything to get you back. If you want me to jump through hoops to prove your power, set them up. I'll start jumping."

"Mac, this has nothing to do with us." My tone was laced with frustration. I didn't bother to try and mask it. "This has to do with Der Keller's future. It isn't personal."

"Sloan, everything between us is personal." He slapped a ten-dollar bill on the bar. "Thanks for the beer. Keep the change."

I watched him stalk to the front door. Had it not been propped open, I had a feeling he would have slammed it behind him. Was I reacting like this because it was personal? No. Otto and Ursula had intentionally given Mac, Hans, and me equal shares of Der Keller in order to keep Mac's spending in check. I needed to talk to Hans.

While I rinsed out Mac's empty pint glass and circulated through the pub to check on the handful of guests lingering over early afternoon beers, my mind kept returning to David. The more I learned, the more things seemed to be stacking up against him. He had planned to fire Mitchell long before arriving in Leavenworth? Regardless of how Mac tried to spin it, he had also made a deal that involved Mac handing over cash in exchange for a role in the documentary. Was David having financial trouble? Money struggles would definitely be a motive for murder, especially if he'd have had to pay out Mitchell's contract. I wondered what Payton knew. She and David had been inseparable. She must know something.

I refilled customers' pints, carefully tilting the glasses under the taps and pouring the beer slowly so as to create a smooth glass with a touch of foam on the top. By the time I had finished delivering drinks to the tables, I had convinced myself that David had to be Mitchell's killer.

CHAPTER

TWENTY-FOUR

THE REST OF THE AFTERNOON passed without incident.
Garrett came to check on me a few times and brought samples of the test batches he was working on. He reminded me
of a mad scientist, with his chemistry goggles mounted on
his forehead and his notes scribbled in his iPad. "I can't wait
to close so you can come brew with me," he said, handing
me a sample of the pine-infused IPA. It would need to ferment for a week before the flavors balanced out. Yet, even
in its infancy, I had a feeling Garrett had brewed a holiday
winner. The scent of pine hit my nose the minute I held the
taster to my lips. He had managed to achieve a subtle earthy
flavor while still maintaining the hoppy finish that IPAs were
known for.

"This is good." I polished off the taster.

"I think it can be better. I took a walk and foraged some
needles from one of the trees in the park." He gave me a
sheepish smile.

"A real taste of Leavenworth," I teased.

"Exactly." Garrett showed me a spreadsheet he had created on his iPad. "See the ratio of hops to pine? I want to up the pine in the next batch and maybe use a combination of hops. What do you think?"

"That could work, but I'm not kidding, I really like this first sample."

Garrett clicked off his iPad. "Yeah, but I want us to do at least three or four unique batches for each holiday brew. Then we can taste and compare."

The joy of brewing smaller batches was getting to experiment. Like Garrett, I enjoyed making minor tweaks to a recipe. Swapping hops varieties or allowing the wort to boil for an extra hour could produce a finished product that was similar in tone, but slightly different in body or color. I was glad that Garrett took extensive notes, as the only challenge in changing up a recipe was that those changes and additions had to be documented in order to duplicate it in the future.

"I'll come join you as soon as the last of the stragglers heads to the festival," I said.

Garrett pushed his goggles back over his eyes. "Excellent. I'm back to the lab."

I was excited to work on the holiday ales with him, but I was also eager to track down David. I wanted to ask him about hiring Mac. Since the pub was quiet, I called Hans. He answered on the second ring.

"Have you talked to your brother?" I shot out the second he said hello.

"Hey, Sloan," he replied. "Good to hear from you, too."

"Sorry. It's just that he stopped by a couple hours ago and told me that he made a 'small investment' in the documentary."

"What?" Hans's reaction validated my concern.

I filled him in on everything Mac had told me.

"No way. We went over this. He can't spend that kind of money without our sign-off."

"That's what I said, but he got mad and stormed out."

"What does he mean by a few thousand dollars?" Hans sounded unsure. "In Mac's mind, that could mean twenty grand."

"I know."

"Don't sweat it, Sloan. You have enough on your plate right now. I'll find him, and he and I can have a chat."

"Do you mind?" I felt bad dumping Mac on Hans. "What about Oktoberfest?"

"It's fine. I'm not on duty until tonight." Hans chuckled. "And I wouldn't have offered if I did. I sort of feel like I'm my brother's keeper lately. And to tell you the truth, it's been kind of fun watching Mac squirm these days. It's good for him."

Mac and Hans had been close growing up, but their adult lives had taken them down different paths. I knew that Hans loved his brother, and I didn't want to come between them. Since Mac had strayed, Hans had been my faithful protector, which I appreciated more than he would ever know. Still I would feel terrible if he and Mac had a falling out over me.

"Thanks." I hung up after Hans promised he would update me once he tracked Mac down. It shouldn't be hard to do. I had a feeling he was probably drinking his worries away at Der Keller's Oktoberfest tent.

The last of the Nitro customers left sometime before five. They polished off every last drop of beer in their glasses, which I took as a good sign that they had enjoyed it. After locking up and wiping down the bar, I went to see how Garrett's test batches were coming along.

I found him in the kitchen, which was enveloped in steam, the familiar scent of malty grains boiling, and the sound of tech beats blasting on the speakers.

"How's it going?" I called over the sound of the music.

It took Garrett a moment to notice me. His attention was focused on a boiling pot of grains on the stove. He had measured out hops on a scale and was adding them by hand.

"Sloan, I didn't hear you come in." He wiped steam from his goggles.

"What are you working on?" I peered into the industrial-sized stainless steel pot.

"Guess." Garrett dried his hands on a towel and turned down the music.

I breathed in the warm steam.

"Don't look," Garrett warned. "I want to put this nose of yours to the test."

"The pressure." I threw my head back and smiled. Then I closed my eyes and took in another whiff. I caught hints of spice—nutmeg, allspice, and cinnamon. A third sniff brought out chocolate and doughy fragrances. "Is this the mulled wine?"

Garrett clapped three times. "Man, you're good. How did you know?"

"Anyone could have picked up the holiday spices in here," I said.

"Right." He made a note with his index finger on the iPad. "Want to sample what I have so far?"

"Of course." I waited for him to extract tastes from the fermenting carboys resting on the counter. The beauty of brewing in small batches was being able to amass such a variety in a short amount of our time.

He made me close my eyes again while I tasted the cranberry sour with a smooth buttery aftertaste, and a chocolate hazelnut stout.

"I think our customers are going to love this idea," I said, polishing off a taster of Christmas stollen.

"I'm having a blast," Garrett replied with a grin. His goggles had fogged over again, and his brow was damp from the heat and steam. "I want you to try your hand at these recipes too. Are you up for an evening of science, or were you planning to hit the Oktoberfest tents again? I've been at it all afternoon, so I can go either way. An ice-cold pint and a plate of schnitzel sounds good. But if you want to start tonight, I'll hang out."

I hesitated. Brewing was in my DNA. The thought of losing myself in the process was tempting, but so was tracking down David. I glanced at the steamy kitchen. Garrett had completed five batches of beer. Quite impressive for an afternoon. "Let's go grab a beer."

I told him about my conversations with Lisa and Mac. Garrett was a good sounding board. He listened with attention. Once I finished, he cleaned his goggles on his shirtsleeve. "Something doesn't seem right about David," he said.

"Exactly. Why would he pay to fly Mitchell here and for the rental property if he planned to fire him?"

"And why ask Mac for an investment in exchange for the role?" Garrett added. "Do you think that Mitchell was helping fund the project?"

I hadn't considered that. "It's possible. What if David's story is flipped?"

Garrett hung the goggles next to the stove. He turned the burners off and placed a lid over the last batch of beer. It would get transferred into a carboy once it cooled. "What do you mean?"

"What if it was the other way around? Maybe Mitchell planned to pull out of the project. Let's say that he was an investor. What if he told David that he wanted out?"

"Now we're talking motive," Garrett said with a low whistle.

I wished I had thought of it earlier. "You know who I need to find?"

"Chief Meyers?" Garrett raised one brow.

"No." I shook my head. "Payton. She's in the middle of this. She must have a sense of the budget and who has invested in the film, as the director, right?"

"Seems logical." Garrett scooped the remaining hops into a plastic container and stuck them in the freezer. "But you're going to keep Chief Meyers in the loop."

"Of course."

An idea began to formulate in my mind. If I could get Payton alone, maybe she would divulge what she knew about David and Mitchell's relationship. She and David had been attached at the shoulder. If anyone knew what was really going on with the production, it had to be Payton.

I helped Garrett pick up the rest of the brewing equipment. He transferred the mulled wine brew into a carboy. "Let me go change my shirt."

We made a good team. I appreciated his input and the fact that he hadn't brought up the subject of Sally's visit. I was happy to bury that conversation for the time being.

A few minutes later he returned wearing a pair of jeans, black Converse tennis shoes, and a charcoal T-shirt that read SAVE WATER. DRINK BEER.

"I like the shirt," I said. "Do you have a massive collection of beer tees?"

He laughed. "Yep. You should see my closet. It's nothing more than jeans and beer shirts. That was one of the good things about working in a city like Seattle and in my industry. No suits required. My beer shirt collection was legendary. I've got more where this came from." He massaged his chest and winked. "You ready?"

"Yep." I followed him through the brewery and outside. The evening air had cooled slightly. Like last night, the sounds and scents of the festival permeated the village.

"Do they pipe in the smell of beer brats?" Garrett must have read my mind.

"I know. I was thinking the same thing." I breathed in a long whiff of the grilling sausages. "It's like a drug."

As we rounded the corner, we bumped into Kat. She clutched a few flyers in her right hand and an empty beer stein in the other. Her cheeks were dewy. "Oh, hey, guys! I was on my way to find you. This is all I have left." She held up the flyers.

"Good work," Garrett said, offering a nod to a group of women in their early fifties who passed by us. He was oblivious to their stares. Yet another way he was different from Mac. I could only imagine that Mac would have poured on the charm if the women flirted with him.

"Should I get more?" Kat asked. Her braids had fallen loose into two frizzy ponytails.

"You've been handing out flyers the entire afternoon. I can't imagine that there's anyone left who hasn't heard about Nitro." Garrett looked to me for confirmation.

"I agree. And the printer is closed anyway." I motioned down Front Street, where tourists danced in the street to the sound of polka music being piped through outdoor speakers on the Kinderplatz.

Kat thumbed through the five or six flyers she had left. "What if I hand out these last few and then call it good?"

"We're heading that way. Want to join us?" Garrett pointed to the tented entrance.

Kat fell into step with us. "I have to borrow a charger from someone," she said to me. "My phone died a couple of hours ago. I bet my friend has texted me back. I took so many pics and posted like a zillion of them on my Instagram. I should have been watching my battery charge."

I perked up at the mention of Kat's friend. "Do you think you can borrow one?"

She nodded. "Yeah. I'm sure there are dozens of people who keep a charger in their purses or backpacks."

"Let me know if you find out who posted that picture," I

said as I handed the alcohol monitor my ID and waited for him to stamp my wrist.

"Will do." Kat waved the flyers. "Double mission—hand out the last of these and find a charger. I'll see you guys soon." She raced off.

Garrett chucked. "You have to give her credit for enthusiasm."

"True." He was right, but I still wasn't convinced about Kat. Her shift in attitude made me question her authenticity. Never once had I seen her chatting with David or Payton. Even Connor for that matter. If she was really desperate for a job in Hollywood, wouldn't she have taken the opportunity to get face time with them? Instead, she had happily breezed off to the festival to hand out flyers for our pub. Something didn't add up.

I paused inside the entrance gates. "Where to? Should we hit the German tent?" One of the tents was reserved exclusively for beers imported from the motherland.

"Sure." Garrett waited for me. "Lead the way."

We squeezed through throngs of beer lovers queued up at beer stands. Rows of German kitsch—hats with built-in long golden braids and shot glasses with the German flag embossed on the front—lined the path to the beer tents. It was like walking through a gauntlet of carnival vendors. I couldn't believe how quickly people were snatching Oktoberfest T-shirts and souvenir mugs. From plush pillows in the shape of pretzels to fake blond braids made of yarn, I couldn't believe the amount of kitsch.

"You want a set of German nesting dolls?" Garrett asked as we passed yet another grouping of vendors peddling wares.

"Aw, shucks. I would, but I already have a collection at home."

He squinted. "Do you?"

I poked him in the ribs with my elbow. "No."

"I knew that." He smiled widely and stopped to try on a pair of beer goggles. "But, man, Sloan, if I find a secret stash of nesting dolls on Nitro's bar, I'm going to have to fire you immediately."

The German import tent was buzzing. It wasn't quite as elaborate as Der Keller's tent, but it was twice the size. Converted semitrailers that had been outfitted with rows of tap handles lined each side. A crowd pulsed to the beat of the music near the front stage, while two rowdy groups of college students danced on top of the wooden tables nearby. "You want to find us seats and I'll wait in the beer line?" Garrett yelled over the music.

"Sure." I scanned the packed tables for an open spot. As luck would have it, my eyes landed on a table on the left side of the stage, not far from the raucous dancers. Payton, Connor, and David were sitting with their heads together as if they were having a deep conversation. This was my chance. I waved to Garrett, who stood at the end of the beer line, and pointed out the table. "Meet you up there," I mouthed. He gave me a thumbs-up.

I made my way to the table. "Hey, mind if we join you?" I had to shout to be heard above the sound of the electric guitar.

Payton looked up and smiled. "Sloan, of course. Sit." She scooted closer to Connor to make room.

He got up. "I want to get some footage of this band, anyway. It's not every day that you see someone shredding the electric guitar in a pair of lederhosen." Positioning the camera on his shoulder, he pushed his way toward the stage.

David shot him a look I couldn't decipher. Then he yelled, "Hey, Connor! Make sure you rotate through each tent."

Connor adjusted the lens on his camera and propped it higher on his shoulder. "You got it." He lumbered toward the stage.

"How's the film coming along?" I asked.

Payton started to reply, but David cut her off. "Exactly as we hoped. This is one of the better shoots that I've been involved with. Not a glitch. Everything is running so smoothly."

Except for the fact that the host of your film was murdered, I thought to myself.

David continued. "I must say that Leavenworth has been a dream. We're going to leave a ton of footage on the cutting room floor."

"I'm glad to hear that." I decided there was no time like the present to ask about replacing Mitchell. "Any luck in finding a new host?"

Again Payton's lips began to move, but David silenced her. "We haven't made an official announcement, as we're waiting for the final paperwork from our legal team in LA, but we have found a replacement who we believe is going to give the film an even more authentic edge than Mitchell would have offered."

Mac was going to give the film an authentic edge? I pressed my fingernails into my thighs in order not to scoff out loud. "That's good news."

The lights flickered when the guitarist hit a high note. We

paused. The crowd went wild, which made the band crank the sound up another notch. I pressed my fingers into my ears.

Payton swirled the inch of flat beer in her stein glass. I got the sense that she wanted to say something.

"Ready for a refill?" David asked, standing and reaching for her pint.

She stared at the glass. "Always."

David excused himself and went to join Garrett in the beer line. I waited until he was out of earshot to launch into my questions. Fortunately, the music had stopped momentarily for the crew to adjust the speakers. I could only hope that they were turning down the sound, but I had a feeling it was the opposite.

"Are things really coming together okay?" I asked, hoping that my approach would put her at ease.

Her eyes followed David. "Yes. Like David said, this shoot has been great. We have enjoyed getting to know the beer community here in Leavenworth." She sounded like she was at a press conference for the documentary.

"I heard a rumor about who you hired as the new host."

"You did?" Her eyes narrowed.

I realized that no one on the film crew likely knew that Mac and I were married. I chose my words carefully. "Let's just say I happen to know the new host."

"You do?" She glanced behind her.

"Can I ask you something?" I lowered my voice. "Is there a chance that the film is having budgeting issues?" My ears were ringing. I tried to massage them with my fingers.

She bit her nail. "Where did you hear that?"

I wasn't sure how to respond. I didn't want to throw Mac under the bus. "This is a very small town. Things tend to travel quickly." I hoped my answer would satisfy her.

She stared at the beer line. "I can't talk about this now."

"Payton, is everything okay?" I patted her wrist.

She sighed. "I don't know, but I can't talk about this here."

"Do you want to go somewhere else? I want to help."

"Not now. It will be too obvious." She chomped on her fingernail and bounced her foot on the cement.

Too obvious. To who? David? From the way her eyes kept darting from me to the beer line, I was confident that I was on the right track. "I can meet you later if you want."

"Okay. Yeah. That would be good. How about in my hotel room? Eleven."

"Sure." Internally I wanted to check my watch. I hadn't intended to stay out late tonight, but I wasn't going to miss a chance to learn what Payton knew.

Garrett arrived with two steins of beer. He sat across from me and handed me a light pilsner. We listened to the band and drank our beers. Or more like tried to survive listening to the band without doing permanent damage to our eardrums. It would have been nearly impossible to hear each other over the sound of the electric guitar and keyboard, but I got the sense that Payton was relieved that it was too loud to speak. She and David left with Connor to check out the other tents after the band wrapped their first set.

"That was weird," Garrett said once they were gone. "I mean, I know it's loud." He stuck his pinky in his ear and wiggled it around. "But they seemed tense."

"Exactly!" I didn't mean to shout. It felt like my ears were stuffed with cotton. I told him about my brief conversation with Payton. "What do you think she knows?"

Garrett shrugged. "I don't know, but do you think it's a good idea to go meet her alone?"

"Payton?" I replied with a chuckle. "She weighs two pounds. I can handle her."

He frowned. "Just be careful."

"I will." We finished our beers and left to go peruse the food vendors. It took an effort to stay awake for the next five hours. I paced myself when it came to beer tasting, preferring to sample small sips of Garrett's imports and switching to coffee around ten.

"Are you going to make it until eleven?" Garrett teased.

"Absolutely." I stifled a yawn.

His face turned serious. "Are you sure you don't want me to come with you?"

I shook my head. "No, I think Payton trusts me. This is a woman-to-woman kind of conversation."

"Text me when you're done, okay?"

My heart thumped. This was the second time in a matter of days that Garrett had expressed concern for my well-being.

His eyes were intent while he waited for my reply.

"Deal." I tried to keep my tone light, but Garrett's gaze was unsettling.

"I'm serious, Sloan. I don't know what I would do if anything happened to you."

I pinched my fingers together under the table. Was there something between us, or was it just my imagination?

"Nothing is going to happen to me. I have Alex to think

about. I won't do anything stupid. I'm going to meet her and find out what she knows about David. That's exactly why I want to talk to her instead of going directly to David. He has to have done it, don't you think?"

Garrett wrinkled his lips. "I don't know, Sloan. Remember, you said you were going to fill Chief Meyers in on everything you've learned?"

"Yeah."

"Why don't you call her before you go?"

"If it will make you feel better, I will."

He looked a bit lighter. "It would."

I couldn't exactly blame him for being overly cautious. He had worked directly with Chief Meyers when a scammer had tried to sell nonexistent hops to a number of local brewers. "Deal. I'll call her on my way to meet Payton." I glanced at my watch. It was almost time to go. I left Garrett with another promise that I would give Chief Meyers a heads-up. Then I left the tent. Was I finally about to learn who had killed Mitchell Morgan?

CHAPTER
TWENTY-FIVE

THE VILLAGE WAS ALIVE WITH laughter and the smell of beer. Festival-goers spilled onto Front Street and packed outdoor tables and pubs where portable heaters and fireplaces glowed with warmth. The party would last until the early morning hours. I wondered whether Garrett and I should plan to reopen next weekend around eleven or midnight for the second wave of the crowds.

I crossed the street toward the gazebo. Children up long past their bedtimes squealed with delight as they bounced in the jumpy houses and chomped on caramel apples. I thought of Alex. One more day. He would be home tomorrow afternoon. I couldn't wait to squeeze him into a hug and hear about his trip. Should I tell him about Sally's visit?

Two kids with caramel apples bigger than their heads raced past me. I paused and watched them jump onto a nearby hay bale and bite into their apples.

No. It could wait. Sally was gone anyway, and I needed time to strategize. There was no point in causing more drama for Alex. He had enough to worry about with his father. However, I had made a promise to Garrett, so I sat on one of the hay bales and pulled out my cell phone. Chief Meyers didn't answer. I left her a detailed message explaining my theory that David was the killer. I told her that I was heading to meet Payton and that I would be in touch first thing in the morning, or sooner if Payton had proof. With that taken care of, I weaved through the Kinderplatz toward the hotel.

Payton was staying at the Hotel Residence. I entered the lobby, where German pastries and late-night coffee service had been arranged in front of the crackling fireplace. Waving to the woman behind the reception desk, I took the elevator to the fourth floor. Payton had told me to meet her in room 412. I knocked on the door.

She opened it immediately. "You're right on time."

I glanced at my watch. It was just after eleven. "Is this still a good time?"

"Yes, yes." She motioned for me to come inside. The room was a suite with a sitting area in the front and an attached bedroom and bathroom in the back. A tray of assorted teas, two teacups, and a kettle sat on the coffee table. "I thought you might want something warm to drink." She poured water into the first cup.

"Tea would be wonderful."

"Do you take cream or sugar?" Payton paused.

"No. Just straight."

She smiled and continued to pour hot water in the mug.

Then she handed me the cup and the basket of individually wrapped teas. I opted for a jasmine peach packet.

Payton didn't help herself to a mug. Instead she crossed her legs. "Tell me what you heard about the production."

I sipped the sweet tea, picking up a hint of something slightly bitter. Odd. I took another taste. Had the water been flavored with lemon? Maybe it needed to steep longer. I wrapped my hands around the ceramic mug. "Nothing concrete. More like rumors."

She nodded. "That's what I'm curious about."

My head felt heavy. I blinked to keep my eyes open. This was why Alex made fun of me. It wasn't even midnight, but I could barely stay upright.

I took another sip of tea. The bitterness lingered.

Payton smiled. "You were saying?"

Why was I having trouble forming sentences? I fought a wave of dizziness and concentrated on Payton. "I heard that David took payment in exchange for giving Mac the hosting job."

She bit her bottom lip. "Really?"

Had I just let it slip that Mac had told me his secret? What was wrong with me? A fuzzy feeling assaulted my head. The room looked like it was tilted on an angle. I took another sip of the tea.

"I don't want to put you in a weird position. I know that David is your boss, but do you think that he's in financial trouble?" Was I slurring my words?

Payton gave me a funny look. "Why do you say that?"

Why did I say that? I felt like I was trudging through a thick bucket of spent grains. What was I doing here?

"More tea?" Payton asked with a strange smile.

My cell phone buzzed in my pocket. I tried to take it out, but my fingers didn't seem to be working.

Payton sat back, watching me struggle.

What was happening? I finally yanked my phone from my pocket. A text message from Kat flashed on the screen. I had to squint to make out the words.

"Text from my friend: Screenshot was from Payton's Instagram."

The picture came up next of Mitchell Morgan, grinning.

"Something wrong?" Payton asked. Her voice was thick with sarcasm.

"You?"

"Me?" She batted her eyes. "Sloan, I think you've had a tad too much to drink tonight. Such a shame. A young brewer. A female brewer, paving the way for hundreds of young girls behind her. Can't control your drinking."

What was she talking about?

The tea!

I swallowed hard. The tea. She had drugged me. What was her plan?

"Alas, we see it all the time in Hollywood. Young starlets. Great actors with such potential whose lives are cut short by drug and alcohol abuse." She stood, picked up the teapot, and poured the water into the sink.

I had to get out of here. I tried to stand, but my legs were like jelly. *Keep it together, Sloan.* What had she put in the tea? Something strong. But I hadn't had that much to drink. Maybe a few sips.

This couldn't be happening. I should have listened to Garrett's warning.

Garrett! He knows you're here, Sloan.

"Gar he—he . . ." My mouth betrayed me as I tried to speak.

"What's that?" Payton asked in a singsong voice as she wiped the teapot clean. "Having trouble getting out your words?" She dried the teapot. Then she picked up my mug and dumped its contents into the sink. "I think you've had enough to drink tonight. That's what the coroner will think, too." She made a *tsk*ing sound. "Such a shame. You stumbled in here completely drunk. I tried to revive you, but it was too late. Not just alcohol in your system, but it turns out that you had a nasty drug habit too."

She was erasing the evidence.

"I—you—I . . ." My tongue swelled.

"Word around Leavenworth is that you've been going through a terrible time. A cheating husband. An impending divorce. Family drama, it gets the best of them." She chuckled.

"It's understandable that you turned to drugs and alcohol to cope." She returned the clean teapot and mug to the tray. "If only you could have left things alone. None of this would have had to happen."

I fought to stay alert. *Think of Alex. Alex,* I commanded myself.

Payton stared off in the distance. She rambled on about Mitchell and how he had ruined everything. My fingers found the keypad on my phone. I had to text Kat a reply.

"He wanted more. He wanted stardom." She let out a cackle. "As if *Wish You Were Beer* was going to do anything for his career."

I typed an "h."

Payton's voice was thick with anger. "He told me to meet him here in this godforsaken village early. Had something he needed to propose. That idiot tried to blackmail me." She shuddered. "He was nothing more than a washed-up child actor. I gave him a break, and the thanks that I get is a freakin' attempt at blackmail. No. I don't think so, honey."

I typed an "e."

"Huh?" I managed to mumble.

Payton didn't acknowledge me. That was good. I typed an "l." Then I tried to hit the "p," but my finger landed on the "o." I pressed send.

"Helo." That's what I sent Kat. What would she do with that? Think I was drunk texting. That would only add to Payton's setup.

"He found out that I'd been skimming. Such an idiot. He wanted me to buy him a vacation property in exchange for his silence. Ha! Like that was ever going to happen. I had no intention of ever giving that man a dime. I have my own plans. After we hit it big with this documentary, I'm striking out on my own. I've had enough of the men in Hollywood calling the shots. It's time for a woman to take charge." She paused and gave me a sickening, sweet smile. "It's too bad that you had to meddle. I really was encouraged to find a woman making strides in a man's field. We have a lot in common, you know."

Aside from the fact that you murdered someone, I thought to myself. My fingers fumbled on the screen. I had to silence the phone in case Kat responded. I found the button on the side of the phone, but I couldn't make my hands move in the way I wanted them to.

Alex. I heard my own voice in my head. *Do it for Alex.*

I flicked the button just as a message popped up. It was a question mark. I typed a "p" in response, praying internally that Kat would figure out what I was trying to say.

"He should have set his sights higher. A vacation property here in the middle of nowhere? That's what he asked for. He could have had me ink out a longer deal, better cut of the royalties, or for more cash, but instead he wanted a cabin? What an idiot. That's what we got for hiring a has-been child star. The world is better off without him and his monstrous ego."

I needed to text Garrett. Why were my muscles not following my commands?

"I suggested that he back off, but he refused. The man got what was coming to him. Who has an ego the size of Texas when they're starring in a documentary? Do you have any idea how many times I had to try and explain the art of the process to him? He didn't get it. He wasn't smart enough."

My eyes drooped.

"Aw, yes, yes, it looks like you're getting sleepy. A few more minutes, and you'll be out like a light." Payton stood and walked to the door.

I used the distraction to flip through my phone. Luckily I had texted Garrett earlier in the day. His name was directly below Kat's. I punched in the letters "h," "e," and "l," but then Payton coughed. I hit send and pushed my phone under my leg.

Letting out a yawn to keep her attention focused away from my phone, I almost fell off the chair.

"My, my, it's working faster than I expected." She returned to her chair and stared at me. Words and letters fused together in my brain. Bright spots flashed in front of my eyes. I tried to open my eyes as wide as possible, but they refused to comply. Then the room went black.

CHAPTER

TWENTY-SIX

THE NEXT THING I KNEW, there was a pounding sound in the distance. Was someone hammering? Where was I? Was that the sound of someone cleaning the mash tuns? What time was it?

"Sloan!"

Was that my name?

"Sloan!"

I tried to open my eyes.

Someone was calling my name. They sounded far away.

"Sloan! Sit up."

A wave of nausea hit my stomach. Everything was dark. Then why did I feel like I was spinning?

"Sloan." The voice was closer now. I felt a cold hand on my cheek.

Sirens wailed. Or was that a baby?

"Is she okay?" I heard the voice ask. Were they talking to me?

Someone shook me gently. While someone else dabbed ice water on my face.

I blinked and tried to move my head away.

"She's coming around," the voice replied.

"Sloan, it's Garrett." His tone was breathless.

Where was I?

I opened my eyes, allowing a slit of light in. Pain throbbed in my forehead.

"Easy, easy," the other voice cautioned.

I thought I might be sick, so I tried to sit up. Hands caught me from behind.

"There you go. Take it easy."

Was I on the water? My head swirled as I forced my eyes open farther.

"Sloan!" Garrett's face came into a hazy focus.

"What happened?" I asked, but I could tell from the look of concern on his face that it didn't sound the way I intended.

A man in a uniform held up a tiny plastic cup of liquid. "Can you drink this?"

I nodded.

"It will help with the nausea." He held my chin as I tried to swallow the liquid.

Garrett wiped drool from the corner of my mouth.

"What happened?" I repeated. This time it sounded more like a coherent sentence.

"Payton drugged you," Garrett said, keeping his arm firm on the small of my back.

"Ketamine," the medic said. "It's a drug often used in date rape. You feel its effects within minutes. Causes distortion of sound and sight, impaired motor function, slurred speech, dreamlike or out-of-body feelings, vomiting, numbness, and memory problems."

That sounded exactly like I felt.

"How long does it last?" Garrett asked.

"An hour. Maybe two. It depends on how much was ingested and whether she had anything else to drink. She's responding well. I don't think she had a high dosage. She's going to be fine."

The memory of Oktoberfest flashed in my head. I was thankful that I hadn't had much to drink.

"Thank God," Garrett said, massaging my back.

They spoke to each other as if I weren't here. "It's a serious drug," the medic continued. "It can cause convulsions, even death. I gave her some antinausea medication. That should help."

"Payton," I said. My memory was starting to come into focus.

Garrett nodded. "Chief Meyers arrested her."

"How did you—"

"Your text. Kat and I were still at Oktoberfest. She showed me Payton's Instagram page. We were already on our way to come find you when we both got your drunk texts. I knew that you hadn't had more than a pint and a few sips of beer. That's when I realized you were in danger. I called Chief Meyers. She was already on her way here. Apparently, she got the toxicology report back. Mitchell was murdered with the same drug. She also received the production company's financial statements. They showed big sums of money missing, which they then tracked to Payton's personal accounts. We arrived at the same time, and we found you passed out on the floor."

"How long have I been out?" I rubbed my temples.

Garrett looked to the medic. "Maybe thirty minutes."

"That long?"

He nodded. "We were with you the whole time. They were watching your vitals."

I looked down to see a blood pressure monitor wrapped around my arm and a heart rate monitor clipped to my finger.

"You missed the fireworks, though." Garrett winked. "It was quite a show. Payton should get an award for best actress. She almost had me convinced that you stumbled in drunk and passed out."

"Really?"

"Well no, because I was with you, but she had given the scene plenty of thought. Chief Meyers was a pro as always. She arrived armed with more than a gun. She had an arrest warrant and a stack of financial records. Payton couldn't argue with numbers. She confessed to everything."

"And I missed it?" I was beginning to feel more like myself. The medication for my upset stomach had quelled my nerves.

"Yep. I almost wondered if she had slipped herself something because she came clean on everything. Told the chief how she had used the same drug on Mitchell. Apparently she spiked his Cherry Weizen at Nitro that night."

No wonder he'd been acting so drunk. I thought about Payton's stash of pill bottles in her purse. Had one of them contained the drug that had killed Mitchell and almost killed me?

"Sloan, I'm glad you were out, because listening to her recount how methodically she had executed her plan was disturbing. She was ice-cold. Colder than any beer we have on tap, while she proceeded to explain step-by-step how she killed Mitchell." Garrett shuddered. I'd never seen him shaken. Payton must have spooked him.

He cracked his knuckles. "After she spiked his drink, she followed him outside and hit him on the head with a growler. To 'finish the job,' in her words. Chief Meyers had the coroner's report with her, which showed that Mitchell had the drug in his system."

"But she told me that they wouldn't be able to trace whatever she gave me." I massaged the back of my head. "She told me that everyone would think I was drunk and passed out."

The medic chimed in. "Wrong."

"So she wouldn't have gotten away with it?" I blinked again, trying to keep the room in focus.

"Not likely." The medic asked Garrett to move so that he could check my vitals again. Garrett scooted out of the way, but kept his eyes on me the entire time.

"How are you feeling? Your heart rate is returning to normal," the medic said, after checking my pulse.

"Better." That was a half-truth. I still felt like I was in a dream. The coffee table where Payton had served me a laced drink kept dropping in and out of focus.

The medic had me follow his index finger from left to right. Tracking it made my stomach swirl. "Do you think you could drink some water?"

I nodded. "Maybe."

Garrett jumped up and returned with a glass of water.

"Sip it slowly," the medic directed.

The cool water slid down my throat. I couldn't believe how close to death I'd come. I had been so sure it was David that I had completely overlooked Payton.

"You have two choices," the medic said after I finished the water. "I can monitor you here for the next hour or so and then send you home under the care of a friend." He nodded to Garrett. "Or we can take you to the hospital and watch you overnight."

"I'll watch her," Garrett offered before I could reply.

I was grateful. The thought of spending the night in the hospital was less than appealing.

They moved me from the floor where I had passed out to the couch. Payton's shrill tone and evil laugh played in my head.

Chief Meyers appeared in the door frame a while later. "Nice to see you upright, Sloan." Her eyes smiled, but her mouth was frozen in a hard line. "Next time wait until I call you back before striking out on your own. Understood?"

I nodded.

She approached me. "You up for a few questions? If not, it can wait till morning."

"I'm fine."

Garrett and the medic huddled on the far side of the room. I overheard the medic explaining any danger signs to watch out for. Chief Meyers clicked a ballpoint pen and proceeded to have me walk her through everything I remembered. I remembered surprisingly much more than

I expected I might. Hopefully that meant that the drug's effects were temporary.

"Not bad for someone under the influence of a nasty drug," Chief Meyers said with a nod when I finished.

"Yeah, except that I had the wrong killer."

She closed her notebook. "True."

"I was so sure that it had to be David. They had acted together years ago, and it made logical sense that if he was producing the film, he had the most to lose financially. When Mac told me that David had hired him as the new host of *Wish You Were Beer*, everything seemed to fall into place."

Chief Meyers's steely eyes landed on a teacup on the floor. She called to one of the police officers standing guard at the door. "You can bag that now." Then she returned her attention to me. "Part of that is right. David did hire Mac, but Payton had a side conversation with your husband"—she paused and coughed—"estranged husband, explaining that David forgot to mention that the job would only be his if he made a minor investment in the film."

"Minor?" I winced.

She sighed. "You know Mac better than anyone. Let's just say that we have differing opinions of the definition of minor."

I gulped. How much of Der Keller's money had Mac lost this time?

"We'll be interrogating David, but at this point we have no reason to suspect that he had any idea that Payton had been dipping into her directorial budget and blackmailing Mitchell for cash for her personal coffers."

"So David is a victim, too?"

"We're operating under that premise for the moment."
Garrett caught my eye from across the room. The intensity of his gaze made my neck burn.

"What about Lisa Balmes? She had nothing to do with Mitchell's murder?" I asked as more of a statement.

Chief Meyers shook her head. "No connection that I can see."

"Other than that he trashed her place. She must have been serious about wanting to perfect her online image. This whole time I've been wondering if she killed him."

"Doesn't appear that way." Chief Meyers flipped through her notebook. "Although I'm not sure that Mitchell trashed the place. I suspect that was also Payton."

"She was looking for something?"

"Most likely. We'll be going through the evidence we collected with a fine-tooth comb, but I'm betting on the fact that Mitchell had documentation of their deal, so to speak. I think she trashed the place to make it look like someone else did it. Perhaps a burglary gone wrong. But her plan didn't work, since he ended up dead a mile away. She might appreciate being locked away for murder. I know I certainly wouldn't want to face Lisa's wrath. She's already hired a lawyer for a defamation suit against Mitchell. I'm guessing once she learns that it was Payton who ransacked the property, she'll go after her too."

The medic came to do one final check of my vitals. "You're a fighter," he pronounced with a grin. "It's likely that you're going to have a doozy of a headache tomorrow when you wake up. Otherwise you've recovered much faster than I anticipated. Take it easy the next couple of days."

Satisfied that I would be in good hands with Garrett, he went over the list of danger signs for what felt like the tenth time and then left.

"That must mean that both Kat and Connor are innocent too," I said aloud.

"No motive for either of them," Chief Meyers agreed.

"Kat is such a conundrum. She was devastated by Mitchell's murder that first night and then had a complete turnaround over the long weekend."

"Youth."

"Maybe." I wondered how much of Kat's distress over Mitchell's murder had been due to worry about where she would land. As for Connor, it appeared that he really had admired Mitchell, regardless of Mitchell's treatment of him. And apparently his felt hat looked just like Mitchell's. I had been sure that the hat was a clue.

"Sloan, you look tired. It's time to call it a night." Chief Meyers motioned for Garrett to come join us. "EMS has given you the signs to watch for. Any of those develop, I want you to get in touch immediately."

Since we were free to leave, Garrett held my arm. "Your place or mine?"

"Funny." I rolled my eyes, which made my head hurt. "Yours is closer."

"Mine it is." Garrett steadied me as we left the hotel.

I felt relieved knowing that Mitchell's killer had been caught and comforted knowing that I was in Garrett's arms.

CHAPTER
TWENTY-SEVEN

AS THE MEDIC HAD PREDICTED, I awoke the next morning with a pulsing headache. It felt like I had chugged an entire keg.

Garrett had tucked me into his bed and was sound asleep in a chair next to me. On the dresser he had left a bottle of Advil, a glass of water, and a note that read "Wake me if I fall asleep."

He had done enough for me already. There was no way I was waking him. Instead I popped two Advil, chasing them with the water, and tiptoed downstairs. I wanted to be alone for a while anyway.

I started a pot of coffee. The lights made my head pulse. I rubbed my temples and tried to blink away the tiny white and yellow dots floating in front of my eyes. It didn't help. I turned off the lights and went to the office to retrieve the file that Sally had left for me.

Once the smell of coffee wafted into the office, I returned

to the kitchen with the file and poured myself a cup. Each page in the manila folder brought back memories of the varied foster homes that I had been placed in. There were brief intake notes for each placement. Things like the foster family's address, adult names, other children in care, and any special requirements. Otherwise there wasn't a single word about my health or wellness. Sally's signature was on the bottom of every page. I thought about her heartfelt apology. Had she felt like she was losing a piece of herself every time she had to sign a new form sending me to yet another home?

Why had someone destroyed my history? The coffee tasted slightly off. Was it a lingering effect of the drug that Payton had given me? I tried to savor it and forget about the bitter taste in the back of my throat as I went through every scenario I could imagine. But every idea I came up with sounded far-fetched. The most likely story was that my parents hadn't been able to care for me any longer. Maybe they lost a job? Or their house? Maybe one of them died?

I was so deep in thought that I didn't hear Garrett come in.

"I thought I told you to wake me." His voice startled me.

I shut the file folder. "You were snoring. I couldn't wake you."

"That's embarrassing. All the more reason you should have woken me." He poured himself a cup of coffee and joined me. I noticed his eyes glance at the file folder, but he didn't say anything. "How's the head?"

"It's been better. I can empathize with the way the frat guys must feel after a night of Oktoberfest fun."

"Yeah, except you came face-to-face with a killer."

"There is that." I smiled, but it hurt my eyes.

"You're taking the day off." Garrett swirled cream and a packet of sugar into his coffee.

"No, I'm fine. Nothing a few Advil won't fix. It's too busy with Oktoberfest. I'm not going to leave you to deal with the masses alone."

"The masses?" Garrett dipped a spoon into his cream-colored coffee. "How many people came in yesterday? Twenty?"

"Thirty-two, over the course of the afternoon."

"My point exactly." He tasted the coffee on the spoon. "Go home. Get some sleep."

I tried to protest.

"Kat already agreed to fill in for you."

"She did?"

He nodded. "In fact, I'm wondering what you think about offering her a more permanent position? She takes initiative, and she mentioned that she really likes Leavenworth."

"That would be great." Having someone to help run the taproom and do odd jobs around the brewery would be a big relief. Garrett and I were way understaffed. "But can you afford it?"

"I ran some numbers and then I had an epiphany."

"What's that?"

He pointed to the ceiling above us. "I have a bunch of empty rooms upstairs. I'm going to offer her room and board in exchange for a small salary."

"That's a brilliant idea."

"I know." He drank his coffee. "It got me thinking that I could put an ad in *Brewer's Monthly*. We might be able to get a brewing apprentice with the same deal."

"Yeah. That would be amazing."

"It's crazy to think that I have all that space going to waste. Why not use it?"

"Why not?" An idea began to brew in my mind. When I was at Der Keller, we always had a waiting list for brewery tours. Garrett could convert some of the old B and B rooms for behind-the-scenes brewing vacations. I had no doubt that we could easily rent out the rooms during Leavenworth's many festivals and to beer aficionados, who would jump at the chance to stay in a real operating brewery. I pitched him the idea.

"Seriously, Sloan. You were drugged and almost killed last night, and now you're coming up with ideas like this. You are amazing."

"You like the idea?"

"Love it." He stood and riffled through one of the kitchen drawers. Returning with a pad of paper and pencil, he mapped out the upstairs floor plan. We could reserve two rooms for Nitro staff, leaving four rooms for rentals.

"What if we decorate each room in the theme of a beer? Have guests stay in the Pucker Up Palace or the Bottle Blonde Bunk."

Garrett made a note. "Perfect. This could bring in a lot of extra revenue. Why didn't I think of this before?"

I shrugged. I felt the same way about not figuring out Mitchell's murderer sooner.

After we had sketched out the Nitro vacation suites, Garrett forced me to go home. I didn't put up much of a fight. I was exhausted and I couldn't wait to see Alex.

Back at the farmhouse, I stored the file from Sally in my

bedroom and took a long, hot bath. Later that afternoon, I heard the sound of a car pulling up the driveway.

Alex!

I hurried to greet him at the door. He had brought company. The entire Krause family piled out of Mac's SUV—Otto, Ursula, Hans, and Alex. "What's everyone doing here?"

Hans balanced a bouquet of pink stargazer lilies and yellow tulips. Otto held up a box of Tupperware, and Alex had his hand wrapped around bright balloons.

"Sloan, we heard about last night. We bring ze dinner and your favorite beer." Ursula limped with the help of a cane.

My heart swelled. This is what it meant to be family.

"Mom, why didn't you call me?" Alex ran to embrace me. Balloons bumped into my head, making my hair stand on end.

I ruffled his hair and held him tight. "What would you have done?"

"Told my coach I had to leave early." He returned my hug—hard. His lanky body collapsed into mine.

"There's nothing you could have done, honey." I kissed the top of his head.

He pulled away and handed me the balloons. "I'm glad you're okay." His voice cracked.

"Me too." I kissed the top of his head. "I have you to thank, you know."

"What? I wasn't even there!"

"I know, but when the drug kicked in, I kept thinking about you. I forced myself to focus on you. You kept me sane."

He leaned in for another hug before heading inside. I couldn't be sure, but I thought I saw him brush a tear from his eye.

Mac helped Ursula up the front steps. Inside he lit a fire, and soon our family farmhouse was filled with the savory scent of German sauerbraten. We gathered around the dining table as we had many times in the past and savored Ursula's traditional Sunday roast and red cabbage. Hans opened bottles of Apple Weizen and passed around a tray of meats, cheeses, and pickles. Thoughts of my past or Mitchell's murder faded away as I shared a meal with my family. I wasn't sure where my search for my birth parents would lead, but this was my family. And nothing could change that.